THE SONG
OF THE
MOCKINGBIRD
A Novel

Bill Cronin

Copyright

Dedication

For Linda; wife, mother, editor, lover, critic, friend, my rock.

For Kay, my sister, whose inspiration was invaluable.

One

Flying Over Philadelphia
1995

My love of writing came from my mother. She was a creative soul who longed to express herself in some meaningful way. She carried around a matchbook with a picture of a dog on the cover and the words, "Can you draw me?" The inside-cover language encouraged the reader to send in a sketch for a free talent evaluation.

"I can draw that," she told me and then sat at the kitchen table with pencil and paper and dashed off four or five flawless reproductions.

"Mother, send them that one." I pointed to a perfect replication from the pile.

She examined the small printed figure on the cover, critiqued her drawing and found some imperceptible flaw. "I can do better than that," she said, and tore the sketches into small pieces and dumped them in the trash, save the one I pointed out to her.

My mother carried the matchbook cover and matching sketch around in her apron like an unannounced winning lottery ticket. But, drawing was not her only creative talent. She could look at a dress in a magazine and make a pattern of it. She had a flair for decorating. I watched her arrange driftwood, shells, and dried seaweed into arrangements. She could take a collection of inconsequential objects collected at rummage sales and redecorate a room with them. I never saw my mother use a recipe. Her ability to create in the kitchen was legendary.

As talented as my mother was, her hunger to write was preeminent, and Ernest Hemingway was her idol.

"Did you know Hemingway used to live right here in Florida?" She talked about him as if he was her closest friend, as though he lived just across the street, and she could've walked down, knocked on his door, and had coffee with him. "He moved to Cuba, in the middle of the Cuban revolution."

Despite her vast knowledge of Hemingway's works and life, she spoke almost singularly and religiously about his "juice." She had read that Ernest Hemingway was a quirky writer, who could only write well when his creative juices flowed. Hemingway referred to this creative stream as "juice." Mother explained this as a creative fountain inside a writer that was either on or off. She further complicated this scenario by adding that there was some mysterious force in the cosmos that determined whether there would be "juice" or not. She accepted this as fact. When she couldn't write, she would throw up her hands and say the juice was gone.

My mother kept the products of her own juice enshrined in spiral notebooks hidden under her bed. I have many pictures of my mother in my memory, but none as cherished or vivid as her seated at the kitchen table, hunched over a spiral notebook, escaping into the land of Juice.

"Mom, this is really good. Why don't you finish it?" She made me read every word she wrote. The long shallow box under Mother's bed contained dozens of spiral notebooks filled with unfinished stories.

"Even Ernest Hemingway has juice problems." She read in an interview that as he got older it was harder for him to get his juice flowing. Standing to write was one gimmick he used, she told me, to spur his juices. Like the matchbook figures she drew, and every other creative venture my mother pursued, it had been clear to every person in my mother's life, save her, that she had immense talent. In all the years Mother labored for her Pulitzer, she never finished one story, never submitted one drawing in the matchbook contest, and never made the first effort to do anything conclusive with her talent.

These were my memories of Mother before she stopped writing, drawing, and lost hope. These were the times before Billie came to stay with us and changed our lives. As fresh and clear as these memories were to me, they are about the times when I was a child and still loved my mother. Since then feelings of anger, resentment, and hatred towards her have haunted me. As the MD88 jetliner touched down at La Guardia Airport in New York, I pictured Mother sitting at the kitchen table exasperated that she couldn't write, trying to force words on paper that just weren't there. I acknowledge that the same unseen cosmic force that robbed my mother of her juice had robbed mine as well. This was no temporary spell of writer's block. Even if I stood on my head, I couldn't write a single word.

New York City
1995

La Guardia had its usual snarl of traffic. Horns blew, people yelled at one another, and the lady behind me in a line for a cab beat me to death with her luggage. Trash swept along by November breezes swirled around the concrete columns, all part of the city's standard welcome.

My cab inched its way to the head of the line. I'd already paired people ahead of me in line with cabs queued for passengers. Normally, I'd end up with a hand-painted ten-year-old Ford LTD, with no hubcaps and a foreign-speaking driver who'd take me to midtown via Newark. I heard the disc brakes scrape as the older Chevy Caprice ground its way to my waiting feet. The trunk clicked open and rose like the lid of a coffin in some Dracula movie. I walked to the back of the cab and loaded a small Hartman overnight bag in a rusted-through trunk. A small piece of army green loop pile carpet covered the gaping hole and separated my luggage from the oil-stained concrete below. Hesitating, I closed the trunk, wondering if I'd ever see my luggage again. I always feel constrained to place my luggage in the trunk of these vehicles that would be in junkyards in any other place in the country. I felt like I was posting bond, to insure payment of the cab fare. It offends me, even though no one has told me that this is an unwritten rule. So New York's first assault against my sensibilities was the announcement that I was not to be trusted. In fairness, I should have kept something of the cabdriver's to ensure I arrived at my destination in one piece.

I opened the rear door to the all too familiar cage that I willingly occupied to my destination. Between the top of the front seat and the roof was a metal and Plexiglas divider that separated the driver from the passenger. The Plexiglas was badly scratched and difficult to see through. I checked the identification of the driver. His first name was Mohammed. I couldn't pronounce his last name. His picture looked like a mug shot taken in a police line-up. A little window could be opened and closed in the Plexiglas. I heard the driver mumble something, and I replied, "Marriott Marquis—Times Square." The rear seat pulled loose from the floor, and my butt slid into the space between the back and bottom of the seat. The compartment smelled of urine. As the cab pulled away from the curb, destined for the bowels of the city, I heard every valve in the engine clatter, as age and abuse had finally taken its toll on the heart of the yellow beast. The engine ran on six of its eight cylinders as it climbed the Tri-borough Bridge headed for Manhattan.

We edged toward mid-town along the river. Graffiti adorned the buildings, overpasses, phone booths, trash receptacles, and even vehicles that had stood in one place too long. Occasionally, abandoned vehicles, long stripped of anything of value, and had stood as sentinels to the entrance of the city. The road was rough, the paved surface replaced long ago by a mosaic of macadam patches, in various halftones of gray and black.

Staying in no particular lane at twenty miles an hour over the speed limit, my cabby demonstrated his prowess behind the wheel. When blocked by a non-professional driver who dared to do the speed limit, he laid on the horn, screamed in Arabic out the half-opened driver's window, and he repeatedly beat the heel of his hand against the steering wheel; each strike sent waves of rattles across the dashboard.

Catapulting across town to Broadway, past the adult theaters that announced our approach to Times Square, we slammed into gridlock just two blocks from the hotel. From the left and rear of the cab, I heard a repeated whistle blow grow louder. Suddenly, the car exploded with a startling thud, and a large, heavy man scrambled across the front of the cab and left a crater in the center of the hood. The official New York City cab medallion on the damaged hood caught the fugitive's old, tattered flannel shirt and ripped off a large square of light-blue and green material. The man bounced off a Jaguar to the right, tore off the ornament, and smashed that hood, too.

Mohammed exploded in anger. His unintelligible ramblings converted to action. He bolted from the car and then he was forced back into his seat by two pursuing police officers who also elected the shortest route to the fleeing man over the top of Mohammed's cab, expanding the huge dent in the middle of the already destroyed hood. Apparently, the officers had discriminating taste. They avoided the Jaguar and opted to bounce across the hood of another cab. The pair bounded to the sidewalk in pursuit of the man with a torn shirt and a gray wool cap pulled down over his ears.

"Sheeeet," Mohammed said in broken but understandable English. He clumsily made his way to the street and joined the drivers of the other cab and Jaguar as they shared their mutual disbelief, anger, and misfortune. The trio stood helplessly as they watched the three-person wrecking crew run down the crowded sidewalk toward the theater district, whistles blew and the crowd separated like the Red Sea at Moses' outstretched arms.

Mohammed inspected the damage done to his already disheveled car as though it had just received its first dent. There wasn't a piece of sheet metal on the car that didn't have either contusions, abrasions, or rust. From where I sat, the readjusted condition of the hood fit well with the ambiance of the cab in general and the city that I had come to loathe in particular. Mohammed was a small, thin man with dark but expressive features. His mood lightened, he still muttered to himself in Arabic, now motivated to move on by the yells and screams of other cabbies and drivers who soon bored of the situation and were ready to move on. Mohammed slammed the car door so hard the glass came off the track and fell inside the door with a crash. He slammed the heel of his hand on the steering wheel again, turned his head in my general direction, and said in his broken English, "I lub dis place." He gave me a grin of yellow-stained teeth via the rearview mirror. Mohammed's smile faded rapidly to a snarl. He slammed the gearshift lever into drive, the car now sputtering toward the Marriott Marquis Hotel, my opinion of Gotham unchanged.

I waited for Lisa Catera, my agent, in the coffee shop at the Marriott. Her office was on the 4700 block of Avenue of the Americas several blocks away. I was surprised she suggested we meet here, since it usually would have taken surgery to remove the phone from her ear at her office. Our once annual in-person conversations were like a poster I saw once that defined management as interruptions interrupted by interruptions. I hated her office anyway. Its appearance would encourage volunteers for a "Save the Forests" campaign. Stacks of manuscripts formed a leafless pine forest of their own, not only in Lisa's office, but in every inch of available space in the agency. Her office was depressing. The dreams of all those writers lay in stacks of white and manila envelopes like so many concrete blocks. It was humbling, too. A reminder of what a small group the published really were.

"Hi, Jack."

I looked up at Lisa, stood, and stretched out a hand. "Hi, Lisa. You look terrific."

She shook my hand in an all too professional manner, and dispensed with her usual warm, friendly hug. Lisa was my age, nearing the half-century mark. She was a woman of the nineties, professional but comfortable. Her short, light brown, frosted hair was cut in Liza Minnelli fashion, and she always wore a severe business suit, complete with dark hose and Reebok tennis shoes.

She hung her backpack purse on the chair directly across from me. "How are you feeling, Jack?" she said, a veiled reference to my current inability to perform to her expectations.

I looked directly at her. "The same."

"Black coffee," she said to the hovering and unpleasant waiter.

"We just have a few moments before Barksdale arrives. I thought it best if you heard it directly from him." Lisa fumbled with the napkin. She looked at everything in the restaurant but me.

I leaned forward, reached across the table, and placed my hand on hers. "What's this about, Lisa?" I was tired of the intrigue.

She looked at me with narrowing eyes. "You have to finish No Place for a Lady. I've already made all the excuses I could think of. He's angry, and you can't blame him. He championed your three-book deal. He put his butt on the line for the one-point-five-million-dollar advance you received. You promised you'd have the second book finished six months ago. You haven't written the first word. He's pissed."

I wrapped my hands around the hot coffee cup as a camper might warm his hands to keep the edge off a cold morning. The gesture did little to remove the chill of her look. I leaned back and looked at the lady who had helped me sell seven novels over the past eight years. Though we saw each other infrequently, we talked every other day. I liked Lisa. I trusted her. Every dime I made passed through her hands on the way to my checking account—minus her ten-percent commission. We were more than friends and business partners. I had to be honest with her.

"I can't finish the book, Lisa."

"What do you mean you can't finish it?" Her face reddened. I had her attention.

"I can't finish it, money or no."

"Sure you can, Jack. It's a good story, a great plot. Right down your alley." She tried to encourage, but her voice was on the edge of anger.

"I'm done, Lisa. I can't even write one simple, lousy sentence. I sit at the computer all day, and not a damn thing comes out. It isn't just the desert story. I can't write anything. I'm through. Do you understand? I'm finished." Months of frustration put force behind my words. I was angry, too, but not at Lisa. I was angry at myself, and the confession to Lisa was long overdue.

Her hands in front of me now on the table turned to tightly clenched fists.

"Jack, if you factor in the first book you finished, there is still nearly a million dollars sitting on the table. You just can't walk away from that. I can't walk away from the commission. Our firm has already deposited and spent our share. It will create a terrible problem if we have to return it."

"I can't help that. I tell you I can't write anymore. When I dig down for the words, they aren't there. If I could change it I would."

I saw the frustration etched in the lines of her thin, elongated face. She brushed the hair away from her forehead. "The medication isn't helping?"

"No." I didn't tell her I had refused the medication. I leaned back in my chair. Lisa looked over her shoulder as though Barksdale would show up at any minute.

"Jack, promise me that you won't utter a word of this to Barksdale. If you tell him what you just told me, his lawyers will crawl all over both of us and demand a refund of the advance. For my sake, I beg you not to say anything. Promise me." She reached across the table, took my hand in hers, and looked at me with panicked, sad eyes.

"Alright. We're just delaying the inevitable. I'll never finish that book—any book."

A waif of a girl, with a bicycle helmet, long stringy blonde hair, black tights, leather finger-less gloves and a worn, brown leather bomber jacket appeared at the table. She barged right in. "Lisa Catera?"

Lisa nodded. The girl handed her a sealed business envelope, with the Reynolds and Ryan logo emblazoned in gold in the upper left-hand corner. "Here, sign this." The girl thrust a form in front of Lisa. The girl, who could have been a poster child for the anorexic, spun on her heels and departed, odors from the street whirled about the table. Lisa trashed the envelope and pulled the handwritten note out with a flutter.

She rolled her eyes and looked at me. "It's from Barksdale. Can't make it. Says you have forty-five days to finish No Place for a Lady, or the contract is canceled and then he expects a check from both of us for one million. Wishes you well. Short, sweet, straight for the jugular." She held the letter out for my inspection. I declined.

I said, "So there it is. Between royalty checks and what I have left of the advance, I should be able to come up with my share. What about you?"

"I don't want to hear this. You sound defeated, like you've given up. This isn't you. Before you quit, I want to know why. You owe me that much."

"I don't know, Lisa. If I knew why, I'd fix it and finish the book."

"Could you change your medication?"

"No," I say, without explanation.

"Are you still going to counseling?"

13

"No. It's a waste of time."

"Something is causing all this. There has to be an explanation."

"There is an explanation. We're just not going to find it in my lifetime."

Lisa dropped her head and clasped her hands. She shook her head slightly as if to say, I can't believe this is happening to me. "You're throwing away a brilliant career." She raised her head and looked at me. She was on the verge of tears.

"You sound like Emily."

"She loves you. She's as concerned as I am." Lisa turned toward the lobby of the hotel, where a throng of conventioneers at the entrance of the coffee shop, waited for the host to show them to their seats. She scanned the line of people as though one of them might have a word of advice. She looked back at me with eyes less emotional. "I'm not just your agent. I'm your friend. You have to resolve this. You have to go back to counseling. You have to find out what's going on. There's a reason for all of this. You can't just give up." She pounded her fist on the table. Dishes and silverware rattled in response.

I was silent. I had no words of encouragement for Lisa. Hell, I had no words of encouragement for me.

Lisa pushed her chair away from the table. She picked up the Barksdale letter and placed it in front of me. "I can't stay. I've an appointment in a half-hour. Have dinner with me tonight, and we'll talk more. You are staying, aren't you?"

Lisa pulled a compact from her backpack, checked her mascara, and tossed the makeup back into her purse.

"I'm not staying. I've had too much fun for one day."

Lisa stood, and I followed her lead. She walked around the table and hugged me warmly. She held me by the shoulders. "Promise me you'll go back to counseling."

"Alright. I'll go. But I can't finish the book, Lisa. I can't."

"Make an appointment with LuAnn. Talk to her. Then call me. I have to go." She hugged me again, picked up her backpack and left.

"Anything else for the gentleman?" the waiter said, clearing off the table. "My, are we busy. Look at the line waiting for tables." He laid the check on the table and scurried off to annoy other patrons. New York, the home of hospitality.

I picked up the note from Barksdale. I recognized his bold, flowing handwriting. I could even picture his large, fleshy, impeccably attired body hunched over the paper as he wrote my death warrant. He probably wrote it with the Monte Blanc gold tip fountain pen he fancied. Forty-five days? I've never written anything in forty-five days, not even a short story. Even with the outline finished, the task was monumental. I was through. No amount of counseling would change it.

I checked my airline guide and found a non-stop flight back to Orlando that left in three hours. Leaving a twenty on the table, I fought my way to the lobby, then down the escalator to the covered entrance. I put the strap of my overnight bag over my shoulder and walked around the corner and out to Times Square. Rush hour neared. Yellow cabs, buses, and the foolhardy snarled the streets. I took a deep breath of the particulate-laden air that smelled of diesel fuel and vented air from the subway system. I felt like the air smelled. Dismal. I wanted to leave for the refuge of Mt. Dora, to sit on my porch, look out at Lake Dora, and drink copious amounts of Cabernet.

I signaled for a cab. From the center lane, a badly damaged relic cut off two lanes of traffic amid cursing and blaring horns and limped to the curb. I opened the door, and the strong pine scent nearly knocked me over. I looked in the front window and a half-dozen of the pine tree-shaped fresheners hung from the rearview mirror. I threw my overnight bag into the back seat and forewent the trunk-clicking routine.

"La Guardia." The cab lurched away from the curb before I jerked the door closed. The smell of the air fresheners was stifling. I found a hole in the door panel where the button to open and close the windows once was. I looked through the wire cage to the black man driving. "Can you open my window, please?"

He spoke to me in a language I couldn't recognize. He flashed me a brown-toothed smile over the seat then focused his attention on wedging the worn Crown Victoria into a spot no bigger than a Yugo in the lane next to us. Fumes from the exhaust system seeped through the floorboards. Traffic was at a standstill.

"God, I love this place," I said to my driver as I laid my head back against the seat.

Two

Mt. Dora, Florida
1995

It was nearly midnight after the three-hour flight and an hour-drive from the Orlando International Airport. I navigated through the small town and on to Lakeshore Drive. I rolled down the window and marveled at Lake Dora bathed in the light of a full moon. With the lake and its many boathouses and docks to my left and elderly but stately homes on the knoll above to my right, I cruised the short distance along the lake to the 1920s home I had bought from the estate of a deceased citrus baron. The crisp November air filled the car and cleansed my senses with familiar sights and sounds I had grown to love. Mt. Dora was as far away from the theme park throngs of Orlando as I could get without forfeiting good restaurants and shops.

As I neared my home, a small yellow moving van stood like a billboard in the moonlight. Every light in my house was on, and someone had parked the truck in the drive, forcing me to park in the street. A burglar was my first thought, until I saw Emily hunched over a heavy box she struggled to carry to the back of the truck. Security lights at the southwest corner of the house washed over the

18

truck like stage lights in a play. She strained to deposit the box into the back of the truck, and then retraced her steps to the house.

As I walked up the drive, heat from the truck's engine compartment felt good against the chill of the night air. I looked in the back of the truck. Various shaped boxes with U-Move printed diagonally across them were haphazardly scattered on the wooden floor. I decided to wait by the truck for the solution to the mystery to come to me. I could hear the door from the house to the garage open and close and then footsteps across the concrete floor. Emily rounded the corner, caught the sight of me, screamed, and dropped a small box, which split open when it hit the ground. Bras, underwear, and nightclothes spilled onto the concrete.

"What are you doing here?" She shifted from one foot to the other, hands on her hips.

"Remember, I live here." I held out my arms toward my second spouse, my faithful mate of eight years. "How about a kiss to welcome your successful author husband home from his trip to Babylon?"

Her eyes flashed, and her brain worked at warp speed for an explanation. She threw her hands to her side. "Shit, Jack. I wanted to avoid this." She began to cry. "I'm leaving you." She bent over, put her now public unmentionables back into the injured box, and tossed it into the truck. Without a word, she twirled on her heels and headed back into the garage.

I grabbed her hand, and pulled her back to face me. "Just like that. 'Oh, by the way, Jack, I'm leaving you.' I can't believe this. You didn't even have the courage to tell me to my face. You waited until I was gone and tried to sneak out in the dead of night?"

She tried unsuccessfully to free her wrist from my grasp. "I'm tired of being the punching bag for your unhappiness. You're depressed, and somehow I'm always the cause. I'm not the cause, Jack. I've gone above and beyond trying to stick it out with you. Not anymore. Now let me go."

Emily yanked free and stomped off through the darkened garage and into the house. In the kitchen, the lights from the fluorescent fixture danced on her hair and skin. She appealed to me more than at any time in recent memory. Light brown wavy hair, brown eyes, and light skin cast a spell on me. Even in this, the most menial of endeavors, Emily dressed to perfection: pearl earrings, brown cardigan thigh-length sweater, matching blouse, and pants.

"I like how we leaped from happiness to separated, and skipped the arguing, fighting, and counseling part. Isn't it written somewhere that we get to talk first before we split up the furniture?"

Hands on her hips, she said, "Happy? Is that what you call this? This isn't happy. This is you miserable while everyone around you walks on eggshells. This is bimonthly sex and romantic starvation. There has to be a relationship before you can talk. There's no relating going on here, Jack. You've crawled into that emotional hole of yours and I haven't seen you for two years. Well, I'm not going to stand around and watch you destroy yourself. And I'm certainly not going to let you destroy my life, too." Tears. Angry tears.

Emily pulled napkins from a holder on the kitchen counter and dabbed her eyes. She took in a deep breath. "I've got packing to do, and I don't want to be all night." She pushed past me, aimed for the kitchen.

I followed the trail of her light perfume. "Will you stop for a minute? You can't just leave like this," I said frantically, my head spinning. The potential of losing my publisher was not totally unexpected. I had many clues the confrontation was at hand. But, Emily. I thought about the events of the past few days. They seemed normal enough. Certainly no signs of her imminent departure. "Can't we talk about this?" I blocked the doorway. She pushed into me with a box and forced her way through the door.

Once in the kitchen, she slammed the box down on the kitchen table and turned on her heels to face me. "We have talked. I'm done talking. I'm tired of you sleeping half your life away. I'm tired of listening to how unhappy you are. I'm tired of watching you throw a fabulous career away."

"Well, we've finally gotten to the nub of it, haven't we? It's the money, isn't it? Everything was great while the money was coming in." I regretted the words as they left my lips.

Anger swept her face. She slapped me hard. Through clenched teeth, she said, "You'd better leave." Her eyes narrowed, and the muscles in her jaw tightened.

"You're doing enough of that for both of us."

She slapped me again. "Get out." She grabbed me by the arm and tried to drag me to the door to the garage. "Now go, Jack, or I swear to God, I'll call the police."

"Alright. I'm going."

"I'll be out by morning. I'll send for the rest of the furniture I want later. You can have your precious little house."

I walked through the garage, past the truck, and down the drive to my car. I leaned against the door and looked out across the moonlit lake. I knew Emily would not be back.

Emily was the long-suffering sort who reached a certain point, then acted. Once she turned a page, she never looked over her shoulder. If it was a job, she moved on. If it was a friend, she permanently wrote her off.

I loved Emily. I felt dead inside. She needed a husband and a lover, and, in honesty, I had been neither. I couldn't have cared for my own needs. I heard her footsteps on the drive, and the thud of a box dropped into the back of the truck, then footsteps back to the house to retrieve another box. I should have been crying, I thought. But there were no tears. I got in my car and reversed my earlier course. I knew none of the motels in Mount Dora would be open this late, so I drove out to the main highway.

At Highway 441, I pulled the car off the road. I had no idea where to go. Traffic was sparse and the moon so bright you could drive without lights. I turned off the headlights and engine and sat in silence. When I was seventeen, my mother had drunk more than her usual share of Chianti. We were sitting at the kitchen table. Through bleary eyes, she had told me she didn't want to live anymore. Her face was as clear in my memory as if she had been sitting next to me now. As a young boy, this was the first time I had felt completely helpless. She had been in pain and I couldn't do a thing for her. I loved my mother deeply and knew I didn't possess the power to make her happy.

As I sat in silence, I felt like that teenage boy again. Helpless. Hopeless. As bad as things had been over the last two years, I had never thought of suicide, until now. I just didn't want to live anymore. I looked toward the glove box. I kept a loaded nine-millimeter semiautomatic pistol there for protection. I contemplated opening the glove box and removing the gun.

As I reached for the glove box, someone rapped on the driver's-side window. The unexpected intrusion made me jump in my seat. I turned and a sheriff's deputy stood a safe distance away and a little behind me. His hand was on the butt of his handgun on his belt. I rolled down the window. I had been so engrossed in my thoughts I hadn't noticed that he had pulled up behind me.

"Everything okay?" the deputy asked, still on alert.

I nodded.

"Would you step out of the vehicle, please?" The deputy backed away from the car.

I opened the door slowly and got out of the car.

"May I have your driver's license, please?"

I turned to the deputy, pulled my license out of my wallet and handed it to him. "My name is Jack McNamara. I just went home a few minutes ago and found my wife leaving me. She asked me to stay somewhere else tonight while she moves out. I'm trying to figure out where to go."

He inspected the license, looked at me, and said, "Could I see the registration for the car?"

I opened the driver's door, crawled across the front seat, blocked the deputy's view of the glove box, and pulled out the registration. I closed the box, backed out of the car, closed the door, and handed the yellow slip to the deputy. He looked at both then handed them back to me.

"Are you okay?" He searched my face for clues. If I looked like I felt, I could understand his cause for concern.

"Yeah, I'll be fine. Thanks for stopping."

"This is not a great place to park. There's a convenience store about a half-mile south on the right. They're open all night."

"I'm thinking about going to Altamonte Springs. I appreciate your help just the same. Thanks."

"Good night, then." The deputy gave me a brief two-finger salute from the bill of his Smokey-the-Bear hat and left.

When I thought about what I had contemplated doing, I thought about my mother. Even though she had been dead for seventeen years, it made me angry that our lives seemed to be so intertwined. I blamed her for the dark side of my life. I knew my troubles were inexplicably linked to hers, a fact that only enhanced my anger toward her. I felt alone, deeply unhappy, and unable to escape.

I started the engine, turned on the headlights, and put the car in drive. As I thought about the unhappiness that filled the remaining years of my mother's life, I decided then that I didn't want to end mine that way. I had been miserable long enough. I had no idea how to pull my life out of a free fall, but for the first time in two years, I wanted to try.

Three

LuAnn Calder's Office, Orlando, Florida
1995

In my twenties, I had this incredibly bright idea to open a bar. It would be a neighborhood joint with red check oilcloth table covers and an antique bar from the gay 1890s. On the weekends, folksingers would entertain. I was going to be rich.

So, I gathered up my dreams and took them to a local banker my father knew. The banker picked patiently at his fingernails while I enthusiastically shared my genius. When I finished, he asked me how much of my own money I would put into the business.

"None," I said. "I don't have any money of my own."

At a very young age I learned the first hard lesson of life. Banks don't lend to people without money. Seeing a counselor is a very similar experience. Counselors don't have answers for people who don't have answers of their own. At nearly a hundred bucks an hour, they listen to your aimless rambling, and when you accidentally stumble onto a nugget of personal wisdom, they say smugly, "There you go. Now you have it," as if they have had the answer all the time and have used their years of training to make you think you have come to this conclusion all on your own.

This is the relationship I had with LuAnn Calder, which was why I quit coming to her. I didn't dislike her, but I wasn't sure I liked her much either. I always felt like a child called to the principal's office when I had done something wrong. I didn't feel threatened. I just felt like I was twelve years old and not the smartest guy in the world.

She asked, "What's bothering you?"

"I'm depressed," I said.

"Why do you think you're depressed?" She drilled right to the core.

"If I knew, I wouldn't be here." I was a smart-ass with my principal, too.

Coming there was like trawling for one particular fish in the Atlantic Ocean with no bait on the end of your hook. The odds were one in a gazillion, but you've convinced yourself there was a shot. So, I submerged myself into an ocean of feelings and searched for the key to unlock my emotional prison. The odds were better winning the lottery.

I hated LuAnn's office. It looked more like a den than an office. The only thing missing was a fireplace. Way too frilly for my taste. When I came there, my mood was dark. I wanted darkness, not little shelves with tiny teddy bears congregated and white flowery wallpaper. She overused vanilla air fresheners. After more than two years of coming to her, I could smell vanilla and I would be instantly depressed. I could tell I had been in counseling far too long when I had begun to look at the counselor's office with ideas for redecoration.

LuAnn was distractingly attractive; mid-thirties, long dark hair, nice figure, friendly face, and a condescending demeanor. I don't know what it was about her, or how she did it, but everything she said came across with attitude. During the couple of years, I'd tried many times to figure how she created this impression. On the surface, she was the nicest person in the world. Sweet. Charming. Likeable, but condescending.

She sat in her recliner. She didn't have a desk; since she said desks made people uncomfortable. She had a little clipboard in her lap and a pen in her hand. She wore a sky-blue pantsuit that matched her eyes.

She cleared her throat and crossed her legs. "What brings you to my door, Jack?"

"Well, yesterday my publisher threatened to cancel my contract, Emily walked out on me, and I seriously thought about blowing my brains out last night. Typical day in the neighborhood, I'd say." A stuffed bear on a bookshelf above and to her left grinned and stared me down with his one remaining black-button eye.

"Tell me about it."

This woman had a heart of stone. Not, "Gee, I'm really sorry," or "I feel badly for you." "Tell me about it," she said.

I looked directly at her for the first time. "Nothing much to say. You know the deal about the publisher. Emily has overloaded on my marvelous personality and disposition. And like my mother once told me, 'I don't want to live anymore.'"

"When did she tell you this?" The word "this" was spoken with an incredulous tone.

"Several times."

"Why didn't you tell me your mother attempted suicide?"

"She didn't try to kill herself. She said she didn't want to live anymore. There is a difference."

My attempt at sarcasm ignored, she asked, "When was the first time?"

I thought for a minute while LuAnn chewed on the end of her plastic ballpoint pen. "I guess I was about seventeen. We were sitting at the kitchen table where we always talked. It was a couple of years after my older half-sister left, or I should say after my mother threw her out."

"What older sister? I thought you were an only child."

"I am. Well, I guess technically I'm not."

"You have me confused."

"My mother was married before. She had a child with her previous husband. Kind of a family skeleton."

"Skeleton?"

"When I was fourteen, my mother got a call from this girl. I answered the phone. The girl on the phone had a thick Southern accent, like Mother's. She wanted to know if Kit McNamara lived there. I handed the phone to Mother. She turned white, broke into tears, and asked me to leave the room."

"The call was from your sister?"

"Half-sister. I didn't know it at the time."

"When did you find out?"

"Later, when my father got home. They had a huge argument. It wasn't until the following morning that my mother told me who it was."

"What about Billie?" Her words had a sharp edge. I knew she was angry with me for keeping all this from her, but I really hadn't given it much thought until now.

"I never knew my mother had been married before. Before that phone call, I didn't know I had a half-sister. My mother said Billie was coming to live with us."

She wrote a few notes on her clipboard and then asked, "Why did your mother throw her out?" She tapped the end of the pen lightly on the edge of the clipboard.

"I don't know. I asked her several times. She wouldn't talk to me about it."

"And this is the reason your mother didn't want to live anymore?"

"I didn't say that."

"You coupled your mother's not wanting to live anymore with Billie's leaving."

"No I didn't. You asked me when she first told me she didn't want to live anymore."

"You don't think these things could be connected?"

"I've never thought about it. Mother had always struggled with depression. After Billie left, she really took a nosedive. Perhaps they are connected."

She shook her head. "I can't believe that you've been coming to me for two years and haven't mentioned any of this."

"It didn't seem important. I certainly don't want to go back and relive any of that."

Her lips tightened into a thin line. She scribbled on her clipboard feverishly. "Tell me about Billie."

"Not much to tell. She came to our home in May of 1961 and left in August, just before school started."

"Were you close?"

I was surprised how hard the question hit me. "Yes, we were." I was not prepared for the emotion I felt at the answer. "Very close." I could see Billie's face, tears streaming down her cheeks on the day she left.

"When was the last time you saw her?"

"When she left in 1961, although I saw her briefly a week before my mother's funeral in 1978."

The answer didn't please her. She uncrossed her legs and pushed herself to the edge of her chair. "This was someone very close to you, a sister, and you're telling me you haven't seen her in over seventeen years?"

I didn't know how to answer her. I had wondered about this myself. After Billie left, she almost didn't seem real to me. In fact, that whole summer was difficult for me to remember.

"Jack, why did your mother hide her daughter from you?"

"I don't know."

"How did you feel about your sister leaving?"

"I was very angry." I stood. Suddenly I felt very uncomfortable. "What made me most angry was my mother's refusal to discuss it with me. I'd asked her many times about it. She just wouldn't talk about it."

"Now, your mother died in 1978. It was cancer wasn't it?"

"Yes."

She flipped through her notes. "Yes . . . and you told me that you were still angry at her when she died. You said the reason you were so angry with her was that she wasted her life on pills and wine."

Suddenly, the picture of my mother's funeral was vivid, eternally etched in my memory.

Orlando Cemetery and Gardens
1978

The cemetery workers manicured the lush grounds with impeccable care. Spanish moss draping from two-hundred-year-old live oak trees danced to the rhythm of the winds. The shade from these living relics made the air feel cooler than it was. A Canadian cold front had swept away the humidity of summer earlier in the day, heralding the beginning of fall. The subtle pageantry of autumn had finally come.

The cool, dry air swept across my face. A break in the canopy created by the giant oaks let a shaft of light through to warm my mood. I tilted my head back and turned my face slightly to take in the full measure of the warmth of the sun.

I said to myself, "Mmmmmm," as if I had just tasted something wonderful, not with my mouth but with my soul. It was then that I first heard the melody. A mockingbird in a branch not far from me sang all the songs it knew. The gray bird with white-striped wings performed his repertoire of songs and drew me into a world of calm beyond my experience.

Earlier that morning, I had eulogized my mother. My father had appointed me, not because of the closeness of my relationship with my mother, but because I would "know the right things to say," and I was a "better speaker" than he. So he shared with me words he wanted me to say, and I added them to my own.

I stood behind the podium in St. Ann's Catholic Church and spoke the words I had written and performed the duties of an only son. I delivered the talk with powerful words and external conviction. But, they were not my words; they were empty of emotion. I could have given this eulogy with the same passion for the women who cleaned the church.

At the cemetery, I stood behind my family, friends, my mother's side of the family, and most of my mother's closest friends. Men in dark suits, with their heads bowed low, hands clasped at their waist, provided a backdrop for the roses, carnations, mums, and gladiola sprays that surrounded my mother's dark brown metallic casket. The liturgical words of the priest and the smell of incense pulled me from that distant, peaceful place. The priest assured us that our prayers, for her sake, would shorten her time in purgatory on her journey to Heaven. I stood in the back because I was ashamed.

There was not a dry eye under the canopy save mine. Sobs of grief and sorrow swept through the small gathering as the casket was lowered into its final resting place. I wanted to cry but couldn't. As workers symbolically covered the hole with green carpet, I hoped no one would see my lack of grief. As they straightened the green carpet, as one might smooth over a spread on a bed, I tried to return to the place of peace I had felt only moments before. It eluded me then and eluded me now. Whenever I heard the song of a Mockingbird, I was reminded of the greatest peace I had ever known and it brought me back to the place of my greatest tribulation.

LuAnn Calder's Office
1995

"Was your anger over Billie the reason you couldn't cry at your mother's funeral?"

I slumped back into my recliner, brought back to the reality of LuAnn's office. I lay my head back against the chair and exhaled deeply. "Sure. I was and still am angry at the way she treated Billie. She abandoned her twice. I'll never forgive her for that. It wasn't just Billie. It was Mother's depression, her drinking, and the endless draining conversations. Mother couldn't talk to my father, so she dumped her problems on me."

Bill Cronin

Looking at her notes, she said, "You told me she started these conversations when you were eleven or twelve?"

"That's when I remember them starting. It could've been earlier. It wasn't until after Billie left that they became marathon, wine-laced sessions."

"Why didn't you just tell your mother that you didn't want to listen to her anymore?"

"I grew up solving my mother's problems. I carried her burdens around like boulders as though they were mine. I didn't know any better. It wasn't until I was almost out of high school that I realized I couldn't help her. Until then, I thought all of her problems were external; my father, her family, circumstances. As she spiraled downward, I realized I couldn't do anything for her."

"So your relationship with your mother changed after Billie left. You never forgave her for what she had done to her. It would be four more years before you left home. Yet you said she continued to confide in you."

"Mother didn't need more problems. She couldn't handle the ones she had, much less rejection from me. Yes, I was angry. At times, I even hated her for robbing me of part of my youth. I couldn't hurt her either. My father was doing a superb job of that. He didn't need any help from me."

"I want to go back to why your mother didn't keep her child. Doesn't this seem a little odd to you? It seems significant that she would hide her child like she did."

"I asked Billie about it once. Her father told her that Mother dumped her when she was two years old after they had gone through a nasty divorce. Shortly after my mother met my father, she supposedly ran off with him and left Billie with a sitter never to return. Billie's father filed with the court for custody."

LuAnn shook her head. "From what you've told me about your mother, this doesn't sound like her, Jack. The bond between a mother and her children is not easily broken. Have you asked your father about it?"

"A couple of times. Nothing. Says it's between Mother and him."

"And how does this strike you?"

"Like he's covering something up."

"Why haven't you kept in touch with Billie?"

"When Billie left, Mother treated her like she didn't exist. Her name was never spoken again. I saw Billie only briefly a week before Mother died. It was only by accident that I saw her. She snuck into town to see Mother. She said my mother had called and wanted to see her. We visited for a few moments, but it was apparent she wasn't comfortable. I didn't push it."

"Sounds like there is more here than you're seeing, Jack."

"I understand. I still can't forgive her for Billie. There is nothing that could justify what she did."

"I'm not asking you to forgive her." She pushed herself up from her chair and began to pace. "First, from everything you've told me about your mother, she doesn't seem like the sort to just walk off and leave her child. She had her problems, but abandonment doesn't fit.

"You were fourteen when your half-sister came to stay with you. That was thirty-four years ago, and you still carry significant anger toward your mother. Before Billie, except for problems between your mother and father, your mother was fairly happy. It was only after Billie left that your mother had thoughts of suicide. It must have been pretty serious for her to come to the end of her life and not tell you about it."

"You think they're hiding something, don't you."

"The real question is what do you think? LuAnn continued to pace with her finger pressed to her lip. I had never seen her as intense. "Jack, you need to find out what happened with your sister. She is the key to the mystery. You need to find out why your mother lost her daughter, and what happened in the summer of 1961 that caused your mother to take such rash action against your half-sister."

"What good will that do?"

"You have unresolved conflict with your mother; an open emotional wound that hasn't healed. You need to find a way past it. The fact that you and your mother share depression and thoughts of suicide has significance. I don't think you can resolve this conflict toward your mother without more information.

"You should go and talk to your father again. If he refuses to talk about it, explain to him how this is affecting you. If you want, I'll go and talk to him myself."

"You don't know my father, LuAnn." I could just see my father talking to a shrink. He already thought I was a "candy-ass wimp" because I couldn't handle my own problems. I could only imagine the things that he used to say to my mother.

"I believe that your own struggles are tied to your feelings toward your mother. You need to find out what happened." She looked at her watch, and like a conditioned dog, this was my signal to get up and leave.

As I walked to the parking lot, I dreaded the thought of dredging up all the wounds of the past with my father again. I feared a future of depression even more. I had always wondered about the secrecy surrounding Billie. In the past, it just made me hate my mother more. Mother's silence was proof that her treatment of Billie had to be appalling for her to go to such lengths to hide it.

I knew LuAnn was right. Whatever emotional short circuit existed, it was tied to my mother. There were times I felt I was reliving pieces of Mother's shredded life, as though I were drowning in her problems. I needed to know what happened. I needed to confront my father. I had to summon the courage to face him.

Four

Orlando, Florida
1995

I had always wished I could connect with my father on some emotional level. We fished together occasionally. Sometimes we drank beer together. Beyond that, I didn't know any of the mysteries of my father's mind and heart. I didn't know if he was lonely since my mother died. I didn't know if he was enjoying life. I didn't know much about the relationship he and my mother had had. We just didn't have conversations like those.

I had needed this support from my father. I had tried over the years to engage him in conversations at this level, but they had always ended up in the same place—he would give me very short answers to my questions or an argument. So we didn't talk. We fished, or we hung out in neighborhood bars and drank. We did anything that would allow us to spend minimal time together without having to talk about anything of value.

Because of this lack of conversational history, I dreaded this talk with my father. Although my father kept his anger out of sight, like the dust balls under his plainly covered bed, it lurked there in the darkness, ready to be exposed if disturbed. When I was a child, I felt the sting of his anger with the length of his belt and was a witness to the damage and existence of his temper by the all-too-frequent black and blue marks on my mother's face. Even in his seventies, I still feared him. I was not only afraid of his potential wrath, which I judged could still be formidable, I was afraid for him.

My father had worked hard all his life to build emotional walls to protect what I had always speculated to be a fragile spirit. When my mother died, he went to pieces, showing weaknesses I had never seen in him before. However, this fragile side was short lived. He mended his wounds, bound up his spirit, and pulled them back behind his well-guarded shell. If I pressed into these well-guarded areas of my father's life on Billie's behalf, I knew my father would defend them ferociously - perhaps angrily. But, he's the only one with answers. It was time for the truth: fear or no fear.

My father's home was in the older section of Orlando, near the East-West Expressway. Built in the 1920s, the house's clapboard siding had long ago been replaced with yellow and green aluminum. Stately oaks with Spanish moss casted comfortable shade across the entire yard. The canopy of trees also made the house very dark. When my father was home, regardless of the time of day, table lamps were on to brighten the house. As I walked up the steps to the front door, I marveled at the healthy state of the ligustrum hedges that my mother planted around the front screen porch when they first moved into the house. Even after all these years, my mother's green thumb was evident. pittisporum, azaleas, and podocarpus formed neat hedges along the walks, property lines, and the driveway. Confederate jasmine consumed the chain link fence that separated the front and rear yards. Although my father was no gardener, or showed any signs of becoming one, he valued the beauty of my mother's creation and paid someone to maintain the ambiance she had created.

From the brick paved street, the home was small but elegant. It was not the home I grew up in, but it would still always be home to me. It was here my mother died. Since her death, my father's house had always been a man's home. Sparse decorations and functional furniture hinted at the absence of a woman's influence. Bare countertops in the kitchen, the lack of knickknacks on coffee tables and end tables, and pictures of his friends instead of objects d'art left the home with a Spartan feel.

My father had always been an ordered man. His years in the navy, confined to the small compartments of a ship, had internalized the rituals of order. He had never been fanatical in his cleanliness. On the contrary, if one looked hard enough one found dust and dirt devils under furniture and adorning most corners. But, his clothes were always hung, and his shoes preserved with shoehorns, and most of his possessions had a place to call home. He liked life much the way he kept his house. On the surface, there was order. When you looked past the facade as few had with my father, only then did you see that his was not a perfect existence.

I moved from Hollywood, Florida to Mt. Dora after college. My parents followed me to Central Florida, but preferred the size of Orlando and its conveniences to the smallness of Mount Dora. Hollywood became a city besieged by unrestrained growth. It lost its small-town charm. My father transferred his business to Orlando after I graduated.

Before I opened the front door, I heard him yell for me to come in.

"Hey Dad," I yelled, not knowing where he was in the house.

"I'm in the bar," he said from the Florida room, once a screened-in porch that he had enclosed.

I walked through the house and out to the bar, where he was sitting drinking a beer and reading the newspaper. "How are you doing?" he asked, getting up to give me a hug.

"I guess I can't complain," I said, searching his face for signs of the mood he was in.

"Emily called me yesterday," he said, letting the statement hang in the air for effect.

"Oh?" I said as I studied the man who took his place on a bar stool next to me.

My father was a fit man for seventy-three. He looked ten years younger. Even at his age his full, thick shock of black hair had not turned completely gray. He was lean, muscular, and carried himself with a military bearing. He wore tan Bermuda shorts, a green golf shirt, and slip-on boat shoes.

"Can I get you a beer?" he asked, then drained the remaining fluid from his frosted mug. I knew the Emily-lecture was on its way. I didn't want to make it any easier by telling him what was going on. He poured me a light beer before I could answer.

"It's a good thing I really wanted one," I said with irritation.

"She's not a happy camper, Jack. I think she's going to leave you."

"Past tense, Dad. She already has."

"You're not going to let her leave, are you?"

"That's not my choice. She has to make that decision."

"What's going on?"

"What did she tell you?"

"She said your marriage was falling apart. That you were on the verge of losing your deal with R and R, and she was not going to continue to watch you throw your life away." The lecture was about to begin.

"We're having some problems."

"What kind of problems, Jack? You'd be a damn fool to let Emily slip through your fingers." Emily and Dad had hit it off from the very beginning. They connected at a level that I never could with my father. She never understood the things that troubled me about him. They were both competitive, and I both hated and envied the easy banter between them when they played pool, shot darts, or competed at anything.

"Actually, Dad, indirectly that's why I came here to talk to you."

"Talk to me? How could I possibly be involved in anything that has to do with you and Emily?"

"I've been seeing a counselor for the last two years . . ."

"A shrink you mean," he interrupted. His words stung.

"If it makes you feel better, a shrink then."

"Lot of good that has done you." He took a long pull at his beer.

"These things take time, Dad."

"Bullshit." He drained his beer, slipped off the stool of the small bar, and walked a few steps to the window.

"What does that mean?" I turned on my stool to face him.

"It means that all this stuff is bullshit." He turned to face me. "Oh, I'm soooo depressed. Oh, I'm soooo unhappy." He held his wrist to his forehead in mock sympathy. "Whine, whine, whine. Jack, I'm sick of your whining. You're a grown man, for God's sake." He walked back behind the bar and pulled another beer and frosty mug from the small refrigerator.

I was silent. While I needed to move the discussion in other directions, he had pushed me into a conversational corner. I felt like I needed to defend myself. That's the way I always felt with him.

Having taken my silence as a sign of progress, he continued. "And Emily. . . I don't understand what's going on there. Jack, she is the best thing that's ever happened to you. I don't understand how you could let her slip through your fingers." He walked around the bar and hiked himself up on the stool next to me. Resting his elbows on the bar, he turned his head toward me.

I remained silent.

He seemed to search my face for clues of my whereabouts.

"I didn't come to talk to you about Emily."

"You didn't? Your wife just left you. There can't be anything more important than that."

I cringed when I thought about his reaction to my next statement. "I want to talk to you about Mother and what happened to Billie."

"Who?" He looked genuinely clueless.

"Billie — you know, my sister. Mother's daughter. Surely you remember."

"That girl is certainly no sister of yours! What does she have to do with anything? More of your shrink nonsense?"

"LuAnn . . . Dr. Calder feels like I have some unresolved conflict with Mother over what happened with Billie."

"Unresolved conflict. Oh, that's good. Unresolved conflict." He jumped off the stool and walked around the small room waving his arms like an overweight ballerina. "The pooooor little boy has unresolved conflict." He sang the words with a falsetto voice. "I can't believe you've bought this bullshit. No wonder Emily's leaving you. That faggot shrink of yours could depress Prozac."

My father's ridicule stung with familiarity. It wasn't only the criticism that singed me, it was the revelation of my stupidity and my lack of value that laced his every word and wounded me to the soul. A novel of words shaped and formed like these, in countless attempts to link with my father, have led to our estrangement. I have often wondered how my father had maintained such an edge in our war of words. I'm paid to turn the unique, witty phrase. When I prepared for discussions with my father, in my practice, I always found the right words. But, when I faced him, I ended up at the place I am now angry, frustrated, and silenced.

Normally, at this point, all my emotional fuses have blown and I have stormed from the house.

Instead, I let silence fall between us. He closed the few paces that separated us and put his hand on my back just at the base of my neck, no doubt sensing my lack of response as an affirmation of his wisdom. I breathed deeply. He returned to his stool.

"I don't want a fight, Dad. I need your help."

"Who's fighting? I just think you're wasting your time with this mental masturbation. I think we can decide whether we are to be happy or miserable. It's a choice. It's as simple as flipping a mental switch. You have the power to either let this stuff eat your life up, or to change it. It's a decision. Only you can make it."

I loathed these "pull yourself up by your bootstrap" discussions. These "I give ulcers, I don't get them" philosophies of my father's. . . They are demonstrated by the emotional debris in the lives of people who orbit him — Mother being the first to come to mind.

My patience thinned. I swiveled my chair around to face him. "I want to talk to you about Billie."

My father's jaw muscles tightened. He started to say something, but swallowed the words before they passed his lips. "What help do you need from me?" His tone was barely conciliatory.

"Tell me about what happened the summer she came to stay with us."

His eyes narrowed into slits. "Where are we going with this?"

"I want to know why Billie left."

"What can this possibly have to do with you and Emily?"

"Nothing. I didn't come here to talk about Emily. I want to know what happened to Billie."

"There's nothing to tell." He looked at me, almost straight through me, as though he were looking back into the past. "She decided she didn't want to stay with us anymore, and she left. That's all there is to it."

"Why didn't she want to stay? She didn't say anything to me about being unhappy."

"She wasn't unhappy with us. She wanted to be on her own."

I remembered the day Billie left. Mother brought her to the paddleball courts to say goodbye. Mother asked me to come with them, but I declined. Mother gave us a minute to be together before they left. Billie told me that the time she had spent with us was the happiest of her life, and that she couldn't understand why she had been asked to leave.

I turned and looked at Dad. "I don't believe that. I know she was happy with us. She didn't want to leave. What's the mystery?"

"There's no mystery. You're trying to make something out of nothing. She wanted to leave, and we gave her a bus ticket and took her to the station."

"Why didn't you and Mother keep Billie when she was a baby?"

"Not this again. I've told you. We've been over this before. Your mother lost a custody suit to her ex-husband. She was well cared for."

"Mom told me once that she left Billie with a sitter when you went off to get married and go on your honeymoon. Billie's father filed for custody because Billie was abandoned. Is this true?"

"I don't know what your mother told you. I promised your mother I wouldn't discuss this with you. This happened a long time ago. Let's just leave it there."

"Can't you just tell me? Is this true or not?"

"Yes it's true. Now, let's just leave it there."

"How could someone get custody of Billie for leaving them with a sitter for a week, Dad?"

"That's the end of this discussion."

"All I want from you is the truth. What's so hard about that?"

"I've given you the truth. Your mother has given you the truth. You just won't accept it."

"If this is the truth, then why did you promise Mother that you wouldn't discuss it with me?"

"I'm going to end this discussion, now. What went on between your mother and Billie were personal things, things she asked me to keep private. I intend to do just that."

"What did she do that was so horrible that she didn't want you to tell me?"

"This conversation is over. Your mother was a good woman. The best. I'm not going to sit here while you malign her."

Dad stood up and walked toward the front door.

I got off the stool. I was angry I hadn't learned any more than I already knew. I walked past him as he stood by the front door to usher me out. "I'm going to find out what happened, Dad. You can't protect her forever."

"Boy, I'm going to give you some real good advice . . ."

I stopped at the doorway. He had one hand wrapped around the doorknob and the other on his hip.

"This shrink has got you on a ghost chase, son. Emily needs you. You should be focused on your problems, not your dead mother's."

I looked at his angry eyes with both frustration and love. I left without saying anything, more determined now to find out what happened.

Five

Orlando, Florida
1995

The meeting with my father left me wounded and angry. My emotional wounds went deeper than this temporary and inconsequential hurt. Ever since I left LuAnn Calder's office the day before, I had been struggling with the grudge against my mother and how it began. I drove around Orlando aimlessly, past Lake Eola Park, through downtown, onto Interstate 4 West toward Disney World and the attractions. As I pulled away from downtown, I tried to think about the times when writing had been exciting, when I could spend hours with a pencil and yellow pad and pour out my soul. I tried to think of the very first things I had written and the joy they had brought me. It was then that I thought of my old friend from my childhood, Malcolm, the doorman at the Hollywood Beach Hotel.

Even more than Mother, Malcolm had tapped into the deep well of my imagination and had shown me the wonderment of the commonplace. With his booming, heavily accented voice he would say, "The best ingredients of stories are those that come from everyday living."

"Well, Malcolm, wherever you are now," — I looked up and away from the windshield for a second — "the only stories that could come from my life right now are horror stories." Right then I missed him terribly. Malcolm had filled my creative tank like no other person in my life.

I turned south on the Florida Turnpike. It had been years since I had visited Hollywood. Since I left in 1966, I had had no desire to return to painful memories. Today I needed to reconnect with those memories. Even though Malcolm was dead, I needed to reconnect with his inspiration.

Hollywood, Florida
June 1961

Normally, my mother looked through the mail as though she was posted in the desert, and the mail was her only source of outside communications with the world. Today she looked for something special.

The table in the small, cramped kitchen was still littered with breakfast dishes, and Mother returned to her chair, coffee cup to the right and ashtray filled with half-smoked cigarette butts on the left. I could hear her two-pack-a-day raspy breath as she excitedly flipped through the stack of mail.

"Oh my God, Darlin', its here." She bolted from the chair and danced around the kitchen shrieking. "It's here. I knew it. I knew it." She held the letter to her chest and looked at the light fixture in the ceiling. "Oh, God. Please. Please. Please."

She opened her eyes and looked down at the envelope. "I'm afraid to open it, Jack."

"Who's the letter from, Mother?"

"Sugar, you know full well who it's from." She started to peel back the corner flap of the envelope and stopped. "I'm excited and scared all at the same time."

"Who's it from?" I asked more forcefully.

"The Tattler, silly."

"Mom, you promised me you wouldn't do it."

"I lied." She spun on her heels with the letter pressed to her chest, like a young girl might embrace a love letter from a distant young man. Lightheaded from spinning around, she dropped to her seat, upset the table and nearly turned over her coffee cup.

"Let's find out what they said." She ripped open the envelope, flipped open the letter, and scanned down the single page. She inhaled deeply, her mouth dropped open, and she began to shriek again and bounced up and down in the chair. "You've won! You've won!"

She jumped from the chair and pulled me up by my shoulders. She danced and jumped around the kitchen and dragged me with her. "Let me read this to you." She pushed me back into my chair and sat down. Her small thin hands trembled as she held the letter up and read it.

"Dear Master Jack McNamara. We are pleased to inform you that your short story, The Doorman, has won first prize in the Hollywood Sun-Tattler's annual short-fiction contest, in the age fourteen-to-eighteen class." She turned from the letter, tears streaming down her cheeks. "Oh, Jack, I'm so proud of you." She continued reading. "'You have won a cash prize of fifty dollars, and your story will appear in a special edition of the paper, the first week in July."

The letter fell to her lap. She reached across the corner of the table and brushed my cheek with the palm of her small hand. "I told you, you have talent. Now everyone in Hollywood knows it, too! Another Ernest Hemingway. One of these days, you'll be a famous writer and win the Nobel Prize for literature, just like he did. God, I can't believe you won that contest. Aren't you excited?"

Outwardly, I was angry Mother had not told me she had submitted my story to the paper. Inwardly, I couldn't contain my joy. "Why didn't you tell me you were going to send them that story?"

"You would've whined and carried on so."

"Well how would you feel if I sent one of your drawings into that matchbook company you're always talking about?"

"There's a big difference between you and me, son. You have talent, and I have a letter here from the Sun-Tattler to prove it. Wait until your father sees this. He'll be so proud." She lit a cigarette and smoke bellowed in the living room.

"I want you to run down to the hotel and show this letter to Malcolm. He'll be so excited for you."

Hollywood Beach, Florida
1995

As I drove through town, I was amazed at the change in Hollywood Boulevard. West Hollywood, which, in 1961, was mostly pine trees, palmettos, and swampland, had been developed with strip malls, housing developments, and apartments from McArthur High School, in West Hollywood, all the way to the Everglades. The filling station I had worked at in Hollywood Hills had been converted to a convenience store. The Florida Theatre, where The Guns of Navarone, To Kill a Mockingbird, and The Great Escape had come to play, had been torn down. When I made the turn around Young Circle and headed east on Hollywood Boulevard toward the beach, I was not prepared for the site of the Hollywood Beach Hotel painted flamingo pink. I would hate for Malcolm to see what they had done to his hotel.

The Hollywood Beach Hotel, opened in 1926 by Joseph Young, rose up on the horizon as the focal point of the drive down Hollywood Boulevard to the beach. The stately royal palms that lined Hollywood

Boulevard between U.S. 1 and the Intracoastal Waterway could not improve upon the ghastly sight. The once splendid and regal white structure that graced the beach skyline was now tarnished and tawdry. The old drawbridge in front of the Hollywood Beach Hotel that had connected the mainland with the beach had been removed and replaced by a high, fixed structure that was tall enough to allow boat traffic underneath and to block the view of one of the few remaining grand hotels in the country. To build the new bridge structure, the state had taken most of the grounds in front of the aging hotel. The once elegant grounds, with the curved pretentious drive to the grand entrance, had been ravaged by pilings and concrete ramps. Now vehicular traffic turned onto A1A on a semicircular ramp within spitting distance of the once splendid structure.

The grounds that weren't taken by the bridge were consumed by a new cinema complex built to the right of the bridge and abutted the now gaudy pink structure. From the signs I could see as I drove by, the hotel had been turned into condominiums and shops.

Three blocks past the hotel, I turned down our old street toward the ocean. The homes along the short block between A1A and the beach looked remarkably the same as they had in 1961 when I left my house to tell Malcolm about winning the Sun-

Tattler writing award. Our old house had been painted a pastel aqua color, but the low one-story bungalow with Spanish arches and white barrel-tile roof had not changed. I parked my car near the Broad Walk, an asphalt walkway that separated the sand of the beach from civilization.

Coconut palms lined the Broad Walk on the ocean side, and shops, apartments, motels, and restaurants lined the other. I turned south on the Broad Walk toward the hotel. Cyclists, rollerbladers, and walkers clogged the pavement. Each street on the beach side dead-ended into the Broad Walk where vehicular traffic was prohibited. Park benches, occupied by the elderly and people-watchers, faced the ocean and served as barricades at the end of each street.

In my youth, well manicured St. Augustine lawns and landscaping decorated the grounds of apartments and motels on the Broad Walk opposite the beach. Now, every square inch of space had been filled with bars, restaurants, and T-shirt shops, giving it the appearance of a true "boardwalk."

Even the commercialism of the Broad Walk could not rob Hollywood Beach of its charm. The Hispanic influence on South Florida was evident. The melodic Spanish language floated through the crowd of passers-by. The dark hair, olive skin, and bold colors of immigrants added to the charm of the place I remembered as home.

As I retraced the steps I had taken as a fourteen-year-old boy bringing Malcolm the good news of my story, my heart sank as I saw the Hollywood Beach Hotel looking very much the whore now.

Malcolm Cambridge, born in Jamaica, was formerly a manservant to railroad empire builder Henry Flagler. Historians credited Flagler with opening Florida to development with the construction of the Florida East Coast Railroad from Jacksonville to Key West. Cambridge was with Flagler at the opening ceremonies of the Hollywood depot of the Florida East Coast Railroad in 1924. Malcolm met the founder of Hollywood, Joseph Young, who was looking for a bell captain and head-doorman for the Great Southern Hotel, which was opened in less than a week of their meeting. Young was so impressed with the black man's demeanor and British-island accent he offered Malcolm the job on the spot. When Young's lavish Hollywood Beach Hotel opened in February of 1926, he moved Malcolm there as head doorman. In 1961, Malcolm Cambridge was the only employee in the hotel who had been there since its opening.

Malcolm's tales of the Hollywood Beach Hotel had set my young imagination on fire. His melodic voice and skills and enthusiasm as a storyteller hooked me as surely as Santiago hooked the great Marlin in Hemingway's The Old Man and the Sea.

The short story, The Doorman, was about the surprise Hurricane of 1926 that hit the hotel and the fledgling, newly-created city of Hollywood only seven months after the hotel's opening. Malcolm was the only hotel employee on site who had any medical training when the hurricane made landfall late one evening in August 1926. A young woman, pregnant and nearing delivery, went into labor spurred by the excitement of the storm. Malcolm was called to assist with the birthing. Even with her contractions increasing in frequency, the young woman refused Malcolm's help because of his color. It was only after Malcolm had fraudulently convinced her that he was part of the royal family in Jamaica, made believable because of his thickly royal accent, did the young woman agree to let Malcolm deliver her child. Only when the woman later saw Malcolm standing at his post at the hotel's grand portico, did she realize she had been duped.

But she did not repay Malcolm's ruse with revenge. Instead, she named her son after him and lavished small gifts upon him at each monthly anniversary of her son's birth until she left the Monday after Easter Sunday, 1927. Malcolm had saved her baby's life. To her, Malcolm was a hero, regardless of his racial standing.

With Malcolm's permission, I recounted the story, changed names and embellished the plot, but stuck to the heart of Malcolm's incredible story of bigotry overcome. The short story came to me at the pinnacle of racial unrest in the South. The newspapers were filled with blatant examples of the injustices perpetrated on the "coloreds."

Malcolm had also provided the plot for one of my first novels, and the Hollywood Beach Hotel was the backdrop. In 1934, Malcolm had been accused of raping a young betrothed woman, a guest in the hotel, who had come from Long Island to marry one of the few stockbrokers who had made money in the stock market's devastating decline. She had had an affair with a black man in Long Island prior to coming south to prepare for the wedding. Her pregnancy sealed Malcolm's fate. Surrounded by family, and in an unfamiliar environment, she had no opportunity to abort the child. Not wanting to lose her fiancé and the wealth he would bring to their union, she set about framing Malcolm to cover her infidelity.

The hotel fired Malcolm immediately. The then bankrupt Joseph Young, who lost his fortune in the stock market crash, had to sell the hotel to remain solvent. Still living in Hollywood, he intervened on Malcolm's behalf with local police. He provided an attorney for Malcolm who demanded the young woman undergo a medical examination. A physician determined that the woman was pregnant and had been pregnant for more than a month before she claimed she had been raped. When confronted with the medical evidence, she confessed the ruse. All charges against Malcolm were dropped, and he was restored to his post.

The first floor of the hotel had now been converted to a small shopping mall. Only the door and chandelier of the original entrance remained. The rest of the lobby had been cut up into shops. Malcolm's station just outside the door, where he stood his post for thirty-nine years until his death in 1966, was one of the few things in the hotel still familiar to me. I could still picture him standing guard at the door of the Hollywood Beach Hotel, dressed in the uniform of a doorman. He wore a maroon, military-type jacket with gold, embroidered epaulets and gold braid. A white, starched shirt and black tie added to the formality of the uniform. Malcolm was meticulous about his appearance. He always had a spit shine on the black bill of his hat and black shoes.

When I brought the good news of the award to Malcolm in 1961, the hotel, shabbily past its prime, was nearly empty, relying on convention traffic to keep the lights on. It would be five more years before Malcolm died from cancer. Malcolm guessed his age in 1961 as 59, but I thought he was probably nearer to 75. It didn't matter. Malcolm was a fixture. As long as the hotel stayed open, he would be the doorman.

Malcolm's wide expressive face, thick formal British accent, and the way the words would roll like syrup off his tongue made me yearn to create and tell stories that would affect others the way Malcolm had motivated me. As I stood on the spot where the old hotel bell stand stood, I heard the cadence of Malcolm's deep and booming voice as he told the story of the Great Miami Hurricane of 1926. I could hear his thunderous laugh as he had spun the yarn of how the hotel had been drafted into the navy and turned into a training facility during World War II. And it was Malcolm who let me roam the vast decaying hotel to search out the stories of its heyday. Malcolm taught me to imagine and dream.

I missed him now. I looked around at what was left of the lobby again. I was saddened that the place that had influenced me so had come to such a sad end. Despite its bawdy appearance, standing in such familiar surroundings made me think of the pure pleasure I drew from my writing then, and the strength I drew from Malcolm's praise as he read through and approved my insignificant stories. It also reminded me of how much my mother supported my writing, and the part she played in solidifying the bond between Malcolm and me. As much as Malcolm provided the inspiration, Mother was an ever present encourager. She created in me an excitement about writing. It was ironic that she had been such a positive catalyst in the embryonic stages of my development as a writer, and now was the cause of my failure.

Six

Hollywood Beach, Florida
1995

I reversed course, left the hotel, and walked north on the Broad Walk. Even in the height of the tourist season, Hollywood Beach was never this crowded in 1961. Hollywood Beach was an idyllic place to grow up and, until Billie changed the course of our lives, it was just a notch short of paradise.

I found an unoccupied park bench along the Broad Walk. Anxious to explore a beach I hadn't seen in more than twenty-five years, I was compelled to sit and drink in the sights and sounds of my youth. Nearing late afternoon, a brisk ocean breeze sent fronds from the palm trees into an un-choreographed dance. Propelled by gusting winds, sand blew in fine trails across the asphalt, collecting in the doorways of the shops. Only a block south of my old street, the moisture-laden air, the smell of briny water, and the sound of chest-high waves as they collapsed on shore triggered memories long forgotten. The smell of donuts frying in a bakery could still bring me back to the mornings I used to fold newspapers for my paper route in front of Watson's donut shop. Carried back by the familiar sensations, I could picture myself as a child as I ran and played at the water's edge, my light brown hair bleached blonde by the sun and salt water. The uniform of the day was bronze skin, bare feet, and a powder blue sun-faded bathing suit.

I had always had a special relationship with the ocean. I had never been successful in living more than an hour's drive away from it. Growing up, the ocean and beach was a playground, a daycare, a companion in the absence of friends, and a place to sit and work out the challenges of growing up. My first kiss, first sexual encounter, and my first proposal of marriage all happened here on the sand of this beach. For more than fifteen of the eighteen years that I lived here, most of life's needs were met here within two hundred yards of the ocean.

But, it is also the place I couldn't wait to leave. It was on this beach that the seeds of hatred toward Mother were sown, the day she threw Billie out. It was on this beach that I wrestled with the many concerns that made mother want to end her life and the guilt of wishing she would.

I looked north on the Broad Walk. It had been a demarcation between my world and Mother's. When I walked down the few doors from our house to the Broad Walk and stepped over it into the sand on the beach, I had found a way to leave the unpleasantness of her world at its edge. Once on the sand, I was protected, shielded. On my mother's side of the Broad Walk, I could only listen to her many emotionally draining problems. On my side of the Broad Walk, I could think more clearly and sometimes find solutions I could offer her. Mostly, as a teen, sitting by the water's edge, my case against my mother was built brick by emotional brick. It became a place of waiting for the day to arrive when I could get away. The Broad Walk was an emotional line not even my father could penetrate. He came very close.

Hollywood Beach, Florida
June, 1961

I owe my love of the early morning to my father. He always arose at 5:30 a.m. and either walked or rode a bike, a ritual that continued for some time. One evening at dinner, I asked him if I could come with him the next morning. He didn't answer at first. He looked at Mother, then at me. "I see no reason why we can't do that."

I could tell he didn't relish the idea. It wasn't until I was older that I realized the value of having time alone. This was his time, and I had invaded it.

"I'm only going to try to wake you once. If I have to fight with you to get you up, I'm going to let you sleep." I was eleven the morning we began this ritual. With his admonition fresh in my head, I was awake the first morning at 3:30 a.m. Afraid that he would leave me, I would be awake every morning when he put his hand on my shoulder.

When I think of my father, these times in the early morning hours are the most cherished. I had him all to myself for an hour or so every morning. If he minded my company, he never said. At times we rode our bikes the mile or two into Hollywood as a break from the routine. On rare occasions, we rode A1A to Hallandale Beach. Most mornings, we walked the length of the Broad Walk.

As often as we watched the sun come up over the Atlantic, I had never tired of it. And, although the event occurred every morning, he would always say to me, "Isn't it beautiful?" Frequently he would follow it with, "You know, just like the prints on your fingers, there are no two sunrises alike."

There was always been a strength in my father that I have admired. A sureness. A true sense of direction. He never ruminated over a decision. His nanosecond decision-making ability was legendary. And once the decision was made, there was no qualitative analysis. "If I made it, it must be right." This cock-sure journey through life was not without blemish or spot. As an executive of the phone company, his superiors promoted him with regularity. His self-starting, self-confident style won kudos for accomplishment. His "my way or the highway" approach to management was not without critics. He was the most positive person I had ever met when it came to his abilities, talents, and prospects. This was not the case with his attitude about the people who surrounded him, at work or home. My relationship with him always had limitations due to this flaw. We didn't have conversations. When we talked, he lectured, and I listened. He had always stated things that had left little or no room for conversation or argument. "Kennedy's a faggot. No balls," he would say. A fan of Kennedy, I would defend my idol, which would be followed by a barrage of criticism, or I could say, "Uh, huh," agreeing with him and avoiding certain confrontation. His island of self-assuredness was surrounded by a sea of incompetence. No one did anything as well as my father. No one understood life quite as well as he did.

On the morning after Mother received notification from the newspaper that I had won the fiction contest we went for our usual walk down the Broad Walk. The memory of this walk with my father had particular clarity. It was on this Broad Walk after we walked its length and reversed direction toward home that the conversation I can recall almost to the word took place. Many mornings our walks were accomplished in almost total silence. Our conversations fell into two categories: small talk or analysis of things I had done or was about to do. None of these left me feeling particularly skillful in managing life's challenges.

"I want to talk to you about this writing stuff." The words came out, "I . . .want . . . to . . .talk . . .to .

. .you . . ." the words punctuated by his 6 foot 2 inch, 225-pound frame as he slammed his feet to the pavement.

I didn't say anything. I just waited. His gait slowed then he stopped. Not in all the mornings that we walked together, even at his most critical appraisal of something I had done, did we ever stop walking. He looked over my head at the sun bleeding out onto the water at the horizon. The air was still, lifeless. Never once, until the very end of his speech, did he look directly at me. He looked either at his tennis shoes, which shuffled on the pavement, or at the ocean painted orange and yellow with fresh sunlight.

"Your mother's a dreamer. She's been filling your head with this writing dream of hers. I don't know." He shuffled his feet as if it could uncover the words he wanted by brushing the sand off the pavement. The silence conveyed his displeasure.

I knew my father did not approve of my mother's flights of creative fancy. Her efforts to draw the animals on the matchbook covers were, in his opinion, nothing more than a fraud perpetrated by some enterprising entrepreneur to part money from the unsuspecting lamb for art lessons. Her fractional manuscripts on which she spent her free time, in my father's opinion, did not have the potential for development. According to my father, they were the principle reason the house was disorganized and meals were not prepared on time.

"I know you like to write . . ."

"I love to write, Dad."

"That's your mother's bullshit, Jackie. You just think you like it. Your mother's brainwashing you with this stuff."

"She's not brainwashing me. I love to write. It's fun, Dad."

"Bullshit. Your mother has been shoving this stuff down your throat. She's driven herself crazy with this junk, and she's going to drive you crazy, too."

Bullshit. Another word for "you couldn't possibly feel that way." Another word for, "that's what you think you want to do." Another word for, "I've decided you're too stupid to know your own mind on this."

"Mom has nothing to do with it. I want to write. I like doing it."

"Most writers are either poor, faggots, or lunatics." Faggot was a term my father used to describe homosexuals, or odd people who didn't fit the mold he considered normal. "Few of them ever succeed."

"Hemingway succeeded. He won the Nobel Prize."

"He's a pervert, and he's as fruity as a Waldorf salad."

"He is not. Hemingway is one of the most respected writers in America." You could never tell my father he was wrong. As soon as the words slipped from my lips, I knew I would regret my indiscretion.

"The poor little faggot is in the Mayo Clinic, suffering from a nervous breakdown."

I could feel the anger build in my throat. "He is not." I paused a second to keep the anger from moving from my throat to my words. "He has high blood pressure."

"I don't want to burst that little bubble of yours, but he tried to commit suicide. The little faggot's depressed. They're giving him shock treatments. He's as wacko as Harpo Marx."

"That's not true." I had read in the newspaper that he had returned to the hospital when previous efforts to cure his hypertension had failed. The Sun-Tattler reported that there were rumors of depression, but both the hospital and the family denied them.

He grabbed me by the shoulders and turned me to face him. It was then he looked at me directly. "Your mother is making herself just as sick as Hemingway . . ."

"How can you say that?"

"I'm telling you, boy, your mother's sick. All she can think about is writing. I've told her it'll never amount to anything, and I'm telling you the same thing. If you persist in this obsession of yours, if you let your mother continue to fill your head with this nonsense, you'll end up as crazy as your mother . . . as wacko as Hemingway."

A wave of courage flooded me. "All Mom needs is some words of praise. All you do is cut her down and criticize her. You make her feel like a failure. That's what makes her feel bad, not the writing." Before the words were completely out of my mouth, I saw the back of his hand come up from his waist. I tried to move my face from its path of flight, but I was too slow. I turned my face just enough to catch the back of his hand with my ear. The pain on impact sent me to the pavement. He reached down and grabbed me by my T-shirt ready to strike again, but he cooled enough to gain his composure. With my T-shirt still in his balled fist, he pulled me close to his face. White spittle adorned the corners of his mouth.

"Don't you ever talk to me like that again." I could barely hear the words for the ringing and pain in my ear. He let go of my shirt, the red slowly flushing from his face. "You persist in this writing fantasy of yours and you'll end up like Hemingway, a nut case."

My father walked off toward the house. We were only a few blocks from home. I crossed the line off the Broad Walk and into the sanctuary of the beach. I sat next to a sandcastle that looked as disheveled as I felt.

Hollywood Beach, Florida
1995

Sitting on the park bench, I could look down the Broad Walk toward where the Casino Pool had been and identify the spot where my father's prophetic and all-too true prediction was made. I had made up my mind then to make writing my life's pursuit. The anger at his words ignited a roaring fire of determination to succeed. Somewhere that flame dwindled away and was extinguished. Then, there seemed to be nothing I could do to get even with my father short of proving him wrong. Now, as I thought about how hurtful his words had been, in some dark and cavernous place in me, as I replayed the scene with my father in my memory, I again wanted to prove him wrong. Though the flame did not roar with the intensity of my youth, I felt the warmth of its existence and drew comfort from it.

Seven

Hollywood Beach, Florida
1961

The walk home after my father's homily about the writing profession left me drained and angry, but determined. The pop on the ear didn't hurt nearly as much as the failure to please him. I felt small, insignificant, and stupid. The day was isn't over yet.

From the kitchen, I could hear the shower running in the master bedroom. I wasn't prepared to face him just yet anyway. A coffee cup, ashtray, pack of cigarettes and a Zippo lighter sat at Mother's appointed station at the kitchen table. This is where Mother and I spent so much of our time talking together. This was her executive workstation and from it, she ran the affairs of the McNamara household.

When she came from her bedroom into the kitchen, her eyes were swollen and red. She marshaled her composure, but barely.

"What's the matter, Mom?" I put my arm around her.

"I'm fine, really." She fussed with her hair and stretched a smile across a face still wet with lingering tears.

"Dad and I got into it this morning, too." I put my hand to my ear.

"He hit you, didn't he?" Her green eyes narrowed.

"It didn't hurt that much." I rubbed my sore ear, the pain fading.

"What did he say to you?" She looked over her shoulder toward the bedroom, but the shower was still running.

"He gave me a lecture about writing and that I'd end up as crazy as Hemingway."

"I don't know about Hemingway, but your father is right when he says that writing is a very difficult business to make a living in."

"He told you to tell me that didn't he?" I could just imagine the lecture he had given her about turning his son into a little faggot.

She pulled at the lapels of her bathrobe, then reached for the pack of cigarettes, and tamped the filtered end on the tabletop, a longstanding habit from smoking non-filtered cigarettes. She popped open a small Zippo lighter with a snap of her fingers, a trick she had learned when she worked in the navy yard. Smoke filled the small kitchen with an acrid smell.

"You have a lot of talent, Darlin'. It isn't just your knack with words. You see things. For a young man of fourteen you have insights into life that many people don't have. It would be a shame to see that talent wasted. I think your father is just worried about your having a career and being able to make a decent living."

"What did he say to you?"

"That's not important."

"He blamed you for my wanting to write, didn't he?"

"Your father loves you very much, Darlin'. He's just worried about you. Wants to make sure you do the right thing."

"Did he hit you, too?"

"No."

"Then why were you crying when I came in? Was it because of me?"

The noise from the shower stopped. I could see Mother tense. She put her unfinished cigarette in the ashtray and headed for the bedroom. I snuck a puff of her cigarette and returned it to the ashtray. A few minutes later she emerged from the bedroom with father behind her dressed in a white shirt and tie, smelling of Old Spice aftershave. He gave me a wary look, kissed Mother on the top of the head, and left.

At thirty-six, my mother was still a very attractive woman. A petite frame, light brown shoulder-length hair, emerald-green eyes, and disarming smile added charm to her beauty. There was an air of graciousness in my mother's ways. She was persuasive and gentle and she made growing up in her home pleasant. As long suffering as Mother was, she had a temper if provoked.

My mother's slovenly ways did not sit well with my father. It was not in Mother's nature to keep a neat house. My mother had to work hard just to keep a semblance of order in our home. And even as hard as she struggled to develop the habits that would please my father, it was never enough. My room was always a source of contention between my father and I, and indirectly a source of friction between my parents.

The week before, my mother's fear of reprisals from my father, and my repeated failure to clean my room as she asked me, sent her into a tirade.

"Jackie McNamara, you get your butt into this kitchen right now!"

I knew my mother was mad and meant it when she called me by my full name. I ran to the kitchen. She fumed, ready to pounce. Mother was four feet eleven inches. Even though I hadn't started my growth spurt that would send me to five foot ten by the end of the summer, I was still a full head and a half taller than she. When I got to the kitchen, she pulled out a stool she used to get to the high shelves in the cabinets, put it in front of me and climbed to the top step. From her perch, she towered over me, and pointed a short slender finger in my face.

She looked toward my room off the kitchen. "That place isn't fit for a pig. Cockroaches wouldn't set foot in that dump in there. I'm at the end of my rope with you, mister. Your father will kill you and me both if . . ."

Impulsively, I reached up and tickled her at the waist before she had the chance to finish her sentence. I already had heard this lecture enough times to know how it ended. She jerked away from my hand, and almost lost her balance. A small crack of a smile appeared at the corner of her mouth, but disappeared quickly as the fire returned to her eyes.

She nearly yelled, "Jack McNamara . . ."

I seized the opportunity and struck again. This time I didn't hold back. I grabbed her at the waist and ground in my fingers, which sent her into a writhing fit. With her standing on the top step of the stool, I had her trapped. It was too far for her to fall, and she didn't have enough control over her body to step down the steps. She was laughing uncontrollably.

"I may be laughing on the outside, Jackie McNamara, but I'm mad as hell on the inside." She sputtered the words out and laughed without restraint. I finally abandoned my assault. She stepped down from the ladder, looked at me, and began to laugh. I was laughing, too, now picturing the absurdity of her standing on the stool and waving that finger in my face. "Stop," she said, crossing her legs at the knees. "You're going to make me pee in my pants."

When I think of my mother, this is the picture I will hold dear for eternity; her bent over at the waist and laughing, wheezing, and coughing all at the same time, worrying she would wet her pants. This was Mother at her best, freed, if only for a moment, of the weight of the baggage of her life. I never saw my mother laugh with anyone the way she did with me. As mad as she got, once provoked, it was gone in a flash.

That morning the tears and the puffiness of her eyes were not the product of anger, but of hurt.

"Tell me what's wrong. What happened this morning?" I sat down at my usual place at the table across from my mother.

She looked at me and tears welled up. She looked away, then back, then down at the table. "I have something I need to talk to you about." She looked at me again, as though trying to gauge my reaction before she spoke. "Do you remember that phone call last night?"

"You mean the one from the lady?"

"Yes." She reached for the cigarettes and went through the ritualistic lighting. She swallowed a large puff of smoke, exhaled, pointing the stream of smoke away from the table and me. "This is so difficult."

"Just tell me. Who is this lady?"

"Before I met your father, I was married to someone else." She paused and let the sentence find root. "I was very young and anxious to get away from a very abusive stepfather. I unwisely married someone to get out of the house. I was only sixteen then." She reached across the table and grabbed my hand, but I drew it away.

"You were married before?" I felt betrayed.

"I had a little girl, Billie."

I couldn't believe the words coming out of her mouth. It was like having a stranger off the Broad Walk come in, sit down at our table, and tell us about their family.

"Who is the lady that called . . .?"

". . . She's your sister." Mother took a long drag off her cigarette and searched my face for clues to my reaction.

"Sister?" I mouthed the words without connection. "I have a sister?"

"She'll be coming to stay with us for a while."

"Stay with us?" It was like a movie, where the voice and picture were uncoordinated. Her revelations were slightly ahead of my comprehension.

All of a sudden, I felt like I was sitting with a total stranger. I thought I knew my mother. She had told me all of her deepest secrets for as long as I had memories. She talked to me because she couldn't talk to my father. Every dream she ever had she laid at my feet, sometimes with unfulfilled tears and at other times with the joy and hope that one day, they would be realized. She never said a critical word about my father, but I knew the pain that he had caused her. I was her closest confidant. This made me feel special, that I had a place in my mother's heart that not even my father could penetrate. Now to find out that there was an entire life that she had not shared with me made me feel as insignificant as my father had made me feel earlier that day.

At fourteen, I wore the virtues of my parents not having had the chance to sew the garments of my own. Since I was old enough to be taught, it was drilled into me by the nuns at school that divorce was wrong and not permitted by the Church. I never gave a thought to the validity of the rule. I never thought about it at all. Now my mother, who had helped me learn my catechism, read me stories at bedtime about Jesus and the apostles, Noah, David and Goliath, who sat next to me in church and took Holy Communion with me, who by her silence indicated her complete and total support for what the Church had taught me, revealed, now, after all these years, that she was divorced.

We sat in silence. I couldn't think of what to say. I didn't feel that important to her or special any longer. I didn't realize I was crying until tears fell from my cheek to my hands folded on my lap. "Why didn't you tell me?"

Even though tears streamed down from her eyes, her voice was calm and level. "When you were younger, I just felt like you were too young to understand. Then it was something that I meant to tell you about, but put it off until the right moment came along. The right moment never came. I'm sorry. I wouldn't hurt you for anything in the world." She reached out to me again, but I wouldn't take her hand. My mother was a toucher. Her affection could only be administered through her hands. I could not think of a time in my young life when I didn't feel completely loved, my mother's touch the only reminder I needed. To deny her the reassurance of a touch hurt her deeply.

"I'm very sorry. I never meant for this to be a hurt for you. It was just something about which I was not anxious to tell you. Please don't be upset with me."

"Who were you married to?" The words were propelled by anger and hurt feelings.

"Bill St. John. I was a waitress in a restaurant. He had a little antique business in Charleston."

"Why did you get a divorce?" I almost spit the word DIVORCE out like the unpardonable sin that it was.

"Darlin', I got married for all the wrong reasons. I wanted to run away from my father. Getting married was the easiest way to do that. After five years of living with a man I didn't love, I just couldn't do it anymore."

"Why did you want to get away from your father?" After the bout I had with my father earlier, I could understand what my own motivation would be.

"I'm not going into all of it, but let me just say that he was a very evil man. I wanted to run away, but we were very poor. I didn't have any money. Getting married was the easiest way out, but a very stupid way to solve the problem."

"Why didn't Billie stay with you?" I didn't know a lot about divorce then, but I knew enough that the children usually stayed with their mother.

"When your father and I got married we wanted to move to Florida, away from Charleston. Billie's father and I went to court both asking for custody. Since most of Billie's family lived in Charleston, the judge decided that Billie would be better off with her father."

"Why haven't we gone to meet them or to see them?"

Mother sat back in the chair with her arms folded across her chest. She seemed detached, withdrawn, mechanically answering my questions.

"The divorce was an ugly one. Billie's father was very angry with me for the divorce and that I wanted to take Billie to Florida. After he got custody of her, he filled her head with lies about me. Your father and I didn't have a lot of money. In those days, after the war, it cost a lot to travel to Charleston. When we did go to Charleston Billie's father made it difficult for us to see her. He had told her so many things about us that weren't true; she was afraid of me. I'd send her letters, birthday and Christmas cards, but I never got a reply. I finally just gave up trying to communicate with her. Divorce is a hard thing, Darlin'. That's why it's good not to get one, because it's the children that suffer the most."

"So why is Billie coming to see you, now, after all these years?"

"I don't know. However, she sounded like she needed someone. She was very upset. She wouldn't tell me what the problem was."

"When will she be here?"

"Tomorrow morning. She leaves on a bus from Charleston tonight."

I couldn't begin to sort through all my feelings. A sister! As an only child, I had thought many times about the possibility of having brothers and sisters. For the first time, I began to think about my mother. Even though she held her emotions tightly, she was visibly shaken.

"Is she what has you so upset?

"This morning has not been good. I'm worried about you and your dad. I'm worried about Billie coming. Mostly I'm worried about how you're feeling. Jackie, I'm so sorry I haven't told you about Billie before this. I hope you can understand that it was something of which I'm not proud. It was easier just not telling you."

At the time, her explanation satisfied me. She was hurting. It was my self-appointed role to be her comforter and encourager. Searching her puffy face and eyes, I hurt for her, and my anger faded.

"It's okay, Mom." I got up from my seat at the table, walked around and put my arms around her. At my embrace, she cried softly, freely.

The moment when my relationship with my mother began to change, was the evening before Billie came. It would begin a summer of bittersweet memories. It was the day I discovered Mother's dark side, a hidden side, the part of her that I would never reach or understand.

Eight

Hollywood Beach, Florida
1961

I had ridden past the bus station at Young Circle on Hollywood Boulevard many times on my bike. No one had told me that the bus was transportation for the poor. I knew it to be so from the people who milled about the station. Brown grocery bags, some with handles, were the luggage of choice for the elderly and the poor.

The inside of the bus station met my expectations. Wooden benches lined the walls. Permanently soiled beige terrazzo floors shone from a recent buffing. A snack bar constructed of stained plywood took up one wall opposite the ticket windows. Father squirmed next to me when a derelict man sat across from him, smelling of the street and stale wine. My father's "don't touch a thing" body language made my mother pay at her insistence that this be a family event.

My mother bit her nails and grabbed my hand. I was surprised how busy the station was. Billie's bus was overdue by ten minutes. In the twenty minutes we had waited, a southbound and a northbound bus had stopped with an urch of the air brakes and deposited their human cargoes at the doorway. Once reloaded, the buses sped from the station with flashes of sunlight reflecting off their shiny metal surfaces and black smoke blasting through the open windows, leaving the smell of unburned diesel fuel.

Mother showed me a picture of Billie when she was seven years old. It was her first day of school. She was dressed in dungarees and a print Western shirt. Her hair was thick, wavy, and long, tied in ponytails high on her head. Her face looked hopeful, excited. The only picture Mother had of Billie was a worn and wrinkled black and white picture she kept in the bottom of her underwear drawer. Billie's bus finally arrived twenty-five minutes late.

I already knew Billie was seventeen years old. Mother said that her 18th birthday was only a few weeks away in July. The only girl to get off the bus stood in the door holding a large gym bag in both hands in front of her. I was amazed at the resemblance to Mother. She was only an inch or two taller than Mother, with Mother's hazel eyes and rounded petite face. Her breasts were larger and her figure rounder, but it was Billie's hair and fair complexion that were most noticeable to me. Short, closely cropped, uncontrolled hair as red as new rust and a freckled, newly sunburned, light skin gave her uniqueness apart from Mother.

"Billie?" Mother stood four paces from the nervous girl.

Billie nodded and closed to within a foot of my — our — mother.

"Give your mama some sugar, Darlin'." Mother bent forward and wrapped her arms around her. Billie still held her bag in front of her. She grimaced at the awkwardness of the hug, until she saw me watching her. A comma of a smile began to appear at the corner of her full lips.

Mother turned and with difficulty draped an arm around Billie's neck and led her to where my father and I still sat. Mother started to cry. I looked at Billie's face. Dark circles under her eyes told me she hadn't slept much on the bus. Rapidly blinking eyes and several hard swallows told me she was nervous, too. I felt badly for her. Badly enough that I overlooked Mother calling her "darlin'," a term of endearment I had never heard her call anyone else but me, not even my father.

As they struggled toward us, I got up from the bench. She put her gym bag on the floor. She was just an inch or two shorter than I was. It seemed natural to hug her. I put my arms around her as Mother said, "This is your brother, Jackie."

She smelled like sweat and cigarette smoke and just a faint remnant of shampoo in her hair. I don't know what possessed me to say it, but before I let her go I said, "We're going to be great friends. I know it." When I pulled away and looked at her face, I knew what I said had pleased her.

"Thank, you, Jackie." Her voice dripped with the same drawl as Mother's only richer. She touched me on the shoulder and looked straight at me. Her eyes, wide a moment ago, softened. She wore no makeup. Her red hair, eyebrows, and eyelashes, fair skin and sun on her face was all the makeup she needed. Her touch conveyed trust, the beginning of a bond.

"And you must be . . . Paul?" Billie took a step toward my father and stuck out her hand.

Father stood and shook her hand. "It's nice to meet you, Billie."

Billie looked at Mother out of the corner of her eye. When Mother turned to look at her, Billie turned away and looked at my father or me. As soon as Mother took her eyes off her, Billie gave her a head-to-toes examination.

We all stood there quietly and uncomfortably until Billie cleared her throat. She straightened her back and looked momentarily at each of us. "I know my wantin' to come here was a surprise to ya'll. But, I didn't know of nowhere else to go. I promise I won't be no trouble. I'll clean house, wash clothes. Anything you ask me to do, I'll do it." I wondered how long she had polished her speech. And while it was apparent she had practiced it, there was no doubt of its sincerity.

"Let's not worry over that now, Darlin.' Let's just get you home."

I grabbed her gym bag, and Mother walked in front of us, holding Billie's hand.

The ride home was quiet. "Wow, ya'll live on the beach?" was the only comment Billie made as we went over the drawbridge onto A1A in front of the Hollywood Beach Hotel and then turned down a side street toward the ocean and our home. I followed Mother and Billie around the three-bedroom house as Mother gave her a guided tour, and then showed her to the guest room.

The few things she had in her gym bag fit into two drawers. Mother asked where the rest of her things were.

"That's it. These are all my worldly possessions. Kinda pitiful, ain't it?"

Mother inventoried her clothing. "Girl, we have to take you shopping."

"Why, I don't need much."

"Where are your pajamas? Are you going to walk around in your underwear in front of Jackie and Paul? No bathing suit? Two days underwear? No clothes to wear to church? Darlin', you need some things. I don't want an argument." Billie looked at me and shrugged her shoulders.

Mother sat on the bed and patted the place next to her for Billie to join her. They both looked at me, my cue to give them privacy.

In the living room, Father slipped on his deck shoes. "You want to go fishing for a couple of hours?" Father had a twenty-five-foot fishing boat docked on the Intracoastal Waterway two blocks from the house.

"Naw, I'll stick around here."

"They have a lot of catching up to do, boy. It would be best to give them a clear path for a while."

"No, I'm going to stay here," I said, impressed, though, with my father's sensitivity.

The door to the guest room was closed. I could hear them talking, but not their words. The sound of crying drifted occasionally from the room. After four hours, I gave up my vigil and walked down the Broad Walk to the shops on Johnson Street. After buying some gum, I started back toward home. I stopped at the Casino Pool on the way. The public pool charged fifty cents per day, collected at a booth very much like a ticket booth at a movie theater. A small marquee announced the formation of diving and swimming teams. The city's recreation department ran the program during the summer months. It would be my third year participating on the diving team. Up until that year, my participation had been limited to the low three-foot board. This year I would graduate to the high board, ten feet above the water.

When I got back to the house, their session had ended. Mother was in the kitchen looking through the cabinets for ingredients for dinner. Billie stood in a corner of the kitchen leaning against the countertop and looking totally out of place.

"Jackie, why don't you show Billie the beach? Dinner will be ready in an hour or so." Mother put her hand on my shoulder and rubbed gently. "She's never been to Florida before. Billie, do you have some shorts you could change in to? You'll be much more comfortable."

"Yes, ma'am." Her voice was soft and smooth.

Billie went to change in the guest room. "Darlin', she's having a rough time right now." She looked over her shoulder toward the guest room. "She needs a lot of family and love right now. Make her feel at home for me, will you?" She hugged me hard. "You're a good boy, ya know that?"

Billie appeared in cutoff blue jeans and a Clemson T-shirt and white Keds. "I'm ready, Mr. Jackie. Show the way."

I retraced my own steps back down the Broad Walk to the Casino Pool. When I explained the swimming and diving program, her face lit up.

"I'm on the swim team in my high school. At least I was on it until a year ago. What dives do you know how to do?" She tried to look through the door to see the pool. It was well after 5:00 p.m. and the pool was closed.

"Front flip with a half twist, gainer, back flip, jackknife — that kind of stuff."

Her smile broadened, and her hazel green eyes danced. "I can't wait to see you do them. My favorite is the high board. I was working on a triple before my sophomore year ended."

"I start the high board this year. I can't wait."

I showed her the shops along Johnson Street and then walked a block to the putt-putt golf and trampoline center.

"You have trampolines on the beach? Have you ever been on them?"

"Couple of times," I said smugly.

"Let's see how much they are." She walked up the steps to the ticket booth and pulled a small purse out of her pocket. "Two dollars for a half-hour." She pulled two bills from her coin purse and handed them to the attendant.

Twelve trampolines made a patchwork pattern in a graveled area next to the miniature golf course. The trampolines were installed so that the surface of the tramp was even with the ground. The earth underneath the tramp was dug out and removed. Heavy red vinyl padding covered the springs around the rugged nylon tramp surface.

Billie took off her sneakers and soon bounced higher and higher. Once she got her bearings, she began a series of forward somersaults, then backward somersaults and then she flawlessly executed a slow lazy forward somersault with a half twist, then a reverse into a layout. I knew enough from diving that she had the grace, style, and body control of a champion: pointed toes, hands and feet together, beautiful execution. She laughed and I knew she felt at home.

Her practiced routine lasted about three or four minutes. By then she had worked up a sweat and stopped. She labored to walk to the edge and exaggerated her steps in her bare feet across the gravel to where I sat on a bench watching.

"Whew, I ain't done — I mean — I haven't done that in a while." She wiped the sweat from her forehead with her finger and shook the base of her shirt to get air circulating underneath. She sat on the bench next to me and rubbed her hair with the palm of her hand.

"You want to try it now?"

"I'm no competition for you." I shook my head, truly impressed with her talent. I didn't know the name of half the tricks she had done on the trampoline. "It's more fun watching you. You're really good. You said you were on the swim team. You aren't anymore?"

"Ah . . . no. I quit school . . . after my sophomore year . . . beginning of last summer. I was on the gymnastic team, the swimming and diving team, and the baseball team, too."

"Why did you quit school?"

Billie looked directly at me and through me at the same time. She brushed a gnat away from her eyebrow and then looked away. "It's a long story." She looked toward the trampoline. Her face cheered. "I got first place in the state finals on the trampoline. Coach said if I worked real hard I could make it to the Olympics one day."

Suddenly, I knew it saddened her that she wasn't still involved in high-school sports. And the trampoline in front of her was now a reminder. "Let's walk some. There is still a lot on the beach I want you to see."

"How did you know I wanted to leave?"

"It just seemed like being here was making you sad."

She patted my arm. "Okay then, let's walk."

On the Broad Walk, we strolled in silence past the seasonal apartments and motels that lined the beach.

"You know John Kennedy's nickname is Jack. Is Jack your real name or a nickname?"

"No. Jack is my real name. Jackie is what everyone calls me, though."

"Billie is my real name. Can you imagine?"

"I like it," I told her, and I really did.

We wended down the middle of the Broad Walk, oblivious to the early evening walkers and bike riders.

I said, "You ever played paddleball before?" We approached Fillmore Street, where the city's paddleball courts were located; another gift to the citizens from the recreation department. The courts were filled. Park benches for those waiting to play lined the side courts. We sat on the bench on the court closest to the Broad Walk. The wop of the tennis ball hitting the concrete wall and the screeching of tennis shoes on the concrete court were all-too familiar sounds to me, and a little intimidating to Billie.

The game was played with a regular tennis ball and paddles fashioned from plywood. There was a wall at one end of the court, but no walls on the side or rear, unlike handball or racquetball. A line across the wall at about the same height as a tennis net served as a net line. The paddleball court was divided in half. The game was played very similar to table tennis, and was scored in the same way.

The serve alternated between two players every five points. The server, from his side of the court, had to hit the wall above the line and hit to the other player's side of the court in-bounds. Once the ball was in play, the ball could be hit anywhere full-court so long as the ball stayed in bounds. Play concluded when one of the players reached twenty-one points and beat his opponent by at least two points.

Billie and I watched two older men play. She was mesmerized by the game and continuously quizzed me about the rules.

"I want you to teach me how to do this, Jackie."

"I love it. I'm here all the time. The older guys run me off a lot, but I can play as well as they can."

"I'll bet you can." She turned and looked toward the ocean. "Let's walk some more." The words some and more slid off her tongue, as 'smore.'

She led me over the Broad Walk toward the water. She sat in the sand just a few feet from the water's high mark. I plopped down next to her.

"Want to ask you something." She turned her head toward me. "What's your mother like?"

The question was too large to answer. "What do you mean?"

"Is she nice or strict?"

"She's nice to me. In many ways she's my best friend. Dad's the strict one. He can be hard sometimes. But they're both great."

"When I was a little girl, I used to lie awake at night and try to picture your mother, I mean, our mother's face. I used to imagine her tucking me in at night, and reading to me, and singing to me. My stepmother never did those things. She didn't like me much. Daddy told me once it was because I favored your mother. So, tell me about her."

"I don't know how, really. No one has ever asked me a question like that." I struggled to find the words to describe her. I looked at Billie's face. Her eyes were wide, bright, and filled with hope. It was Mother's face. The lines were softer, the skin smoother, the features a little rounder, but it was

Mother's face. There was openness about Billie that I liked immediately.

"She's a toucher, isn't she?" Billie drew little circles in the sand with her finger.

"Yep, she's that."

"Since I got off the bus, her hands have been all over me. She's held my hand, rubbed my back, touched my cheek. A toucher."

Mother couldn't talk without putting her hands on you. It was as if she transmitted love through her fingertips. I had the flu once, burning up with fever and the touch of her hand on my forehead and cheek was more comforting than a chest filled with medicine. "Yes, she is a toucher. She is very affectionate. Get used to her hugs. They are as much a part of her day as breathing."

"I can't remember when my stepmother hugged me. Daddy, too." She was silent for a moment. She looked at me and smiled like she had awakened from the most pleasant of daydreams. "Tell me more. I want to know everything."

We sat huddled on the sand, and I shared all I could about Mother. Mostly it was Billie asking questions and me filling in the blanks. What I noticed most about her was how easy it was to talk to her. Conversation flowed like we really had been brother and sister all these years. From that moment, until she left that summer, I can't think of a time when she didn't make me feel special. Having her there sitting next to me was as natural as the incoming tide.

Hollywood Beach, Florida
1995

From the park bench on the Broad Walk, I looked at the spot on the sand where I first decided that I liked Billie some thirty-five years ago. I could still picture her closely cropped red hair blown by the sea breeze and her face all freckled and cheerful, eager to make up for lost time with Mother. And it was there on the sand with Billie, where my life collided with hers, that I began to face my mother's secret past. It was also the first time that I confronted the fact that Mother had let Billie slip through her fingers as a toddler, and I wondered for the first time how that could have happened. Like then, I still wondered.

Nine

Hollywood Beach, Florida
1961

"What's with you?" Billie flopped on my bed next to me.

"Nothing." I laid flat on my back with a towel wrapped around me, legs dangling over the edge, still dripping salt water from the pool on the hardwood floors. I had just gotten home from my first day of diving lessons.

"Well, how'd it go? Did you get to go off the high board?"

"Naw. We're still doing stuff off the low board. Next week."

"Is that what's bothering you?"

"No."

"Then what is it? You look so low you'd have to stand up to see over a street curb."

"It's nothing, really." I lifted my head off the bed, stretched to make eye contact, and gave her the best "lay off me" look I could muster.

"Is it me? Did I do somethin'?" The words singsong, as if we had just begun a new game.

"No, of course not."

"Your mom or dad?

"No." I said no, in two syllables, mimicking the melody of her tune.

She was contemplative. Drawing circles around her lips with her finger, she shifted on the bed to face me, the game entering a new phase. "Alright. It's not me. It's not your parents. It isn't the lessons, 'cause that's where you just come from. Well, what is it then?" She slapped her hand on her knee and pointed at me. "It has to be a girl!"

I tried to look totally disinterested in her analysis, but I couldn't believe she had guessed correctly.

"Ah, ha. That's it! Your face is as red as a tomato." She bounced up and down on the bed and came in for the kill. "That's it, ain't it?"

Heaven and earth couldn't keep the smile from my lips.

Billie scooted herself closer to me, anticipating my full and complete confession. "Tell your older sister the whole sordid mess."

"It's nothing, really. I met this . . . well I didn't really meet her. I didn't even talk to her."

She tried to tickle me. I jerked away from her hands. "Don't stop there. I want details."

"There are no details. There's this girl in my diving class."

"Ah, you men are all alike."

"And I suppose at seventeen, you're an expert on these things."

"I know more than you do. Now tell me about her, you little twerp."

"What's to tell?"

"What color is her hair?"

"Blonde."

"Ooooo. A blonde. And she has blue eyes, too?"

"Brown."

"Short?"

"Tall. That's the problem. She is almost a head taller than me."

"Why's that a problem?"

"Come on. Be serious. I'm a midget compared to her."

"At fourteen, size isn't that important. Even when you get to be my age, there are plenty of taller girls going out with shorter guys."

"Right." I gave her my best sarcastic look.

"It's true. It ain't the size that counts anyway. It's the type of person you are. All you have to do is talk to her, and she's yours."

"Right. I can't even say hello to her. Even if I got hello out, I'd make a fool of myself."

"Hey, you're the writer. I've read some of your stuff. You're good with words. You'll find the right things to say."

"I don't know what to say to her. I don't even know if she would talk to me or not."

"I'm a girl. We talk all the time. What do we talk about?"

"That's different. You're my sister." When the word sister came out, I realized that it was the first time I had called her that.

"Oh, Jackie, that sounds so good." She pulled me up into a sitting position and hugged me ferociously. "You're one of the nicest things that ever happened to me."

The emotion of the moment caught me. "You too, Billie." I returned her hug and a warmness overtook me.

She grabbed my hand. "Let her do the talking."

"How?"

"Just ask good questions. When you can't think of something to say, try to find out something about her. I always know when I'm going to like someone when they want to know something about me instead of talking about themselves."

"You mean like asking her about school and stuff?"

"Yeah, but try to make your questions a little more personal. Like, what do you like to do? What is your favorite color? Do you like rock and roll? Who's your favorite star? Questions like that. The key to good conversation is the questions you ask."

It occurred to me that Billie asked me many questions. Somehow, I was the one who always ended up doing most of the talking. And, it made me feel good that she wanted to know about me.

The next morning, Billie asked me if she could come to the pool with me. She sat in the bleachers that lined either side of the pool. When lessons were over, when everyone was standing around drying off, I looked at the bleachers and Billie was gone. I looked around the pool and saw her standing next to Jody Holland, the girl I had told Billie about. Billie walked out the back entrance. Without trying to be obvious, I looked over at Jody, who grinned broadly.

I was so angry. What had Billie said to her? What gave her the right to stick her nose into my business? I toweled off, pulled on a T-shirt and headed home. I was too embarrassed to look at Jody again.

Billie sat on the steps to the front porch waiting for me. As I approached, she patted the step next to her, inviting me to join her.

"I can't believe you did that." I paced back and forth in front of her.

"Jackie . . . "

I wouldn't let her finish. "You had no right to do that without telling me."

"Jackie . . ."

"She must think I'm a real retard that I have to have my sister talk for me." My pacing increased in intensity.

"Jackie . . ."

"You had no right . . ."

107

"She likes you." She almost had to yell over my ranting.

"You had no . . . She what?"

"She likes you. She told me she has been trying to find a way to meet you, to get someone to introduce you, but she's new in town and doesn't know anyone."

"New in town?"

"She . . . thinks . . . you're . . . cute." She almost sang the words. Her broad grin told me she enjoyed this immensely.

I swatted her on the shoulder. "But, you should've told me you were going to do that."

"Uh-huh, and what would you have said?" In a falsetto voice she continued, 'Oh, please don't do that, you'll embarrass me.' Her voice dropped to normal. "And it would take you another month to work up the courage. And you would've never known that this girl wants to meet you just as bad as you want to meet her."

I surrendered. She was right. I sat on the step next to her in pleasant defeat. "So what else did she say?"

"You're not angry at me anymore?"

"I . . . guess . . . not."

"Good. I told her we would meet her at the ice cream shop on Johnson Street at three o'clock. I jumped to my feet again. "You what? That's two hours from now."

"Relax. If you waited to see her until you went to the pool in the morning, you'd feel even more uncomfortable. You'd lay in bed all night long thinking about what you're going to say. Then you'd be a nervous wreck. It isn't good to let a lot of time pass on love."

I knew Billie was right. Now that Jody knew that I liked her, it would be awkward at the pool. "But what am I going to say to her?"

"Questions. Think about good questions. Quit worrying. I'll introduce the two of you, get the conversation going and then you're on your own."

That sounded too easy.

Two hours passed in a second. Jody was sitting in a booth in the ice cream shop when Billie and I came in. Her short, curly blonde hair was dry and combed out. In place of a swimsuit, she wore a sleeveless white blouse, yellow shorts, and a pair of white Keds.

When I saw Jody sitting in the booth, I almost forgot Billie was there. I walked up to the table. Her eyes followed me until I stood next to her.

"Hi, I'm Jack." I pointed to the empty seat across from her. She nodded her head toward the empty seat.

"Well, I guess you guys won't need me anymore." Billie leaned over and whispered in my ear, "Questions." She patted Jody on the shoulder and then backed up a few steps as though unsure of what to do, then she turned on her heels and left.

"Your sister seems really nice." Her hands were folded in prayer in front of her on the table. Her knuckles were white from clasping her hands so tightly.

"She is."

"She said you lived on the beach."

"Yeah, I only live a couple of blocks from here, just off the Broad Walk."

"You don't have an accent like your sister."

"She's from South Carolina. She just came to stay with us a few days ago. She's my half-sister. My mother was married before. Billie came to stay with us for a while."

"You know, I love to listen to her talk."

Questions. I repeated Billie's admonition in my head. "Yeah, I really like her. Billie said that you were new in town. Where did you move from?" This was the first chance I had had to look at her closely. Her eyes were light brown. They were so light you could see the flecks of brown and black in the color. Her light yellow blonde hair was teased slightly, and her skin tanned dark. I liked to watch her full lips as she talked. I wondered what it would feel like to kiss them.

"We're from St. Pete. My father's an engineer. His company moved him here to work at Port Everglades."

"What kind of an engineer?"

"I really don't know what he does. He has something to do with gasoline. He works for one of the oil companies at the port." Jody unclasped her hands. She brushed at the edges of her bangs with her finger then pulled at a pewter football charm on a silver chain around her neck.

"Where do you live?" Billie was right. I felt like I was in control. I just hoped I didn't run out of questions to ask.

"We're staying at the Sea Ray Motel, just a couple of blocks from here on the Broad Walk. My folks bought a house on Pierce Street. We move in in a couple of days. At the Sea Ray we have an efficiency and three regular motel rooms."

"You bought that big two-story about halfway between the Broad Walk and A1A?"

"That's it."

"Wow. That's a big place. You could put our house into that one two or three times. You have a big family or something?"

"There are seven of us. Mom just had a baby about six months ago. I'm the oldest of five. Mom's in the hospital right now. I have to go in a few minutes to watch the kids. My grandmother came to stay with us. She's got to go grocery shopping and all."

"Is your mother okay?"

"After Robert was born, that's the baby, she's been real sad and all. Sleeps a lot. Doesn't feel like doing much. Cries a lot, too. Dad took her to the doctor and he put her in the hospital to rest. Dad told me that some women go through this after they have a baby. Post-parta something. I can't remember the name exactly."

"When will she be home?"

"Tomorrow, I hope. With her gone, the rest of the kids keep me pretty busy and all. Grandma does a lot. She can't do a lot of lifting and cleaning. I have just enough time right now to go to diving lessons. I had to practically beg Grandma to let me come here. I had to promise her that I would be home by three thirty. That gives us five minutes."

"Gee, I'm sorry you have to leave so soon."

"Yeah. Me, too." She reached over and gave my hand a squeeze. "I'd ask you to come over to my house tomorrow, but we don't have it yet."

"Won't your mom be coming home tomorrow?"

"Yeah, that's right. But, I'll see you at the pool day after tomorrow." Jody stood up. "I have to go, or Grandma will be ticked off. I'm glad we met and all, Jack." She reached out and shook my hand.

"Me, too. See you Wednesday."

As Jody walked to the door, she reminded me of a foal walking on legs too long for its body. Her body had matured, but she had not yet found the way to carry her femininity.

The half-hour vanished so quickly I didn't even get a Coke or ask her if she wanted something. I looked out the window of the ice cream shop, and I just caught the sight of her running up Johnson Street, then turning north at the corner on the Broad Walk.

When I got home, Billie was sitting on the steps waiting.

"Okay, Romeo, spill your guts."

"There's nothing to speeeel."

"You makin' fun at the way I talk?" She grabbed me by the hand and pulled me to the step beside her, then wrapped her arm around my neck and put me in a headlock. "Don't you be makin' fun a me, bowey, or I'll whoop yo butt," she said, her accent exaggerated.

"Okay, okay. Let me go."

"Well then, tell me how it went." She released me, and I rubbed at my ear, reddened by the rough play.

"I did just like you told me. I just kept asking her stuff. It worked great."

"What did you ask her?"

"I was so nervous, I can't remember everything."

"Another thing you need to learn about women is that we need details. What did you find out about her?"

"She lives at the Sea Ray Motel. Her father's an engineer. He works at the port. She has four brothers and sisters and she's the oldest. Her mother's in the hospital and gets home tomorrow, she thinks. And her grandmother stays with them to help Jody take care of the kids. She could only be gone a half-hour. That's it."

"She's a pretty one." Billie had made the mistake of feeding the seagulls on our doorstep. Now three of them congregated, pecking around for food. I stomped my foot, and they sprang to flight like a covey of quail flushed by a hound. They escaped only a few feet, then landed and hobbled back within breadcrumb-throwing distance.

"Don't do that. I like them."

"You keep feeding them, and we'll have a city block of them. Dad's going to love it when he has to clean all their crap off the stoop." I sprang to my feet, flailing my arms and smacking my tennis shoes on the pavement.

"Ah, you scared them off." Billie threw the remaining breadcrumbs onto the street away from the sidewalk.

I looked at Billie as she brushed the remaining crumbs from her hand. I knew so little about her. The reason she was here seemed such a mystery.

"Billie, can I ask you something?"

"Sure."

"Did you run away from home?"

114

"Did a couple of years ago. Me and Ella, my stepmother, don't get along. She's even turned my daddy against me. I was fifteen. Just a year older than you."

"Where did you go?"

"My daddy's an antique dealer in Charleston. He buys a lot in New England and Europe. He doesn't need her to, but Ella travels with him most times. So they hired a governess to look after me while they were gone. Stella was young, more of a mother to me than Ella. I loved her very much. Ella knew it and hated her for it. Ella turned my father against Stella and had her fired. When she left, I left with her. She took me in."

Except for the first day that Billie arrived, she had always been a fountain of cheerfulness. Always up, always encouraging. Now her forehead was wrinkled up, and her eyes red. Suddenly, she looked tired, and I was almost sorry I had opened up the subject.

"Stella ran into money trouble and couldn't support both of us. So I had to leave. Actually, we got kicked out of our apartment when the rent wasn't paid. I had nowhere to go. That's when I called your mom."

"Our mom," I corrected her.

Now the tears began to flow. The veneer of happiness cracked. I had pierced the veil between our world and hers. "She may be the woman that had me, but it's hard for me to call her my mother. She had a choice. She could've kept me when I was a baby. She didn't. As far as I'm concerned, she hasn't earned that yet."

"What do you mean she had a choice?"

"I promised your mother I wouldn't talk to you about this. I gave her my word."

"What do you mean she had a choice? She gave you up for adoption, didn't she?"

"No. I told you, Jackie, I can't talk to you about this. I promised."

"Then what?"

"One of these days, I will tell you the whole story. Not here. Not now. I gave my word."

Hollywood Beach, Florida
1995

I stood across the street from our old house. The steps that Billie and I had sat on were now repainted with gray deck paint that had peeled. I could still picture her, the only time that I had seen Billie upset, the words resonating down through the years. "One of these days, I will tell you the whole story." I had to find her. At every turn there seemed to be much my mother didn't want me to know."

Ten

Hollywood Beach, Florida
1961

"Hey, you." Jody tapped me on the back. I was taking off my shoes and shirt by the side of the pool. Diving lessons would begin in five minutes.

Jody had a throaty voice. It wasn't masculine or deep but sounded as though it were on the verge of laryngitis. The sun was bright behind her and set her light yellow hair ablaze.

"Hey to you. Is everything okay?"

"Why?"

"Well, you haven't been here for a couple of days."

A broad grin spread across her face. "We've been moving."

"Yeah, I know. I came by the motel day before yesterday when you didn't show up for lessons."

"Why didn't you come in to see me?"

"Well, your dad was yelling at your brothers, and I didn't think he was in the mood to meet a boyfriend."

Jody's eyes widened and a comma appeared at the corner of her mouth. "Is that what you are, Jack? My boyfriend?"

Embarrassing. "You know what I mean. Did your mom come home yet?"

"Yes, yesterday. I'm so excited. We moved into our new house and all. But, I just told you that. See, I said I was excited."

Coach blew a whistle signaling the start of the session.

"What are you doing this afternoon?" I picked up my shoes and shirt and put them in a pile on the bench.

"Well, I thought about asking you to come over to see our new house and meet my mom. Then we can do anything you want. Is one o'clock okay?"

"Are you sure it's going to be okay with your mother just getting home?"

"I was telling her all about you. She was the one who suggested it."

Coach impatiently blew the whistle several times. Other kids scrambled to their predetermined meeting places around the pool.

Jody placed her hand on my bare shoulder. It was cool compared to the sun which had just cleared the coconut palms that lined the Broad Walk.

"Okay. One o'clock." I watched her pad to where the other girls gathered. Turning the corner at the end of the pool, she looked back and caught me watching her and smiled.

"McNamara. Are you going to join us today?" I turned and looked at my class who were assembled around the coach and looking directly at me.

The big two-story house on Pierce Street had been completely redone. The front had been given a facelift, and the asphalt shingle roof had been replaced with galvanized steel, in the style of the Florida Keys. White aluminum clapboard siding covered old wood siding, and the front porch, which had been screened, was now open. Pastel green wicker furniture and large Boston ferns resting atop matching wicker end tables added contrast to the otherwise sterile white porch.

Jody sat on the wicker loveseat and had donned her adopted uniform of the beach: white tennis shorts, a white T-shirt, and white Keds, which made her tan look all the darker.

"Hey, you."

"Hey," I said, ascending the stairs from the sidewalk to the porch.

I sat next to her. "I like your house. What a difference!"

"The builders finished just in time for Mom's homecoming. Even though Daddy had to make all the remodeling decisions, Mom really likes it."

"How is she?"

"She's seems fine to me now and all. Not completely herself yet. But, she's doing better."

I had explained to Mother the affliction Jody said her mother had and the symptoms she described. Mother said she had never heard of such a thing. "You're enough to depress anyone," she had said and winked and then had given me a swat on the butt.

I wanted to ask Jody more about her mother's hospitalization, but her mother came out the front door and onto the porch before I could ask.

Jody's mother was a slight, frail woman, as short as my mother but much thinner. She had Jody's blonde hair and brown eyes, but not her full lips. It seemed an effort to stretch her thin lips over large, square, ivory-white teeth too large for her small thin face. Her smile was broad, warm, and sincere.

"And you must be Jack." Extending her hand, she walked the few steps from the front door to where I sat. Before Jody could get to her feet and introduce us, her mom said, "I'm Jody's mom. Just call me Helen."

I snapped to my feet. "Hi. Nice to meet you."

"Has Jody offered you anything to drink? A Coke? Some tea?" She looked at Jody and raised an eyebrow.

"Just got here . . . didn't have a chance . . . No, I don't care for anything."

"Sit. Sit." She waved her hands as one might shoo away a dog. She pulled a wicker chair from the wall and placed it in front of the loveseat with the back of the chair to the street. We all sat down to creaks from the wicker furniture.

"I understand from Jody that you live on the beach, too."

"Yes, ma'am. Only a couple of streets from here."

"Any brothers or sisters?"

"Sister."

"You don't have to be so polite, Jack. Just call me Helen."

"Yes, ma'am . . . I mean . . . Helen."

Helen Holland. I repeated the name to myself several times like one might say a tongue twister and tried not to let my amusement show.

"It's nice that Jody's had a friend here, while I've been gone. I'm afraid Jody's had her hands full filling in for me." She reached across and laid the palm of her hand on mine. "Thanks for being such a good friend to her."

I looked over at Jody, who looked pleased at her mother's compliment.

I was too embarrassed to say anything.

"Let me see . . ." Helen drummed her fingers on the arm of the chair. "Jack McNamara. A week or so ago I read in the newspaper about a Jack McNamara who won a writing contest of some kind. Any relation to you?"

"Yes, ma'am. That's me."

"They said they would publish the story in the newspaper."

"The second of July."

"So, I'm sitting in the midst of a famous author." She looked at Jody and grinned before turning back to me. "And what's your story about?"

"The doorman at the Hollywood Beach Hotel is a friend of mine. He's always telling me stories about guests in the hotel. I took one of his stories and put it on paper. No big deal really. It wasn't even one of my stories. I didn't even enter the contest. Mother sent it in without me knowing about it."

"Well it must have been well-written. I understand the judges had thousands of submissions. Still pretty impressive."

Helen looked almost childlike. She was so short her feet didn't touch the ground. Her blonde hair was short like Jody's, but thinner and curlier. Her face was expressive, and her eyes danced.

"Thanks."

"Do you want to be a writer?"

"I think so. But my father isn't too keen on the idea."

Her eyebrows furled and the tight skin of her forehead wrinkled. "Why not?"

"He says it's a hard business to make a living in." I was embarrassed to tell her his other observations.

"Well, your father's right. For some it is a hard business to make a decent living. It's like most anything in life. If you have talent and work hard, you'll succeed."

"Mom's a writer. She works for a magazine."

I turned from Jody to Helen.

"Freelance writer. A mother of five doesn't have a whole lot of time. Before I got married, I worked full-time for them. Then, as I started my family, I started my freelance relationship. I'm anxious to read your story. Do you have a copy I could look at?"

"Sure."

Helen pushed herself out of the chair. "Would you like to see the house?"

"Yes, ma'am. I mean, Helen."

Helen gave us a tour of their home. It was typical of many of the homes along the beach built in the twenties and thirties. High ceilings, large rooms, dark hardwood floors and plaster walls. But, Jody's house was unique. During remodeling, extra windows, skylights, and ceiling fans were added, which brought light and breeze to every part of the house.

What I noticed most about the tour was the graciousness of this small almost frail woman. Unlike Jody's father, who had an obvious temper, Helen was cool and unruffled. When she looked at you and talked to you, she listened to every word, caught every nuance, and noticed every minute gesture. When she talked, she searched my face for understanding, and repeated something until she was sure I understood. Whether by heritage or training, Jody had this same precious quality. When you were with her, she made you feel that no one in the world mattered to her, except you.

I stood in the doorway leading to the porch, Jody beside me. Helen held out her hand.

"It was a pleasure to meet you, Jack. I'm serious about your story. I'd like to read it."

With that, she disappeared into the house and left Jody and me on the porch.

"You didn't tell me you liked to write." Jody grabbed my arm and led me down the stairs of the porch and turned toward the beach.

The passers-by on the Broad Walk dwindled to a trickle. The sand was pocked with footprints from the day's beach-goers. By morning, city tractors would smooth the sand clean. The ocean breeze, usually light in June, blew strong in gusts.

Jody crossed her legs Indian-style and found a clean spot in the sand among the seaweed near the high-tide mark. "Let's sit here." She pulled at my hand until I sat down next to her.

The breeze blew her bangs off her flawless, smooth, tanned forehead. She said, "Does your mom ever get depressed?"

"Yeah, but not very often."

"Has she ever had to go to the hospital for it?"

"No. She'll get into one of her sad moods, but it only lasts for a day or two. Is that what's been wrong with your mother?"

"If my dad knew I was talking about this he would be upset. He doesn't want anyone to know that doctors treated her for, you know, mental problems."

"She seemed fine to me. She didn't seem sad."

"Well it's like living with two different people. Some days she's fine. Just like today. Happy. Gets all dressed up. Ever since she had Robert, there are times when she'll stay in her room for days at a time. She doesn't eat, doesn't get dressed, she just hides in her room with the door locked. I almost didn't graduate from grade school this year since I missed so much school taking care of the kids."

"She's better now, right?"

"I asked Dad the same question. She seems better to me. He said that mental illness is not the same as a regular physical illness. When you go to the hospital, they have these sessions where you talk to the doctor."

"You mean like a psychiatrist?"

"Yes. She still goes to see him. And will probably have to go for a while." She scooted around in the sand to face me. "I read an article that said in some hospitals they put this hat-like thing on the patient's head and give them electrical shock. I asked Dad about it, and he said they only do that with people who are severely depressed."

"Did they do that to your mother?"

"No. I heard Dad explain to his Grandma on the phone that some company is working on a pill you can take to help with depression.

"It must be hard on you, having to take care of your brothers and sisters so much."

"It's hardest on my dad. His favorite saying is, 'We'll just have to wait and see.' I feel bad for him. He hates to take me out of school to take care of the kids, but he's lost so much time from work that he's afraid he'll lose his job. And he won't admit to anyone the kind of sickness my mother suffers from, especially not the people at work." Jody pulled a knee to her chin and doodled in the sand with her finger. When she looked up at me, she was crying.

Instinctively, I gave her a hug of reassurance. She inched closer and laid her head on my shoulder. Her crying finally subsided.

"I'm sorry." She straightened up and looked at me, but didn't move away. I could smell the shampoo in her hair.

"I know it's hard. I wish I could do something."

She reached up and touched my hand. "You just did." And then, she kissed me. She pulled away, but only by inches, and looked at me. And, I kissed her. It was a longer kiss. I explored the pillows of her lips with my own. Despite the hours of worrying about how it would happen with Jody, it was the most natural thing I had ever done. I could taste the salt from the tears on her lips still wet from crying. I felt like I had known her for a lifetime.

Eleven

Hollywood Beach, Florida
1961

It was dusk when I left Jody and headed the two blocks home along the Broad Walk. Billie sat on a park bench at the head of our street. She sat on the top of the seat back with her feet on the seat. Her arms rested on her knees. She looked east over the beach and scanned the horizon. I joined her on her high perch.

"I don't think your father likes me." She looked down at the bench seat.

I said without thinking, "There are lots of times I wonder the same thing."

"I'm serious. I wonder if it was a mistake coming here."

"How could it be a mistake?" I was a little disappointed. I wanted to tell her all about my time with Jody. "What did he do that makes you feel this way?"

She hopped down from the bench and looked around the beach as if trying to find an escape route. "I shouldn't be talking to you about this."

From my perch on the bench, I said, "And why shouldn't we be talking about this?"

"I'm the outsider here. He's your father. He's your blood."

"And we aren't.? You're my sister."

"Half-sister. And a distant half-sister at that."

"What did he do?"

She threw her hands down to her sides in desperation. "He hasn't done anything. That's the point. He treats me like I'm not even here, like someone who won't be stayin' long. The way you might treat a stray cat or somethin' that you don't want to stay. It's the same way that my stepmother made me feel, like an unwanted pet."

"That's just Dad. I guess he could make the Pope feel worthless, too." I could tell my reassurance did little to assuage her concern. I knew how she felt. I felt many times like an unwanted obligation, or that's how he made me feel. Mother had always assured me of my father's love. I wanted to believe her. His actions were evidence against him. I felt tolerated. I felt like my mother's possession and that my father tolerated me because of that affiliation. And there were times when that didn't carry much stock.

I didn't know how to respond to Billie. If I told her how I felt, it might make her feel worse. If I defended my father too strongly, it might create false hope.

"What were you expecting?"

"What do you mean?"

"When you came here, how were you expecting Father to act?"

She paced in front of the bench. "I don't know really. I hadn't thought about it."

Suddenly I became uncomfortable sitting at the end of our street. Father would be home soon and I felt guilty talking about him. "Let's walk down the beach." We turned and headed down the Broad Walk toward the Hollywood Beach Hotel.

"Okay, put yourself in my father's shoes. What do you think his feelings are about your being here?"

"Well, I guess I don't really know."

"Malcolm told me once that if I wanted to make a character come to life in a story I had to crawl into the head of the character and try to think the way the character would think. Now, my characters aren't real to me unless I can become them in my imagination. Try to crawl inside my father's head, and try to think what he's thinking."

"Who's Malcolm?"

"A friend. He's the doorman at the Hollywood Beach Hotel. Now pretend you're my father."

"You mean, now?"

"Yeah, tell me what you think is going on with him."

Billie stopped walking, grabbed my shoulder, and spun me around to face her. "This is silly."

"No it's not. Try to think about his side of you being here."

She raised an eyebrow and shook her head and started walking again. "Well, here your dad is happy as a new minted penny, and I show up at his door. A new mouth to feed. I eat like a horse, sit in his chair, and run my mouth all the time. And I'm constantly spending time with his wife." We stopped again. She turned and looked at me with widened eyes. "I'm consuming your mom's attention. And your dad likes to be the center of attention."

She said it so matter-of-fact, as if commonly known. "He likes to be the center of attention." Whether she came to this conclusion on her own, or this was a mother's revelation to her daughter, I don't know. But it was the first time someone had defined my father in a way that finally made sense to me. He had to be the center of attention.

"He's jealous! I came into his home, and took away the attention that your mom usually gave him."

I agreed with this conclusion immediately. We began to walk again. We fell into silence while she continued to mull over his perspective. "I guess I would be guarded, too. Here I have this new person in my family, and before I put too much of my heart into things, I would want to see how things went for a while."

"Is that what you're doing? Waiting to see how things go?"

She put both of her hands over her heart. "Me?"

Billie was animated. Always. Her enthusiasm was infectious. There was an excitement and hopeful edge to her that filled my tank when I was around her. Even now at one of her low points, she was hungry to turn this setback into a victory.

"Is that what you think I'm doing?" It wasn't as much a negative reaction as it was her chewing on the possibility.

"I think he's probably doing that too. He'll come around. Just give him some time."

"I've been spending so much time with your mom he probably thinks I don't want to be around him."

"You have so much personality. Work some of that charm on him."

"Make him the center of attention?"

"Something like that."

We stopped walking again. She hugged me ferociously, and kissed me on the cheek. "Thanks, Jackie. I'm the big sister. I'm supposed to be helping you, not the other way around."

"You did. You've helped me a lot."

"What did I do?"

"Jody?"

She put her arm through mine and we began to walk again. It was dark now and the Hollywood Beach Hotel lights spilled out onto the Broad Walk.

"I didn't do anything. Just gave true love a push."

"Have you ever been in love?"

She turned and looked at me. I knew instantly that I had touched a hurtful spot.

"Yes. Very much in love. The best feelings I have ever had. And they have been the worst, too."

"How could being in love be bad?"

Billie pulled me off the Broad Walk and onto the sand. We found a spot near the water and sat in one of the cabanas in front of the hotel. Her face reddened, and she became tearful. I regretted taking our conversation in this direction.

"There is no joy equal to someone loving you as much as you love them, especially if it's the first time. And there is no hurt greater than not having that love returned. The deeper the unreturned love, the greater the hurt. When someone rejects your love, it can be very painful."

I knew then that Billie came to be with us not only because she had no place to go, someone had hurt her very deeply. She had come to heal. She had come to her mother because her heart was broken, and she needed the love that only a mother could give. I could think of nothing to say that would console her except, "I love you, Billie." I said the words meaning them. There was a tenderness and openness about Billie that endeared her to me.

"You don't know how much those words mean to me." She hugged me for the longest time without saying anything. I wondered who had hurt her so badly. I thought of Jody. I couldn't imagine that she would hurt me like that. I had to admit that there was much I didn't know about her either.

When we returned home, Mother was just putting dinner on the table. She shuttled food from the kitchen to the table: roast beef, mashed potatoes, green beans, and corn on the cob. Father sat at his place at the head of the table and hid behind the newspaper. The scowl on Mother's face warned of a storm brewing below the surface. As she ferried food from the kitchen to the dining area, she glared at my father, who knew better than to catch her glance. The silence of the room was foreboding. I looked at Billie and knew she understood the need for silence.

I went to bed early. Rarely did my parents fight in front of me. Often their spats vaporized with the daylight. At about 10:30 p.m., yelling and the crash of pots and pans yanked me from a sound sleep. I ran from my room. Billie was already in the hallway peering around the corner in the direction of the kitchen, afraid to interject herself into the melee. I instructed Billie to stay where she was, and I went into the kitchen. The first thing that caught my attention was the smell of liquor. My mother stood in the middle of the kitchen, holding an iron skillet like a tennis racket. Her face was swollen and red just below both eyes. She was hysterical and screaming, "You touch me again and I'll kill you." The words came out in a rush of wind and spittle.

My father had a knot on the side of his forehead the size of half a baseball. His face was red. His hands shook violently, hanging to his side in clenched fists.

My father noticed me standing between him and my mother. "Get out of here!"

I was frozen in fear. I was afraid of what my father might do to me if I stayed, and afraid of what they would do to each other if I left. I held my ground. I couldn't bear the thought of Father hitting my mother again, although from the looks of the knot on the side of my father's head, Mother appeared to be holding her own.

When I wouldn't leave, Father's resignation wavered. His anguished face softened, and his heaving chest slowed. He looked around the kitchen as if to get his bearings and then just walked out of the kitchen, leaving Mother to find another head to hit with her frying pan. When he left, she wilted, handed me the skillet, and then dropped tearfully into her chair at the kitchen table. She wiped the tears from her eyes, but they were quickly replaced. Now she abandoned her attempts to hold back, and cried uncontrollably.

"Go to bed, Darlin'. It's all over now." She slurred "Isallova" into one word.

"I'll just sit with you a minute."

"I'm fine, really." She grabbed a napkin from the holder on the table and mopped up the tears mixed with mascara that had drained in crooked creeks across her face."

Father passed by the kitchen with a pillow and sheet, heading for the couch.

"Here, let me get you into bed," I told her. "It's been a long day."

"I'm fine," she repeated, then got up and let me lead her into the bedroom anyway. Billie gestured that she could help, but I waved her off. Father would see her help as taking sides, which wouldn't help her situation at all.

I aimed Mother toward the bed, which was now partially unmade from Father's scrounging. She fell into bed and was out before her head hit the pillow. I took off her shoes and covered her. The places under her eyes where Father had hit her looked like cheese pizza. They'd had their spats before, and my father had hit her before, but nothing like this. I turned off the light on the nightstand and went to console Billie.

I whispered, "It's okay. Everything is fine now."

"It doesn't look fine to me. It sounded like they were trying to kill one another."

"It's okay, Billie." She looked frightened and concerned. She turned on her heels and headed to her room. I knew my reassurance did nothing to calm her.

In the morning, Mother was at her post, sitting in her chair at the kitchen table, coffee on the right, ashtray on the left. She smelled of a shower. She combed her hair back into a stubby ponytail, and she had put on makeup, in a failed attempt to cover two black eyes. I sat at the table opposite her and tried to hide my reaction to her pummeled face.

"I'm a mess aren't I?"

I didn't say anything.

"Well, this time your father doesn't look any better. He was lucky I didn't bust his skull wide open."

I looked around for his coffee cup that he always took with him on his way to work.

"He left before I got up this morning." She paused to light a cigarette.

I wanted to ask her, what happened, but I waited to see what she would tell me first.

"I'm sorry you had to get in the middle of it, Jackie." She took a sip of her coffee. She liked it black and strong. She reached in her bathrobe and pulled out a piece of paper and handed it to me. I opened it. It was a copy of a bar tab from O'Brien's

Bar and Grille, my father's hangout. I looked at Mother, questioning its importance.

"Turn it over."

I turned the receipt over. A simple note had been written in pencil: "Why didn't you call me?" It was signed simply, "S." I still didn't comprehend the significance.

"Your father is seeing someone." She looked at me and realized that I still didn't understand. "Your father has a girlfriend. He's cheating on me."

"Was that what the argument was about? You think Dad is cheating on you?"

My words had an edge of disbelief.

"Your father denied that it was from a woman. He said it was someone that he worked with. But what man would write a note like this to another man?"

My father had his strengths and weaknesses, but cheating on Mother was not one of the things I would suspect of him. Take her for granted, yes. Not pay her attention, yes. Lord it over her, yes. But never infidelity.

"Then it wasn't about Billie?"

"He's not crazy about her being here, but, no, it wasn't about her." She flipped a long ash from her cigarette into the ashtray. "Look at the handwriting. Does that look like a man's handwriting?"

"I write like that, Mother. There are plenty of men who write well."

"That isn't the only thing, Jackie. A woman knows when her husband is cheating."

"He loves you. He wouldn't do anything like that."

"Your father stopped loving me long ago. He tolerates me. He lives with me. Love?" She dismissed the notion with a wave of her cigarette. "I cook for him, clean his house, and take after you. Love stopped being a part of it long ago."

I scratched around for evidence of his love that I could present to her, but none immediately surfaced. "Mom, you're the best. He could never find anyone like you. You're beautiful, talented, and fun to be with. How could he not love you?"

"Oh, you're sweet, Darlin'." She hugged me and told me that I had a way of making her feel special. But I knew my words held no impact.

Hollywood Beach, Florida
November, 1995

Standing in the street, in front of our old house, I could picture Mother sitting in her chair in the kitchen as though it were earlier that morning. What I remembered about that morning was that Mother first suspected Father of cheating on her, and it was on that particular morning that my relationship with my mother turned from being a child to her confidant. It was that morning when my mother lost faith in my father, and lost faith in everything else, including herself. From this point forward, I would become her counselor and virtually her only source of encouragement. Little did I know, sitting across from my mother with blackened eyes, that if she were looking for signs of an improving relationship with my father, there would be little ahead that would console her.

Twelve

Hollywood Beach, Florida
July, 1961

"Hey you. Waiting on the paper?" Jody stood in front of me and hooked her blonde hair behind her ears.

"Why? Do I look that excited?"

She sat close to me on the stoop, smelling of a bath and newly washed hair.

"You look like a cat ready to pounce on his prey. That newspaper delivery boy won't have the newspaper out of his bag before you have the paper open to that story of yours."

I looked away from the street where I knew the delivery boy would be coming and looked at Jody instead. Her brown eyes danced with delight at my impatience.

"Well, I guess I'm pretty excited, alright. The whole thing has been a little hard to believe, and July 2 has seemed so far off to take it seriously. It really didn't mean a whole lot until the paper called Mother this morning and asked if she wanted additional courtesy copies of the paper for family and friends."

Jody slipped her arm inside mine and gave it a hug. "I'm excited, too! So is my mother. She made me promise to bring you back to the house after the paper comes. She has something for you. It's a big secret and all. Won't say a word about what it is."

I don't know which felt better, her so close to me, or the realization that soon my story would be in the newspaper.

"Jackie, did the paper come yet?" Mother's voice boomed from inside the house. The screen door popped open. "Has it come . . . Oh . . . I didn't know someone was here."

It had been several days since Mother and Father had had their "discussion." Mother's eyes were no longer swollen, but they were still bruised, and even heavily caked makeup did little to hide the battle scars.

"Well, Darlin', this must be Jody." Mother wiped her hands on her apron, and reached down to shake Jody's hand. Jody stood to intercept.

"Mrs. McNamara. Pleased to meet you."

"What's such a pretty girl doing with the likes of my son?" Mother winked at me.

"Well, Missus McNamara, your son is a famous writer, and all. That makes it hard for a girl to resist."

"Well my famous writer-son is about to bite off every fingernail he has waiting for that newspaper to come. This is the same famous writer who got so upset when his mama entered one of his stories in that contest. Isn't that right, Darlin'?"

"Don't listen to a word of it, Jody. She's more excited than I am. She even walked down to the corner store to see if the paper came earlier there. You'd think it was one of her stories."

"You write too, Mrs. McNamara, don't you?"

"Call me Kit, girl. You make me sound like a grandmother. And yes, I write some. But, it's Jackie here who has all the talent. I just helped refine some of the genes on the way to him."

"Jack has told me how well you write. It seems to run in the family. Did he tell you that my mother writes, too?"

Mother stepped down from the doorway onto the step and sat between us. Mother had cleaned up, fixed her hair, and put on perfume. The smell of her drowned out the subtle smells of Jody. To Jody she said, "I have always dreamed of a job like your mother's; to write for a New York magazine and stay at home with Jackie. Now that would be an answer to my prayers. Now how did she pull that off?"

"Well, she worked there when she met my dad. And when Mom started to have her family the magazine still wanted her to write for them, so she freelances."

"Freelance. Even the word sounds like a vacation."

I heard a familiar car door slam. I looked down the street and saw my father parking his 59 Ford Sunliner and then he locked the door. He, too, sported the wounds of Mother's wrath, but partially covered it with a Yankee's baseball cap. He carried what appeared to be several copies of the newspaper. When he got within earshot, he said, "I thought you'd be anxious for this, so I stopped at the newspaper on my way home and picked up a few copies."

Mother was the first to her feet. "Oh, Paul. That was so considerate of you to do that." She hugged him, and hopped on her toes to kiss him on the cheek. "Did you look? Did you see his story yet? Where did they put it? Let me see!"

"Before I give you this paper, I want to warn you. There's some news in here you're not going to like. In fact, it's bad news."

"Well, what is it for heaven's sake?"

"Kit, I've been warning you about this for a long time. I told you this guy was a flake."

I couldn't contain myself any longer. I jumped from the step and pulled a copy of the paper from under my father's arm. Across the very top, above the masthead, "Winners' Submissions to the Sun-Tattler Fiction Contest Inside." But below the masthead, below the headlines, a sub-headline read, "Nobel Winner Dead at 61." In a smaller headline, "Widow says, self-inflicted gunshot wound, accidental."

I let the paper fall to my waist and turned to Mother. "Hemingway's dead. It says he died cleaning a shotgun."

Mother grabbed the paper from me, and gaped at the headlines. "This can't be."

"These headlines are garbage." My father's tone was all knowing. "I heard on the radio. It was suicide."

"But Paul, it says right here it was accidental." Mother pointed to the newspaper, the places under her eyes bruised from my father's backhands, puffed up and turned red.

"Heard it on the national news. They say he put the barrel of a shotgun to his forehead, pulled the trigger, and blew off the top of his head."

I could tell my father enjoyed sharing his little bit of news.

Mother slumped to the step in disbelief. "He was such a brilliant man. It just had to be an accident."

"I warned you, Kit. The guy is — I mean was — a flake." Then my father looked at me. And the look said without a word spoken, "You'll end up just like him, if you keep on with this writing stuff." Aloud, he said, "Here, I thought you might want some extra copies." And then he walked in the house to leave the small Jackie McNamara fan club to commiserate.

Jody stood near Mother, unsure of what to do. She put a hand on my mother's shoulder and remained silent. She knew my mother and I were fans of Hemingway, but had no idea the depth to which my mother's fantasies of the future were tied to him. And until my father said that Hemingway's death was suicide, I had no forewarning of how profoundly I would feel his loss. I didn't want to believe what Father had said about him, but I knew, deep down, it was true.

At that moment, it was difficult to separate the accuracy of Father's prediction of my own fate from the accuracy of the news shared about Hemingway's death. I looked at the small bundle of newspapers and knew that the evidence that my life would follow Hemingway's, if I continued to write, laid between the pages of the July 2, 1961, Hollywood Sun-Tattler.

Mother must have sensed the hole that Father had punched into my still small and fragile ego. Seeing my sickened reaction, she slid on the step closer to me, reached over, and put her arm around my shoulder. "I'm sure what your father said about Hemingway wasn't true. But even if it was, nothing can take away from his tremendous accomplishments. He was a great man."

The screen door opened and slammed closed. The late afternoon sunset set Billie's red hair afire. She bounced off the stoop and onto the walk. "Why's everybody so glum? Let me see the paper." She grabbed a copy from the bundle in my arm, sweeping the pages back until she found my story. "Master Jack McNamara. There's that name in lights where it ought to be. Wow. To think you're my brother. Jody, did you see this?" Then Billie opened the paper and showed my story to her.

Jody noticed Billie's upbeat reaction. "Oh, this is so cool. I've never known anyone famous before. Miss Kit, you should be so proud."

"Darlin', you know how proud I am, don't you? I want you to promise me that you will not let your father discourage you from writing. You have talent, boy, and I don't want you to forget it. Now let's go inside and celebrate."

Jody stepped around my mother and kissed me on the cheek. "You listen to your mother. You do have talent. My mother said you do. She loved your story. When I brought it to her the other day she just went on and on about it."

We all stood and pushed through the creaking screen door and celebrated with Black Cows, vanilla ice cream in root beer.

Hemingway was such an icon in my life it was difficult to imagine the horrible things they were saying about him on television that evening. The television news anchor Walter Cronkite confirmed what my father had said earlier, that Hemingway had died from a self-inflicted gunshot wound. After our family celebration, she led me to her house to visit with her mother. Cronkite was on the television when we walked in the house. I was glad that I was watching the television at Jody's. Had we been at my house I would no doubt be browbeat with 'I told you so" from my father.

The anchor said, "The nation has lost one of its prize literary possessions. Hemingway rose to fame in America mastering the simple declaratory sentence, and re-wrote the rules of prose for the next generation of writers. His often raw and controversial work captured the imagination of a generation hungry for details of distant worlds. He wrote with the language of the common man, and the common man took him as his own."

"Sad isn't it?" Helen Holland's small voice floated on the air as she entered the room. Jody walked behind her.

"I told Mom how fond you were of him." Jody sat next to me on the couch, and Helen sat next to the television after she turned down the sound. Images of Hemingway's life flashed on the screen.

"Jack, Hemingway was a very sick man."

"Yes, I know. My father says he's wacko, a real fruitcake."

"And do you believe that?"

"I don't want to."

"When I worked in New York, I made a good many friends in literary circles. Hemingway's short stories often appeared in monthly magazines. Ours was one of them. So, our magazine developed a relationship with Hemingway's agent. My editor has kept in close contact with A.E. Hotchner, a close friend of Hemingway's, so I know what I am sharing with you is true.

"Hemingway was involved in two airplane crashes. He suffered significant internal injuries from which he never fully recovered. After the crash, his health declined. Doctors forbade him from drinking, and his travels and physical activity were severely curtailed. Hemingway was an outdoorsman, Jack. Fishing, hunting, and drinking were part of his persona. He had a deep need to live life on the edge, and he did so his entire life. If he wasn't in the Florida Keys fishing for marlin, he was in Wyoming and Idaho, hunting. When he wasn't in the States hunting, he was traveling throughout the world, seeking excitement at new and different levels.

"But all that changed when he was in the plane wreck all that changed. He was no longer physically able to live that lifestyle. He became an imprisoned man. I suspect that Hemingway had a rather fragile spirit. There are many who speculate that he lived his life like he had something to prove. And the confinement drove him over an emotional edge. He began to suffer from depression and, later, paranoia.

"Depression is an awful state of mind. In very severe cases, electro-shock treatment is used on the brain. It often leaves mental functions in a confused state, and very often, the patient loses memory functions. Hemingway's depression became severe enough that they admitted him to the Mayo Clinic after it was feared he would attempt suicide. He was released briefly, and the shock treatment left him in such a state that he could no longer write. At this stage, virtually everything that Hemingway had enjoyed doing, everything that he lived for, had been taken away. He had no hope at all. None. He tried to take his life several months ago, but the family and his doctors kept it out of the papers. They returned him to the hospital for more treatments, but it probably only worsened his condition."

"Then my father was right."

"If you mean that Hemingway was crazy, yes, he was probably right. I would prefer to think of him as a very ill man. Ill as he was, he was one of the greatest writers of this century. He was a very gifted man. And he's still worthy of your admiration."

"I'm sorry, I just can't find a single reason that would justify killing yourself."

"I know you don't understand it, but Hemingway reached a point where there was nothing in life left to live for. You stand here with a brilliant future ahead of you. With a little luck, you may well exceed his success. From that vantage point, I can understand how hard it would be to understand his plight. But enough of Hemingway. I want you to continue to honor him in the work you do. Nothing has changed. His words and life are not altered an iota by his death.

"Now for some news. I liked your story so much I sent it to the magazine for their review. We feature short stories in every edition. They're always looking for something unusual. Although their editorial calendar is full until next year, they want to feature your story in the spring edition. They won't pay very much for it, and we'll have to clear it with the local newspaper to make sure they don't claim ownership, but it's a great opportunity."

"Mom, why didn't you tell me about this?"

"Because I knew as soon as I told you, Jack would know in five seconds. I wanted it to be a surprise."

"They really liked it?" It didn't seem real. It was just a story I wrote while playing around one night when I had nothing else to do. It was like a game, writing a story to see how Malcolm would react to see one of his stories in print.

Helen smiled. "They liked it a lot. These were their words, not mine. They said, 'Maybe we have another Hemingway on our hands.'"

"Thank you, Helen. I don't know what to say."

"The expression on your face is thanks enough. But I want you to promise me something." She looked over at Jody, and then back at me. "Promise me that you will continue to write. Promise me that you will give it your best effort."

"I will."

"Promise me."

"I promise."

"Even though there may be people around you who will try to discourage you?"

"Yes, I promise."

"Good. Now I'm sure the last thing you guys want to do is hang around me." She got up, switched the television off, and left the room.

Sleep was hard to come by that night. My father's predictions about Hemingway stung, and Hemingway's death was a blow. Everything I had read about him suggested a man of courage, a man's man. As an ambulance driver, he was shot on his first day of combat. In fact, he went into the battlefield knowing the dangers he faced. At every turn in his life, as a fisherman and hunter, and an aficionado of bullfighting, he appeared to show little fear. How could a man of such virility, such courage, want to take his own life? It seemed cowardly. Hard as I tried to give credit to him as Helen Holland suggested, I could not shake my disappointment. But as deep as my feelings of disillusionment about Hemingway were, I tried to understand the ramifications of my story appearing in Lifetime magazine. While Hemingway may have been an idol, Helen Holland was a benefactor in person. She was not some distant figure, but someone who had taken an interest, someone who had put herself out

Bill Cronin

on my behalf. As disappointed as I felt that night, I was deeply indebted to Helen Holland for her unsolicited support, help, and kindness.

Thirteen

Hollywood Beach, Florida
November, 1995

I got a room at the Vagabond Motel, its only redeeming feature a small courtyard that abutted the Broad Walk. The small porch had two vinyl-web chairs with a small corroded aluminum table between them, just large enough for a couple of drinks. The motel sat at the end of the street that I had lived on as a child. The grocery store down the street sold cold beer and I took my position on the porch in the late evening sipping a cold light beer and thinking of Emily. A small group of Latinos had gathered just off the Broad Walk in the sand. They danced and sang to Latin music from a boom box. One couple in their late twenties danced sensually to the music; the intensity in their eyes hinting at the passion they would show each other later that evening. It reminded me of Emily and me in days before we were married.

Emily had only worked for me for a short time. I had just hired her as an editor and I asked her to accompany me to a writer's' conference in Muncie, Indiana, to handle conference details. I had been the keynote speaker.

Until then, we hadn't really talked about anything beyond work. When we got off the plane, I was just her employer. She drove from the airport in Indianapolis to the hotel in Muncie. By that evening, we were dancing to a small band in the hotel and looking at each other with the same excitement and anticipation as the Latino couple across the Broad Walk. Our relationship did not cross the physical boundary until much later, but what I remember most about that trip, was our conversation in the car on the way back to the airport. The topics progressed from writing, my recent book, to our recent divorces, to love, then to our sexual preferences in less than thirty minutes. Now, as it did then, my conversation with Emily about sex reminded me of Billie and the first time I had ever discussed sex with anyone.

Hollywood Beach, Florida
July, 1961
Following the huge fight my mother and father had, Billie seemed more withdrawn. She was still a fountain of positive energy, but less hopeful, less sure of the future. Despite my assurances that their fight had nothing to do with her, she was unconvinced. I could see her enthusiasm for our home change to a restless uneasiness. I had wanted to share with Malcolm the good fortune of Lifetime publishing the story. I was still healing from Hemingway's fall from grace and my mother's general melancholy at his departure. I didn't want to

be cheered up by Malcolm. Despite my resoluteness to remain in the doldrums, I knew Malcolm would not permit me to remain there. I was happy wallowing in my unhappiness.

My mood finally brightened, and the usually cool and bright morning on the beach and the sounds of the ocean restored me. It was about ten in the morning when Billie had finished her shower and sat at the kitchen table with her emotional chin on the table. Her short red hair had been roughly dried with a towel and still flew off in all directions. I sat at the table with her, but she wasn't there.

"You, okay?"

"Yeah, I'm alright. A little homesick, I guess."

"Tell me what you miss."

"I miss my friends and familiar surroundings. You know? You don't spend seventeen years in Charleston, without missing it."

"I'm family, and I'm your friend. And I'm right here."

"I know. And if it weren't for you, and your mom, I would really be having a hard time."

"I want to go see Malcolm and share the good news about the story appearing in the magazine. Would you like to go with me? You said you wanted to meet him."

"Well I'm certainly not going looking like a shredded carrot. Can you wait a few minutes for me?"

When Billie came out of her room, it was the first time I had seen her with makeup. She had her hair parted on the side and combed back over her ears, donned dangling black and gold earrings, and had sparingly applied orange-red lipstick and mascara. She wore a white sleeveless blouse tucked into jeans that fit snug at the waist.

"Whoa. You look pretty good."

She smiled and curled her hair behind her ears. "Thanks. I didn't want to embarrass you. So I thought I'd get fixed up a little."

"You don't have to worry about Malcolm. He's as plain as a grocery bag."

"Well, it don't hurt a girl's mood to get gussied up every once in a while. And today I needed it."

"If my friends see me, they'll think I snagged me a high school girl."

"Ooooh, what a nice thing to say. Well, I won't tell them if you don't."

Malcolm was helping a cantankerous old woman out of an airport vehicle that had Dade County plates. The van had brought her up from Miami International Airport. She was alone, hunched over at the waist. She was irritated about something and shook her umbrella at Malcolm, and raised her voice.

"If you think I'm tipping you, you're nuts. You have my bags up in my room before I get there or there will be hell to pay. Do you hear me?" Then the old woman looked at Billie and me. "What are you two looking at?" She set her jaw, aimed for the main door, and stormed off.

"Yes, Miss Helms. I assure you everything will be taken care of, Miss Helms. Don't you worry yourself about any of this, Miss Helms."

Once she passed, Malcolm smiled and shook his head. When she was out of earshot, a deep laugh started at his toes and rumbled up through his chest, until his black mouth was filled to capacity with white teeth, and both of his massive hands were on his knees as he tried to gain control of his composure.

"Master Jack, I have not seen much of you lately. The whole hotel staff, they are talking about your wonderful story in the newspaper. 'When will Jack be by?' they keep asking me. Soon. Very soon, I tell them. They want to share their joy with you, young man. This must be your sister. I'm Malcolm." He extended his massive black hand to her. "Malcolm Baldridge." He bowed his head slightly and touched the end of the bill of this hat with his thumb and forefinger.

Billie nodded to Malcolm. "Jack tells me his story was based on you, and the hurricane of 1926."

"Master Jack tells the story much finer than I." He extended his arm and waved it across the entire front of the hotel. "The building is filled with thirty-five years of stories and memories. When you walk down its halls, the building speaks to you about all the people who have come and filled this old place with life.

"Our charming Miss Helms has been staying at the hotel since it opened. She comes three times a year, for two months at a time."

My visits with Malcolm always went this way. Within a minute or two, he would be spinning a yarn, telling a tale, or filling me with the history of the place. He backed up to a stool near the taxi stand and sat on the edge, half sitting and half standing. Billie and I stood between Malcolm and the curb in front of the main door. The door flew open and a black bellman found Miss Helm's bags, and then disappeared into the lobby, no doubt given the same stern lecture that Malcolm had received.

"Now you take Miss Helms. A widow, you know. She is a bitter woman to be sure. She can be very cantankerous. After you hear her story, you might not judge her too harshly.

"She and her husband Herbert began coming to the hotel even before it opened. Mr. Young, the original owner and builder, had constructed a tent city on the beach all around the hotel grounds to handle the tourists who flocked to this area during the winter before the hotel was finished. The Helms' began coming to the hotel for the winter in 1925 and moved into the hotel when it was completed. Even came back after the Miami Hurricane nearly destroyed the place in 1926.

"Now when they began coming here Miss Helms was in her early thirties and Mr. Helms was almost fifty. They had only been married a few years. What we did not know, and what Miss Helms did not know, was that Mr. Helms also brought his mistress to the hotel each year, even back in the tent-city days. So from 1925 to 1930, Mr. Helms had his dual living arrangements without the knowledge of Miss Helms or anyone else for that matter.

"In 1930, Mr. Helms suffered a heart attack and died in the room of his mistress. Miss Helms was heartbroken and never recovered.

"As it turned out, Mr. Helms had early connections in the oil business and died leaving Miss Helms a considerable fortune. She came to the hotel manager and negotiated to rent both hotel rooms permanently, the room that she and Mr. Helms rented, and the room that he died in.

"The mistress' room, number 825, has not been opened in thirty-one years. Her room, number 630, has never been renovated, although the hotel has been renovated several times. Even during the times when the hotel was taken over by the navy during the war, the hotel owners continued to let Miss

Helms keep her rooms, undisturbed as she requested.

"Even with all that money, she has made herself a prisoner, locked into a time in her life when she was happy. She and this old hotel are similar in so many ways. Both are long past their prime. Both happier in times past, trying to survive in a future that neither one of them want to be in."

"She never remarried?" Billie was now concerned for the old woman.

"No, Miss Billie, she never did. And she was a beautiful woman. She could have had her pick of men who swarmed around her. But she spent most of her time in her hotel room, locked away with her memories."

"Sounds like you care about her a lot." I knew that once Billie met Malcolm, she would fall prey to his spell, too.

"Oh, yes ma'am. She yells and screams and carries on so. But, there has not been a Christmas since 1930 that she has not remembered me financially. There have been times that just her generous gift alone has made the difference financially between my staying and leaving this place. The hotel has never paid that well. There are others that work at the hotel, old timers, who she has cared for, too. And, over the years, as occupancy has declined at the hotel, there haven't been enough in tips to keep a church mouse alive. If it was not for Miss Helms, I could not have afforded to stay. It is the people like old crabby Miss Helms who keep me here. They are like family and the hotel my home."

A tour bus pulled into the circular drive spewing black smoke from the diesel engine into the white oleanders that lined the drive. The forward door flew open and the driver announced its arrival at the hotel. The bus shifted from side to side as passengers queued up to depart.

"Well, back to work. Miss Billie, it was most agreeable meeting you. I'm happy for both of you that you found each other. Say hello to your mother for me, Master Jack."

"By the way, Malcolm, I just wanted to tell you that our story is going to be published in the Lifetime magazine. Be out in the spring next year."

"That is just about the most amazing thing. Before you know it you'll be pulling up in front of this door in a limousine, and I will be waiting on you."

Suddenly I felt guilty that it was Malcolm's story, and I was getting all the attention for it. "Really, Malcolm, your name should be on the story, too. After all it was your story, all I did was put the words on paper."

"Now you listen here, Master Jack. There are two types of people in this world. There are doers and there are talkers. That is the difference between you and me. All my life I have talked about all the things I would do if I had the chance. But I never have done any of them. But not you. You had the gumption to write that story down and make something of it. I'm proud of you. You're not afraid to do. And all I will ever do is talk. That is the difference between you and me. It's a good difference. You can have every story I have, if it will help you. It is enough for me that you think they have any value at all. Now I have a little work to do." And he moved to the bus to escort an elderly gentleman down the stairs.

"He is such a sweet man, Jack. And he's been there since the hotel opened?"

We walked around the hotel to the Broad Walk and turned north toward home. "It's so hard to believe that he's been there so long, doing the same thing. I'd go out of my mind if I had to do the same job for thirty-five years."

Once we turned onto the Broad Walk, the wind had turned strong from the south and sent Billie's red hair flying. "What's hard to believe is that old woman has never remarried."

"Who would want to marry an old battle-ax like that?"

"I'll betcha she was a vixen."

"What's a vixen?"

"A woman who can wield her sexual charms like a weapon."

"How would she do that?"

"Hasn't your mother ever had a talk with you about sex?"

"No. Did your mother ever tell you about sex?"

Billie furled an eyebrow and moved her upper body away from me. "Wait a minute, I asked the question first."

"Did . . . your . . . mother . . . ever . . ." Jack drew out the words.

"No."

"Then how did you learn?"

"What is this all about anyway?" She was acting the way Jody might act if I dropped a spider in her lap.

"You brought it up."

Billie clammed up. We walked past our street and stayed on the Broad Walk. The crowds grew along the macadam strip as the noon hour approached. For several minutes, we walked without saying anything.

"Have you ever had sex with anyone?" I tried my best not to laugh.

"Slow down, sport. Where are you coming up with these questions?"

"Your face is getting red. I'm not trying to embarrass you. You're the only one I know to ask."

"Why don't you ask those nuns where you go to school?"

"That was last year. I'm going to public school now. Besides, a question like that would have gotten me the strap."

"I wish I had one myself right now. I'd say those nuns have a pretty good idea there."

"Come on, Billie. Tell me."

"Don't you think this is something you should be talking to your dad about?"

"You're serious?"

She looked at me out of the corner of her eye. "Yeah, I guess that wouldn't be such a great idea."

"Then you'll tell me."

"Why do you want to know, now? You're not planning to do anything are you? You're a little young to be thinking about sex, aren't you?"

"Well, how old were you when you had sex for the first time?"

"That's none of your business!"

"Then you've had sex then."

"Whoa, slow down, boy." She moved farther away from me.

"What was it like?"

"Now stop this. I'm not the right person for you to be talking to about this."

"Why not? You're my sister. My older sister. If I can't talk to you about it, who can I talk to?"

"Your mother would kill me if she knew we were having this conversation, much less my telling you about sex. And your father would put me on the street."

"Come on, Billie. Details. The boy needs details."

"You promise me you'll never tell anyone we had this conversation?"

"Boy, I sure have made a lot of promises lately."

"What promises?"

"Never mind. I promise. I promise I will never tell anyone that we had this conversation."

Billie pulled me off the Broad Walk, and we sat in the sand under a coconut palm. Billie answered almost all of my questions. Honestly. Truthfully. And in detail.

"So how old were you when you had sex for the first time?"

"There are some things that are just too personal to share with you. One of these days, you'll understand. But, I will say this. Sex is an expression of love at the very deepest level. While it is easy for me to explain what sex is and how it works, no one can tell you when the time is right for it, and whom to have it with, except you. Sex is a beautiful thing, Jack. It's worth saving for the right person. And it carries with it a lot of responsibility you won't be ready for, for a long time.

Hollywood Beach, Florida
November, 1995

No one had ever talked to me the way Billie did. She treated me like an adult. I felt closer to Billie, at times, than I did to my own mother. We shared things that I could never share with another soul.

Although I had been married before, there had never been anyone since Billie that I could talk to with such candor and intimacy until Emily. There was nothing I couldn't share with Emily. Maybe that was the problem. Maybe I shared too much with her, more than I needed to. Watching the Latino couple spin the web of lovemaking that would end later that evening, made me miss Emily. Our own lovemaking knew no boundaries, until the quagmire of my own depression took that desire away, too.

Sitting on the porch of the Vagabond, I couldn't recall a time when I felt emptier, more alone. I did not want to relive the events of that summer. But I knew that the keys to unlocking my own emotional prison lay within the folds of those memories.

Fourteen

Hollywood Beach, Florida
July, 1961

It had been three weeks since Hemingway committed suicide and my story appeared in the newspaper. On this particular morning, Father was out of town, and I slept in. This was the time of the year I loathed the most. The jalousie windows in my room were wide open, and the sheets were damp from the humidity. The nighttime lows rarely dropped below eighty degrees. There was no escape from the heat.

"Jackie, come here quick." Mother was at the door to my room. It was rare to see my mother so agitated.

I jumped from the bed.

"What's Jody's last name?"

"Holland."

"Darlin', this isn't good."

The CBS affiliate in Miami had a reporter on Hollywood Beach. They were interviewing a woman, and the building behind it looked familiar. The camera panned back to the reporter, and behind her was Jody's house.

"For those of you who may have just joined us, a Hollywood woman is in custody after allegedly shooting her entire family. The woman's name, which is being withheld until next of kin are notified, is reported to have shot all five of her children and her husband with a .38 caliber revolver. Before she could reload the gun to take her own life her oldest daughter, who was not fatally wounded, successfully wrestled her mother for control of the gun. The girl – the only survivor — was taken to Hollywood Hills Hospital, where she is in stable condition. The children ranged in age from six months to fourteen years."

The picture returned to the news anchor. "Hollywood police and detectives from the Broward County Sheriff's Department are investigating the shootings. . ."

"Oh, my God, that's Jody's house." I sprang from the chair and ran to my room, put on the clothes I had taken off the night before, ran back into the living room, and stopped at the television, somehow hoping that what I had just heard was not true. "I'm going over to Jody's."

"But, son, why don't you wait for a few minutes? There may . . ." I heard my mother's voice trail off as I bolted through the front door and up to the Broad Walk at a dead run. I closed the distance to Jody's quickly. Police barricades blocked the street, and the area immediately around the house was roped off. Police vehicles from the city and the sheriff's department clogged the small street. A policeman stood at the steps to the front porch guarding the house.

"My name is Jackie McNamara. Jody, the oldest girl, is a friend of mine. Do you know if she's okay?"

"No, I have no idea." Then one of the plainclothes detectives walked out on the porch, his eyes red. He looked like he had been crying. The policeman guarding the door said, "This young man is a friend of one of the children."

"I'm a friend of Jody's. I just wanted to know if she is okay?"

"Is she the oldest girl?"

"Yes."

"Yes, she is at the hospital. That's all I can tell you, though. If you call them later in the morning, they should be able to give you some information. Now, you're going to have to move outside the roped-off area, son."

I backed up and stood behind the barricades along with other neighbors and the curious. I couldn't believe what was happening. Why would Helen want to kill her whole family? How could anyone do such an awful thing? The youngest was only a baby.

I heard the click of a camera behind me. I turned and a man was standing behind me.

"Hi, I'm with the newspaper. Did you know the Hollands?"

"Yeah, Jody, the oldest girl, is a friend of mine."

"What did the police tell you? I saw you talking to one of them on the porch."

"They said that Jody is at the hospital. But they don't know how she is."

"I just called the hospital. They said she's okay. Pretty shook up, though. You know the mother?"

"Yes. She was a nice person."

He asked for my name, said that he hoped Jody was okay and then disappeared into the throng of policemen.

I stood in disbelief. It seemed like an eternity. Then I felt a hand on my shoulder, then an arm around my shoulder. Then a hug. It was Mother. "The hospital called. Jody is asking for you. They wondered if you might come up to see her. She's very upset. They thought you being there might calm her down."

"Can you take me?"

"Well, Darlin', I just want to make sure that you feel comfortable about going. This is a pretty awful thing to have happened."

"What do you think it's like for Jody, Mother? I want to go see her. Can you take me?"

"Yes, of course."

At the hospital, Mother escorted me to Jody's room. The nurse suggested that Mother wait in a waiting room down the hall, while she and the nurse accompanied me to Jody's room.

"Before we go in, I want to ask you to do a few things for me, okay?"

"Sure."

"Jody is very upset. She has a bandage on her head. Don't make a big deal about it. It's just a grazing wound that will heal up in no time. But she has been through a horrible experience. She has been asking for you since the ambulance brought her here. When you go in there, just listen. If she wants to talk, talk with her. If she wants to cry, let her cry. If she just wants to sit with you and say nothing, just sit with her. Don't try to get her to do anything, okay? Just follow her lead. Do what she does."

I nodded. Then she pushed the door open and led me in.

It was a regular hospital room with a bed and two chairs. Jody sat in one of the chairs, looking out the window. When she saw it was me, she jumped from the chair and flew into my arms and began to sob uncontrollably.

"I'll leave the two of you alone for a while."

I could hear the door close behind me.

Jody clung to me and cried deeply. I hugged her fiercely. I didn't know what else to do.

She cried for a long time. My heart broke for her.

"Jack, it was awful. I managed to get the gun away from her before she shot herself . . . blood

172

everywhere . . . she even shot the baby . . . and Dad didn't have a chance. Jack, I've have no one. My family is gone." She cried again, louder, more strongly, longer.

"My aunt from Atlanta is coming to get me. She is going to take me back with her."

I cried with her. "Don't you have any relatives here to stay with?"

"No."

"You could stay with me. We have room at our house."

"They say I'm underage, and I have to go with relatives. I've lost my family, and now I'm losing you, too."

"You haven't lost me. I'm right here. I'm not going anywhere. When is your aunt coming for you?"

"Today. I have to talk to the doctors. They want to make sure I'm okay. They told me that I'll be leaving with her tonight or tomorrow. Oh, Jack. This is so hard. I love you so much. I don't want to leave you."

"I love you, too, Jody. I love you, too."

The nurse appeared in the doorway. "Jody, we have tests to do. You're going to have wrap up your visit."

"Can't Jack stay just a little longer, please?"

"Okay, ten minutes. And then the doctor needs to see you."

I tried to be as strong as I could. But when the nurse left the room Jody clung to me even tighter, as if by exerting her sheer force of will she could keep me there forever. And I returned her affection gratefully. We both cried, and held each other, not saying anything. She dealt with the grief of losing her entire family and I dealt with the grief of losing her. The nurse returned and, like a referee in a prizefight, divided us and escorted me out of the room. As I left, Jody looked at me, tears streaming from her eyes. "Jack, I'll never forget you."

Mother met me in the hallway, and I crumbled in her arms. The emotional encounter with Jody had drained me. I felt sick to my stomach and couldn't stop crying. Mother never said a word. She just held me, walked me to the car, and took me home.

I called the hospital when I got home to try to talk to Jody again, but they told me that she couldn't take calls — doctor's orders. I slept most of the day and tried to call again around five. They told me that she had checked out of the hospital. I never saw Jody again.

That evening, the Sun Tattler ran the story of the shootings on the front page. "LOCAL WOMAN SHOOTS FAMILY OF FIVE. Suffering From Depression, Helen Holland Discharged from Mental Hospital Less Than 14 Days Ago." In the center of the page there was a picture of me standing behind the police barricades with my head hanging down. The article described the shooting as one of the worst mass-murders in Florida's history. Doctors had tried to dissuade her husband from releasing her early from treatment, but were unsuccessful. Had she remained in treatment, the article said, the violence might have been avoided.

Hemingway's death had been a significant blow. The circumstances of Helen Holland's depression had been unfathomable. Both ripped apart by an unseen and otherwise untreatable demon; depression. It seemed as though my father's admonition that I would end up like Hemingway if I pursued writing as a career, was underscored with Helen's horrible tragedy and failed attempt to take her own life. But what really sidelined me was losing Jody.

For months following, I would lie awake at night and think of her kisses and the physical closeness we shared. All the other loves of my life had the opportunity to run their natural course. But with Jody, and the horrific circumstances of her departure, our love had always had a place in me.

Even when we received the letter that Lifetime magazine had formally accepted my story and returned an agreement for my mother to sign which gave them rights to it, I could not shake the fear that I would now suffer the same fate as Hemingway and

Helen Holland. Billie helped me sort through my feelings of fear and sadness.

"I'm beginning to worry about you." She stood at the door, her shoulder leaning against the doorjamb, with her arms crossed at her chest. "Scrooge seems like a happy person compared to you."

"I miss her."

"I know you do. So do I. And there aren't that many people I think are worth missing either."

"First, I lose Hemingway then Jody then they haul Mrs. Holland off to a mental hospital. It's like everything that means anything to me has been taken away. And I know that Jody is hurting, and I can't be there to help her."

"She has family, and they love her, too. They're going to take good care of her."

"Helen Holland seemed so nice. She was so good to me. Why would she do something like this?"

"She wasn't well. Only a person who is sick would commit such a desperate act."

"She seemed fine to me. The times that I visited with her, she seemed normal."

"She was sick mentally, Jack. I don't know a whole lot about mental illness. But, people who have problems like that are just like you and me. Sometimes you just can't tell."

She made semi-circles on the rug with the toe of her Keds. "A mother would have to be very, very sick to kill her children."

"She had the same problem Hemingway had — depression. Father warned me that Hemingway was a wacko. He said the same thing would happen to me. Then, Mrs. Holland kills her whole family and tries to commit suicide. She was a writer, too."

"Whoa." Billie crossed the room and sat on the corner of my bed. "Hold on a minute. I know what your dad said to you, but I don't think he meant that everyone who writes is crazy or will end up like Hemingway. Not everyone who writes suffers from depression, any more so than every doctor ends up with heart trouble. The fact that Hemingway committed suicide and Mrs. Holland tried doesn't mean that you will. Suicide has nothing to do with your profession. Now, I don't know a whole lot about it, but mental illness can strike anyone."

"I just hurt inside, and it won't go away. I can't stop thinking about what happened to Jody. I can't stop thinking about what she must be going through. I only lost her, and I know how horrible I feel. She lost her whole family. I can't imagine how she feels. It must be awful. And I feel helpless."

She put a cool hand on my cheek. "I know what it's like to lose someone that you love deeply. I still wake up at night and hurt because my real mother didn't love me enough to want to keep me. I still hurt when I think about how my stepmother hated me and has turned my dad against me. Someone that I love very much went away, without me. I know how much these things can hurt."

I looked at her and knew that my hurts didn't begin to compare to hers. "Why do things like this happen? Did I do something wrong?"

"Now I don't go to church a lot. In fact, I haven't been since I left home. Even when I did go I didn't pay it a whole lot of attention. One morning in Sunday school, they were teaching out of one of the books in the Old Testament. The teacher said the Bible says that, 'It rains on the just and the unjust alike.' I was feeling just like you, that maybe I had done something wrong to deserve all the stuff that was happening to me. When I thought about that verse, I had to admit that it was true. Bad stuff happens to everyone. Good folks and bad. Now even though I know this is true, late at night, when I can't get to sleep, I sometimes begin to think that I'm being punished for something I've done."

"And that's supposed to help?"

"I'm not doing a very good job of explaining, am I? But I do know this. You're one of the nicest people I know. You have a talent, Jack. Your mom, the people at the newspaper, the people at Lifetime magazine and even Helen Holland have all recognized this ability. Now I'm not the smartest person in the world, but I know that what happened to Hemingway and Mrs. Holland had nothing to do with their writing. They were just sick people who happened to be writers. Your being a writer doesn't mean that you will end up like them. You have a lot of talent. Don't let anyone take that dream away from you."

She put her arm around my shoulder and looked directly at me. "The feelings you have for Jody, I can't help you with that one. It's going to hurt for a while. Trying not to think about it won't help either. The more you try not to think about it, the more you will. It'll just take time." She hugged me. "I wish I could help."

I put my arms around her. Just having someone to talk with had helped a lot. "You have helped. Thanks."

"I know I haven't said this to you, I didn't want to say something I didn't mean. I love you, Jackie. I couldn't have wished for a brother any better than you. You have a good heart. And sometimes a person with a big heart hurts more when it's broken."

Billie always seemed to know the right thing to say to me. It was hard to believe that she had only been there a couple of months, and that I had come to depend on her so. I suspected that soon that would change, too.▨

Fifteen

Hollywood Beach, Florida
August, 1961

The paddleball courts on Fillmore Street were jammed with the young and old. During the weeks of summer, the retired and teenagers queued up equally for a court. It was only 9:30 this particular morning and the wait for a court was an hour or more. Players of all varieties, ages, and descriptions sat on park benches, plywood rackets in hand and at the ready.

The older man next to me had just asked me to play with him when I felt a hand on my shoulder. It was Mother. She had been crying.

"Did he hit you again?" I stood up ready to defend her.

"No. He didn't." She sopped up the tears on her face with Kleenex she pulled from her apron. Can you come with me for a minute, please?"

I left my racket with the old man and followed her out of earshot from the other players-in-waiting.

"Billie is leaving." Mother looked out at the ocean, the sun still low in the sky, turning the ocean yellow. "I'm taking her to the bus station and I wanted you to say good-bye to her."

"Leaving," I said in a half-statement, half-question. "Why?"

"Things are just not working out, Jackie." She wouldn't look at me. She looked at her feet, the ocean, people that walked by, but not at me.

"What do you mean?" I did a quick mental inventory of all the things that had happened since Billie's arrival. Not only were there no incidents that would indicate a problem, but things had been going exceedingly well. "How haven't things worked out?"

Mother would turn her face as people walked by, not wanting them to see her crying. "There is so much you don't know. This is not the time to talk about any of this. I just didn't want her to leave without you saying good-bye to her."

"Why? All I want you to do is tell me what's going on."

Mother stiffened and turned toward me red-faced and teeth clenched. "We're not going to discuss this, boy. Now you either come say good-bye to her, or I'm leaving. Now what is it going to be?" She walked past me toward the parking lot behind the paddleball courts and didn't wait for a response.

Reluctantly, I followed.

Billie leaned up against the car, arms folded at the chest and legs crossed at the ankles. As I came closer, I could see her reddened face she held to the wind defiantly. Mother circled the car and sat in the driver's seat. I stood directly in front of Billie. She didn't move an inch. Her face still turned away from me.

"Are you going to tell me what's going on?"

Nothing. Not a muscle moved. Disheveled red hair flew in the strong on-shore breeze.

So I just stood there. I wasn't going to beg her to talk.

Finally, she looked down at her shoes, and then at mine, then slowly to my face. By the time our eyes met, her granite face softened, and reluctantly she reached out, put her small hand on the back of my neck, and pulled me to her. She sniffed back tears, and when our bodies touched, she was trembling.

"I knew this would happen." She wiped her cheeks and eyes on the shoulder of my shirt. Even though her head lay on my shoulder, and I couldn't see her face, I knew the words came out through gnashed teeth.

I pushed her away slightly. "What's going on?"

She shook her head, and the face of stone returned. "Nothing you would understand. It's just not working out."

The words my mother had used. "What isn't working out? I thought things were fine. Did I do something?"

She grabbed me by the shoulders. Her hazel eyes turned to fire. Mother yelled it was time to go. Billie looked at Mother and then at me. "Now you listen to me. You're the first person in my whole life that I truly cared about. This has nothing to do with you. Do you hear me? Nothing! I want you to remember that I love you very much. I can't remember a summer when I've been happier. This has nothing to do with you. One of these days, I will tell you the whole story."

She hugged me as tightly as I can ever remember anyone hugging me, kissed me on the cheek, and got in the car next to Mother on the front seat. She looked up at me from the car window, held up a hand to wave, but put it to her lips and she began to cry. The car pulled away from its parking space, out of the parking lot, and down A1A. I didn't see Billie again until just before Mother's funeral.

I left the paddleball courts and walked north on the Broad Walk until the macadam ended then crossed the beach to the water's edge and walked until the beach was deserted. I needed to talk to someone, but Jody and Billie were gone. I remembered Helen Holland's words about Hemingway, that he reached a point in his life when everything that was important to him had been taken away. He came to a point in his life where he had no hope. Sitting on the sand by myself, I began to understand what Hemingway and Helen must have felt, and for the first time in my life I felt the weight of that hopelessness.

I sat down in a spot I found in the sand, wrapped my arms around my knees, laid my forehead on my knees, and cried. I don't know how long I was there or how long I cried, but I kept thinking of Hemingway and Helen Holland. If they had felt like I felt now, then I could understand why someone would want to die, why he or she would be willing to end their life.

I thought of Jody and wondered where she was, and if she felt as despondent as I did. As I thought about the horrific events of recent weeks involving her family, my burdens paled in comparison. I was only losing a sister. She had lost her entire family. I thought of her enormous grief. And I ached for her. I wished she were here with me now, so we could hold each other and be of comfort. I closed my eyes and tried to remember the first time we had sat on the beach and embraced and kissed for the first time. I could smell the soap on her skin and the shampoo that she used in her hair, and I was there languishing in her affection once again. Jody showed me what love was. While circumstances may have broken my heart, she didn't. I'd never had the kind of feelings Jody brought out in me. They were fine feelings, amazingly deep feelings, feelings I knew she felt for me, too. Although she was not here, I knew that I would never forget her.

As I listened to the waves, I watched the pelicans soar just above the tips of the waves hunting for food, and I thought about Hemingway. I tried to understand what it was about his loss that grieved me so. Was it Mother's adoration that had rubbed off on me? While I credited her with my initial interest, it was his work that drew my admiration. His sentences were so plain, yet the words so well chosen. The "The Old Man and the Sea" brought images from the page to the mind like nothing I had ever read before. After having read it for the fourth time, I wanted to paint pictures with words so real that others would react to what I had written in the same way I reacted to Hemingway. Hemingway, despite his problems, despite the things that people had said about him, created in me a desire to write. While other boys my age were reading the Hardy Boys, my mother hooked me on Ernest Hemingway, and he opened a gritty world of war, love, hunting, fishing, and lust for life beyond my experience.

When people asked me if I wanted to be another Hemingway, or they compared my meager style to his, it only solidified my admiration. I wanted to write like him. I desired to create the emotions in others that he created in me. I longed to visit the places he had visited and to share my experiences with others through the things I wrote. I understood now what it was like to lose people that were important to me. I had lost Hemingway, Helen Holland, Jody, and now Billie.

Sitting on that beach, I hurt beyond anything I had ever experienced. But, unlike Hemingway, I could still write. I could still escape into faraway places. As hopeless as things seemed then, I could still pour myself out on the page and sweep out the darkness from my heart into my stories, instead of keeping my feelings a prisoner. If I had lost my writing maybe, I wouldn't want to live anymore either. I hurt, but I still had hope. I could write.

My dad may have been right about Hemingway. Maybe he was wacko. Maybe I would be, too, if I had lost what he had lost. If I had to choose between writing and not writing, I think I would rather be a writer and chance it making me crazy than not to write at all. And if that's what it took to write then so be it. I wanted to write. No one would dissuade me.

I didn't know enough of Helen to understand what deep losses she may have had that would have driven her to the depths of personal and familial despair. She couldn't have been herself, for the person I knew was both caring and considerate. The desperate act of mass murder and attempted suicide only indicated to me the depths of her despair. I hated what this had done to Jody. I hated that Helen's desperate act took Jody from me. Maybe Helen, like Hemingway, lost something in her life that made her happy, and took her hope away. I didn't know a whole lot about depression, but I knew how awful I felt at the losses of the past month and the feelings they created in me.

She had taken an interest in me, and unselfishly cared enough to send my work to someone else. It was an incredible act of kindness. That was how I wanted to remember her. I wanted to live up to her confidence in me, and to continue to write.

Perhaps of all the disappointments, losing Billie was the greatest. With each of the others, I had felt like I had lost something. With her I felt like I had lost part of myself.

The sandpipers pranced along the edges of the surf looking for food but feared getting wet. They reminded me of her. Billie was never afraid to get wet. She dove into our family headfirst, gambling everything she had emotionally. Ever optimistic, always the encourager, I grieved for her the most, for it was she who had so much to give and so much to lose.

I felt more alone than I ever had. I thought about Billie being alone on a bus headed somewhere, feeling like me, and wondered how she would survive. As she had demonstrated repeatedly, she would bounce back. She would wipe the tears from her face and try to find the good in the situation and focus her thinking on that. I couldn't bear to think of any other outcome. I tried to think like Billie. Difficult as it was, I tried to focus on the good that had come from all of this. It came down to my writing. My story would soon appear in the

Lifetime magazine. I had to look forward to that. But, I still didn't know why Billie had left.

Maybe she didn't want to be there anymore. I dismissed this immediately. I could read Billie well. If she hadn't been happy, I would have known. Even though she hadn't been there long, she was happy. Of that, I was sure. Then something must have happened, something between her and Mother. What could she have done to have angered Mother that much? What could she have done that would have earned her immediate expulsion from our home?

From the looks of the sun and the tides, I had sat there on the beach most of the afternoon. The Australian pines behind me sang soprano in the strong sea breeze as the late afternoon sun settled behind them and the humid air-cooled. I brushed the sand from my shorts and wished I could brush my current hurts from my heart as easily.

When I got home, the house was silent. I searched for Mother and found the door to her room closed and locked. I called for her several times. Either she was asleep or she refused to be bothered.

Not long after I got home, Father came through the front door. His search for Mother had the same result. He came into the kitchen. "Have you seen your mother this afternoon?"

"No."

With no reaction, he headed to the living room, and turned on the television and watched the evening news.

When my father went into Billie's room to go to sleep, my mother finally came out from her room, went to the cabinet, and pulled out a bottle of Chianti. She was in her bathrobe, no makeup and she had pulled her hair back into a ponytail. She sat at the table, lit a cigarette, and poured a liberal amount in a glass that once held Donald Duck grape jelly. I sat down at the table next to her.

"Before you say anything, I'm not good company right now. And I definitely don't want to talk about today." She looked up at me through blood-shot eyes and I knew she was serious.

When I got up the next morning Mother's head was on the table, her hands in her lap, and she snored loudly. I checked Billie's bedroom and the living room, and Father had already gone to work foregoing our normal bike ride. This was the first time I had ever seen my mother drink like that saving the night she used a frying pan on my father.

Hollywood Beach
November, 1995

From the patio of my room at the Vagabond Motel, I tried to think of events of that summer beyond the day that Billie left. None came to mind.

Except that this was when my mother had begun to drink heavily and our long sessions at the kitchen table had been initiated. Mother was convinced that Father was cheating on her, and she felt helpless to do anything about it. She even followed him on some of his evenings out with his friends. Although she never found evidence, it never assuaged her suspicions, which she discussed in detail with me all-too frequently. I had asked her many times about Billie and why she left. Mother would only answer that it was too painful to talk about, and that one day she would tell me.

Sixteen

Savannah, Georgia
1995

Mother's parents passed away before she did, and not long after her older sister succumbed to bone cancer. She had two younger sisters Ruby and Glory Jean. Ruby was a Bible-toting Baptist. Glory Jean was the total opposite of Ruby, a wild free spirit whose flamboyance knew no bounds. I hadn't seen her since Mother's funeral, but she had faithfully sent me greeting cards on all the major holidays. Although I had been to Savannah many times, I had never taken the time to visit her. Guilt filled me as Interstate 16 deposited me into the middle of the old section of town.

I had only met Glory Jean twice in my life, once when I went with Mother to my grandmother's funeral in Charleston and then when Glory Jean came to visit Mother shortly before Mother died, and then she stayed for the funeral. I didn't remember much about her other than a ridiculous hat she wore, a purple monstrosity with an ostrich feather in the band and wild-colored clothing. I also remember she made my mother laugh. As sick as Mother was when Glory Jean came to visit, she brought brightness to the closing moments of Mother's life. I will always remember Glory Jean for that. Try as I did to bring a smile to my mother's frail face, I had failed. It warmed me deeply to see, one final time, the glow in my mother's dancing eyes brought on by Glory Jean's brashness and wit.

Both times, I'd met Glory Jean, I remembered her laugh. It was a wheezing affair, which began with a snort at her nose, a cough, and a sputter until she was out of control. When you heard her laugh, it infected everyone. I tried hard to pull a picture of her into my mind as I watched the house numbers descend to hers.

Savannah had always been one of my favorite places, even more than Charleston. Savannah was a city of dreams still remaining. When I drove her streets and inventoried the many stately homes in disrepair and I thought of what the city must have been like during the boom years of King Cotton and all the history dying with the decaying structures. I imagined the lavish lifestyle of the gentry after the Civil War and saw the warehouses along River Street brimming with white gold. Sailing ships of European lineage clogged the wharf their sailors filled the pubs and inns along the waterfront. Money flowed, and the new rich of the developing American South lined Savannah's newly built streets with their architectural dreams.

The elegantly restored homes gathered around Savannah's many squares provided but a hint of the elegance of the city past. But it was the old, unrepaired, and unloved, clapboard structures with multistoried columns and priceless gingerbread in disrepair that made me wish I lived here. I would buy one of the unwanted treasures and build my life around its restoration and maintenance. I would sit on the wraparound porch in the waning hours of a summer's day and drink mint-iced tea.

I found, in my life, that it was not the things I had accomplished that brought me the most joy, but dreaming about the things I still had left to do. To oversee the reconstruction and renovation of one of these queens-of-the-city, would indeed be the fulfillment of a lifelong dream.

As I pulled up to my aunt's home, I was exhilarated and brought low at the same time. The sheer beauty and charm of Savannah in contrast to the depression one feels as priceless architectural relics die helplessly along many of her streets left me feeling that I should do something to stop the decay.

This sense of duty gnawed at me as I pulled my car to the curb in front of a two-story home of gray unpainted clapboard. My aunt's home was somewhere between renovated and a ramshackle. Freshly painted, crooked, pink shutters framed windows with cracked or broken glass. The porches on the first and second floors sagged, and the disheveled railings on both floors were missing many spindles, but the gaps were filled with bright red geraniums in terra-cotta pots. Lush Boston ferns, hung with macramé, brightened the rotting porches.

I carefully stepped across dry-rotted boards of the porch to the front entry. The screen door looked like the rest of the house. Fresh white paint covered the door, but the metal screen was badly rusted and had been ripped away from the frame at top and bottom opposing corners. The front door was open. A breeze blew from somewhere in the structure out through the screen. Smells of breakfast bacon found me before I knocked on the screen door. I didn't knock hard for fear of unhinging the old door.

I yelled, "Glory Jean. You home?"

From the back of her home somewhere came, "If that's you Jackie, come on in here. If it's a salesman, get off my porch before I call the police. I don't want any."

Rusty hinges creaked as I pulled on the screen door to enter. The inside of the home looked much like the outside. The first floor had a shotgun design: living room, then the dining room, then the kitchen. Peeling ancient wallpaper and sagging plaster ceilings were accented with beige freshly painted wood trim and doors. Aging threadbare furniture in the living room was covered by knitted throws, and gaily embroidered pillows.

The dining room table and hutch I remembered from my grandmother's house in Charleston. A turn-of-the-century solid black walnut set with hand-carved trim barely fit the room. Through the doorway to the kitchen, I could hear Glory Jean padding toward me. She shuffled through the door. Nothing I had imagined prepared me for shock of seeing her. The woman standing in front of me looked much older. She was the personification of the house; a blend of extremely old and poorly applied new.

She could not have been more than a hundred pounds. Wild, rust-colored hair flew out in all directions, a la Phyllis Diller. Thick makeup, the goal of which was to add a youthful appearance to her deeply crevassed face, made her appear more clown than debutante. A brown cardigan sweater hung almost to her knees and a purple print housedress tried to hide itself under the sweater. Purple Birkenstock sandals and flesh-colored support hose completed the ensemble. She approached me, arms outstretched. She said, "Aren't you the picture of your mother."

"I love the house, Glory Jean."

"You don't need to turn on the charm with me, Jackie. We both know the place is falling apart. It's sad really. I wish I had the money to do something with the old place. I'm afraid the house and I are dying together. I just wish I was going as gracefully as the house." She winked and brushed a spray of rusted hair from her furrowed brow.

"She must have been beautiful in her time."

"Me or the house?" she asked with a mischievous smile at the corner of her thin mouth and lips.

"You're still beautiful," I said, trapped.

"Well, I'll say this. You have your mama's charm and your daddy's bullshit." Her eyes squinted into a smile. "If I'm so beautiful, why am I alone? Why am I cooking breakfast for you and me instead of rolling around in the sack with the man of my dreams?"

Before I could speak, she continued. "It's like this house, Jackie. No amount of paint can return her to her youthful beauty. Only major reconstruction could make this house beautiful again. And only re-incarnation could do a thing for me."

I could see an older version of my mother in Glory Jean's face. Her sharp hazel-green eyes and wide expressive brows made me hungry to see Mother again. Glory Jean searched my face, looked up and then back down into my eyes.

"Besides, the only men who have any interest in me . . ." She held up a withered hand, and raised her index finger straight and firm, then slowly curled it over limp — "too old to satisfy the needs of this old woman."

I laughed.

"You don't think a woman my age still has needs?" She was defiant.

I howled.

Her smile originated in her eyes, sending an explosion of wrinkles across her heavily made-up face. She laughed a deep-throated wheeze, slapped the Formica-topped table with the palm of her hand and winked at me. "What brings you to my door, Master Jack?"

Her forthrightness gave me pause. I said with hesitation. "A bit of a family mystery."

"It has to do with Billie, doesn't it? How do you want your eggs?" She turned on her heels and headed to the kitchen.

I said to her back, "Please, nothing for me. I ate before I came. How did you know this was about Billie?"

Glory Jean led me to the kitchen, her sandals slapping against the floor as she walked. "When you called yesterday, I knew it was about her. From the time your mother left home, Billie has always been the only thing that has tied me to her. It's sad really. All those years your mama and I could have been close. And Billie was the only thing that kept us connected."

"Why didn't she try to stay in touch?"

"Your father didn't have much use for your mother's red-neck relatives, sugar. It was only a twelve-hour drive to Charleston, but your daddy wouldn't let her come." She turned the gas off on the frying pan and offered me a seat at the kitchen table. "She called me once, and we talked for over an hour. She wrote me a note that your daddy exploded when he found out how long we had been on the phone. The poor darlin' tried, but . . ." She looked to her right to the window as if a photograph of my mother could be found there. "In the whole time your mama was married to your daddy, I only saw her three times. One of them was just before she died, when her brain was half-eaten with the cancer."

It reminded me of a morning when my mother was driving me to school. She began to cry, so hard in fact that she pulled off the road. I asked her what was wrong. She told me that she missed her mother and sisters and wanted to go see them. But Father wouldn't let her go. She said they didn't have the money. Mother found a receipt the next day on Father's dresser for a deposit for a deep-sea fishing trip in the Keys. The amount of the deposit was nearly the same as the cost of a bus ticket to go to Charleston.

"Why did he want to keep Mother from her family?"

"Part of the mystery, Jack." She got up from the table. "I'll be back. Pour yourself some coffee."

Glory Jean shuffled out of the kitchen, her sandals slapping against the hardwood floors. She was bird-frail, but her eyes were clear and bright. The coffee on the stove, a strong Louisiana blend with chicory, brought back memories of Mother. She occasionally drank the same muddy, bitter, concoction. Like grits, collard greens, hush puppies, and okra, coffee with chicory were ties to my mother's Southern heritage, a lineage my father could not tolerate, a bruise to his Northeastern upbringing. But on rare occasion, she would brave his tyrannical objections and fill the house with the acrid, defiant aroma. Over Glory Jean's percolator, I inhaled deeply. I never understood how my mother drank the stuff. I wondered how to beg off without hurting Glory Jean's feelings.

"I found it," she proclaimed with a shaky loud voice from the back of the house. "I want to show you something, sugar." She appeared at the kitchen door, excited as a child.

She labored to sit at the table and held the picture between bony, arthritic fingers for my examination. "Anna, your mother, Ruby, and myself, just before your mama moved out. I remember the occasion of the picture like it was yesterday. We were sitting in a booth at the Pilot Restaurant, on King Street in Charleston. Bill St. John was struck with your mother. He took our picture to impress your mama with a camera he had just purchased.

The grainy black-and-white photo, taken in the thirties, showed the four sisters huddled together in a booth. Mother sat in the middle. It was amazing how much the four favored each other; wide expressive mouths, narrow small faces, full thick wavy hair, and a smile that was Mother's most valuable asset.

I examined the picture closely. Anna had her arm around Mother's shoulder and Mother had her arms folded with her left hand holding the bicep of her right arm. Glory Jean hugged one of Mother's arms and Ruby had her arm around Glory Jean. On Mother's left hand was an engagement ring, the focal point of the picture.

Glory Jean leaned over the table toward me. "Your mama was so happy then. She certainly had a glow about her." She looked at me and raised an eyebrow.

"She was pregnant?"

"Yes," she said, still hunched over, leaning toward me, pinching at the corner of the picture.

She looked at me for a long time. "She was only sixteen then, Jackie."

When Billie came to stay with us that summer, I had already done the math, calculating how old my mother was when she had Billie. But it wasn't until now that the full weight of her age hit home. "Sixteen. Why so young?"

"Here, take your Aunt Glory Jean for a walk. They say that it ain't safe for a lady to walk the streets of this part of Savannah alone. I've walked these streets alone for years since Jasper died, and I haven't yet been sexually assaulted." She winked at me, pinched a spray of red hair with her fingers and pulled it off her forehead, then pushed herself to stand. "Your mama had a hard childhood, sugar. The Depression in the 1930s was hard enough, without adding all the other woes your mama had to deal with. She did the best a young girl could do."

"I've interrupted your breakfast." I looked to the stove with cooked bacon in the iron skillet.

She looked over at the stove, and at the bacon still sitting in the pan.

"No you haven't. You're taking me out. If you think I'm missing the opportunity for a young good-looking young man to take me out to eat, you're sadly mistaken. But, when we get to the restaurant, I don't want you to tell a soul you're my nephew. It'll drive 'em nuts trying to figure out who you are. Let 'em talk."

I escorted her through the living room toward the front door. "Why did she get married so young?" I asked again.

"We all make choices in life, Jackie, sometimes unwisely so. Even as old as we are now, we are still capable of making poor decisions, even though we have the experience to know better. A girl sixteen, still a child really, doesn't have a chance. She isn't old enough or has enough experience to understand the consequences of decisions made in haste. She has the body and the desires of an adult, but lacks wisdom. In your mother's case, one very poor choice she made without the benefit of experience or wisdom, plagued her for the rest of her life. In my mind, some of the poor choices she made she made trying to fix the first mistake. Sad really. She could have avoided so much heartache had she never slept with Bill St. John."

I had so many questions. Although I could feel my impatience building, I tried to wait for her to explain in her own way and time.

She put her arm through mine and gave it a squeeze. "You're taking me to my favorite place to eat. Would you like to do that?"

"It would be my pleasure."

Seventeen

Savannah, Georgia
1995

Glory Jean hobbled down the steps of her porch. Lined with ancient live oaks flying Spanish moss like ice cycles on a Christmas tree, her street was a worn-down museum of Savannah's architectural past. Although some of the one-hundred-and-fifty-year-old homes had been restored, the majority along her street had been cut up into apartments and left to decay.

Her gait was slow and labored, but determined. With her arm slipped under mine, I could feel the effort that went into each step. If she hurt, as I suspected she did, she never complained.

We came to one of the many small squares in old Savannah and sat on a wrought-iron-and-oak park bench. Behind us, a small fountain bubbled. Shaded by a sprawling live oak, azaleas filled the square, which would have made a picture in bloom; the red, pink, and white blooms against used brick that paved the walkways on the square.

Glory Jean pulled on my arm for balance as she sat and then pulled at me to sit next to her.

"You won't understand what happened to your mama, sugar, till you grasp what happened to our family."

She looked around the square at the homes that had been magnificently restored and I looked with her. Protected by walls constructed of red brick and black wrought iron white clapboard homes trimmed with black shutters lined the streets around the square. If you ignored the cars and noise from trucks making deliveries in the old city, you could imagine it was 1850, and hear the horses clacking down these cobblestone streets pulling fine carriages. It was these departures from reality, inspired by the imposing beauty of parts of Savannah, which made this one of my favorite places.

Chilled by the cool shade, Glory Jean pulled the old cardigan tightly around her shoulders and bunched the lapels up tight around her neck.

"You see, it was like this. Daddy — his name was Chester...Chester Poorie — was a merchant marine. He was a navigator, and he worked the radio equipment, too. Until the Great Depression, he made good money. We had a nice home in North Charleston, but we didn't see him a lot. He might be home for a month or two each year. But Mama, her name was Adie, took good care of us. When the Depression came, and business dried up, so did the shipping business."

She was shivering. I coaxed her up and toward a bench about twenty yards away in the sun. Once we settled in and she assured me she was warmer, she continued. "It's hard to remember details, but I think it was 1934 when Daddy's employer went bust. He was in Auckland, New Zealand when bankers seized his ship. They didn't even give him money to come home, just kicked him off the vessel without a penny. He tried to find work on another rig there in Auckland, but the shipping business was bad there, too. By then the U.S.'s money trouble had spread to the rest of the world. He had to use most of our savings to buy passage home.

"He found work in North Charleston, but it was mostly day-labor. It was enough to put food on the table, but little else. After only a few months, he became depressed. I remember the morning he left. I was always up early, earlier than anyone in the house. I could hear a door close as I came down the stairs to the kitchen. On the table, Daddy had written a note on the back of a page ripped from the calendar Mama hung from the wall in the kitchen. 'Adie, if I stay another day I'll go crazy. In the envelope is every penny we have. I'll try to send more when I find work. Let the girls know how much I love them.'"

"I could see him off in the distance as I ran from the house into the street. When I caught up with him, he acted surprised that I was up.

"I told him that I had read his note. He said that he regretted that I had read before mama. He explained that he had to be on a ship going somewhere. He was a sailor and that he had to be a sailor. He said he told mama when they first got married, that he was married to the sea, too. He made her promise that she would never ask me to quit it. But, she did. He said he just couldn't stay any longer. He felt like he was in prison.

"I asked him about me and my sisters. I told him we needed him and that we didn't make that promise. He said again that he couldn't stay and hoped one day I would understand.

"He pulled me to him and hugged me fiercely. He said that he loved me. He asked me to promise I would be good for mama. Then, he was gone.

"I knew that was the way Daddy was. When he was home, he would usually stay for a month or so. Two months was the longest he ever stayed. By the second or third week, he was itching to leave. Mama used to say that Daddy had seawater for blood, and breathed through gills behind his ears. When Daddy said it was hard to understand, he was right. It was hard then and hard now. I never felt that he really loved us very much. If he had he would have wanted to stay."

"What happened to him?" I shifted in my seat so the sun wasn't in my eyes.

"A few days later the police came to the house. Daddy had been seen in the marina on the Ashley River the night a sixty-foot sailboat had been stolen. Several businesses had been burglarized for provisions. Since he had disappeared, the police assumed he was responsible."

"Did they ever catch him?"

"Nope. And we never heard from him again. Mama made excuses for him. Oh, he was a man of the sea, she said, and once the sea was in the blood, it couldn't be removed. Nonsense. He dumped us. Ran out, the little bastard."

She fell into an uncomfortable silence. She looked troubled. I let the time pass and waited for her to continue.

"That's when our family troubles began. Mama didn't have any skills, 'cept raising children. It wasn't a month after Daddy left that the bank took our home. They even sold off our furniture to pay past due payments. We got to keep our clothes and money Mama had hidden when Daddy left.

"After begging and borrowing from family and friends, in 1935 Mama finally found a job waiting on tables at the Pilot Restaurant. Anna was sixteen, Kit was fourteen, Ruby was twelve and I was eleven then. Mama swapped room and board for twelve-hour shifts cooking in the kitchen and waiting tables. Anna and Kit had to work too. We had a two-room efficiency apartment on the second floor. That's when Mama met Joe O'Connor."

Mother had never talked about her family. Occasionally she would talk about her sisters, Ruby and Glory Jean in particular, never anyone else. At first, I began to listen as Glory Jean talked about her family. Then I realized that she was talking about my grandfather. This was my family history she shared. Glory Jean reached out and took my hand and pulled it into her lap and held it.

"Joe owned a filling station and garage on Chadd Street, one of only two filling stations south of Broad Street. While the Depression raged, Joe's was one of the few businesses that prospered. There may have been a car in every garage in Charleston, but they spent more time in Joe's garage being fixed than they did in carriage houses of Charleston's rich.

"Joe came into the restaurant every morning for breakfast. He was a loud fat little man with atrocious manners who took a shine to Mama. It was after we had been at the Pilot for a year that Joe started pestering Mama about marriage. I never did like Joe O'Connor. He made my skin crawl. When Mama wasn't around I saw the way he looked at Anna, Kit, and Ruby always grabbing at them and pestering them.

"Mama was desperate. She didn't figure that any man would want her, especially with four kids; grown ones at that. So she was flattered when Joe paid her attention. And she was practical, too. When Joe asked her to marry him, she accepted. She saw his house on Queen Street, and the wad of bills that he carried around in his pocket, and fell in love with security. It wasn't until after they returned from the honeymoon and we moved into his home that we found out what Joe really wanted.

"I didn't know this at the time, but we weren't in the house more than a month when he started visiting Anna's room at night. After Anna ran away from home a year after we had been in Joe's home, she warned me of what was going on.

I knew what Joe was up to. It wasn't a month after Anna left when Joe came to my room. I had gotten a butcher knife from the kitchen and hidden it under my mattress. I expected him to smell like booze and grease, but he smelled like soap and toothpaste. He pulled the covers off me and he was just about to crawl into my bed with me when I pulled the knife from the mattress. Oh, Jackie, I was so scared. I had been practicing what I would say and do for a week, because I knew he was coming. I told him if he put one finger on me and I'd cut his gadget clean off. I said that if he stopped me from doing it now, I'd do it some night when he was asleep. I must have been a sight, the blade of the knife pointed at his crotch, the blade shaking more than the hand that held it. I know I was crying with fear, but I held it back and held my ground. He slowly backed out of my room. It wasn't until Kit married and moved out that Joe and I had a rematch.

"I suspected that Joe had more success with Kit. But it wasn't until the day that the picture I showed you was taken that I knew how serious the consequences were and why your mama was so willing to marry Bill St. John."

Suddenly, I didn't want to hear any more. Glory Jean must have sensed my uneasiness.

"Life isn't always as pretty as the stories you write, Jackie. Your mama was dealt a crummy hand. She did the best she could with it, poor thing."

I was angry. "Why didn't you or Anna go to your mother and expose him?"

"Anna tried before she left. But Mama didn't believe her. Joe had Mama convinced that Anna had come to him and tried to seduce him. When he spurned her advances, she concocted this story to get even. It wasn't until Kit married St. John and moved out, and Mama caught Joe trying to attack me that she discovered the truth. By then it was too late for Kit."

"What happened to Anna?"

"Anna fared better than your mama did. Anna was strong, a fighter. Her scars were temporary."

It was approaching the lunch hour and I suggested to Glory Jean that she show me the restaurant she wanted to eat at.

The building looked like it might have been a corner drug store long ago, not a quarter of a mile from Glory Jean's home. There was no sign on the front of the establishment, but by a quarter till twelve, the small place was nearly full.

"Ah, the sexiest woman in all of Savannah. And who is this handsome man with you, Glory Jean?" A balding man in his sixties, with a white long-sleeved shirt, black pants, and a white apron greeted us.

She put her arm in mine and pulled me close to her. "A friend, Carlo." She drew the word friend out slowly.

"You mean there is another man who competes with me for your affection?" Carlo winked at me when Glory Jean looked away. "And you have the brass to bring him here, to my restaurant, to flaunt him in front of me? I'm truly hurt." Carlo pouted.

"I couldn't wait for you any longer, Carlo. The only woman in the world you care about is this restaurant. I'm growing old waiting for you. I had to move on." She gave me a nudge in the ribs with her elbow.

Carlo reached for her hand, pulling the back of it to his lips. "You know that you're the only woman in the world for me, Glory Jean."

Then I noticed that most of the patrons were elderly.

"What about me, Carlo? Am I the only woman you care about, too?" a woman with another man in the rear of the restaurant yelled to him.

Carlo turned. "Yes, my dear. I love only you."

"And what of me, Carlo? Am I still the only woman you love?" pleased a silver-haired woman joined by others her age, pleaded.

"You are all my only love." With a sweep of his arm, he bowed low.

Glory Jean slapped at his arm. "We're hungry. Got a table?"

And, the patrons laughed and threw their hands at Carlo and went back to their conversations and food. He showed us to a table by the window. The inside of the restaurant was a harsh white. The forest green carpet did little to relieve the hospital feel. Only the assorted flowers in vases on the tables brought any color to the place. It was clear that Carlo was the draw. I hoped the food had the same charm.

I looked around and many of the older women pointed at me and talked in whispers to others at their tables.

"They're all dying to know who you are."

"Do you know them?"

"This is an elderly neighborhood. Carlo takes good care of us. He's been here for years. The city tries to get us to go to the community center. We come here. These are my friends, good ones at that. Your visit will keep them buzzing for a week. Oh, I'll tell them eventually who you are. But not today. Let 'em drool."

The menu was split between a collection of blue-plate specials on one side of the menu, and diet-type dishes on the other.

Carlo strolled to our table. "Glory Jean, I have not seen you for days. Have you been okay?"

"Trying to make the check stretch." It was approaching the end of the month.

"You know you can come here anytime. Money is never a problem here."

She dismissed his comment with a wave of her hand. "How about your meatloaf?"

Carlo looked at me.

I said, "Meatloaf sounds good to me."

Carlo scribbled a note to himself. "Two orders of meatloaf it is."

"So tell me about the day the picture was taken."

"Anna, Kit, Ruby and I were at the Pilot the day after Bill St. John asked Kit to marry him. St. John was also a patron of the restaurant, an antique dealer in his late twenties, who had built a rather substantial business on King Street a few doors down from the Pilot. Kit had just turned sixteen and he was smitten with her. It was the first time the four of us had been together since Anna left. Kit vehemently denied that Joe had forced her to have sex with him. Anna continued to assure her that it was alright to talk about it, that he had forced himself on her and that Kit needed to talk about it. But she continued her denial.

"You think she was pregnant when that picture was taken?"

"I didn't know that for sure then. It wasn't until I visited your mother just before she died that she confirmed my suspicions. She said O'Connor had threatened to kill her and her mother if she told anyone."

"Billie is Joe O'Connor's child?"

"Yes. I thought so then. But Kit never would admit it, even when she ended up delivering a seven-and-a-half-pound baby girl six and a half months after marrying Bill St. John."

"Didn't he suspect that the child was not his?"

"Yes. Kit, bless her heart, never changed her story that Billie was Bill's child. Their marriage began to crumble when Billie was born. Bill knew that his namesake was not his child. It wouldn't be until 1945 when Kit was nineteen that she filed for a divorce."

Carlo delivered our lunch. While Glory Jean occupied herself with her meal, I thought about what I had just learned. The fact that Billie was Joe O'Connor's child could explain why Mother had abandoned her as a child. I would think she would be a constant reminder to her of the treatment she received from Joe O'Connor. While this might be a reason, I still had a hard time imagining Mother leaving Billie behind. There had to be more. There had to be a better explanation.

Eighteen

Savannah, Georgia
1995

Glory Jean picked at her food and then finally pushed her plate away. "The divorce between your mama and Bill St. John was difficult. I was living in a small apartment building. She moved into the apartment upstairs from mine. The state awarded her Billie, but St. John got out from under alimony and paid only minimal child support. It wasn't that he couldn't afford to pay her. I think he wanted to put her in a financial position where she couldn't afford to keep her, hoping to get her back. But Kit was a resourceful woman.

"The war was at its end when your mama filed for divorce. During the war, the navy shipyard hired women from all walks of life to be welders, riveters, plumbers, and electricians. Kit went to welding school, and worked in dry dock repairing battle-damaged ships. She hired a woman to sit for Billie and managed to make ends meet. That's when she met your daddy, just as the war was ending. Do you remember what it was like when you fell in love for the first time, Jackie?"

I nodded, thinking of Jody Holland.

"Remember your mama had never been in love before. She never had a chance. Before St. John, she had worked almost every waking hour. When she was married to him she had a small child and a husband to care for, when other girls her age were going to proms and dating. And when she left him, she had to go to work immediately to care for her child. And let me tell you, the work at the navy base was hot, miserable, hard, physical work, twelve hours a day, six days a week.

"Your father was a Lieutenant JG assigned to oversee the repairs to the ship while in dry dock. He met your mama when she worked on his ship, and invited her to the Officers' Club for a drink. That's all it took. She was deeply in love. Sugar, your daddy was a handsome man; an educated man, too. He swept your mama off her feet. I don't know how she did it, working all day, going out with him every night, and caring for Billie. But she managed.

"The war ended before repairs on your daddy's ship were finished. Then the shit hit the fan so to speak.

"Your daddy was being discharged from the service. Kit was heartbroken. She was sure he was leaving to go home, and she'd never see him again. Then he asked her to marry him. But things were not quite that simple.

"Your daddy was Catholic, and Kit was a divorced woman. Today that would be easy enough to fix. Annulments are pretty easy to come by. Not then. They wanted to get married in the Catholic

Church but found out it wasn't possible without a lengthy process. They eloped and got married by a justice of the peace. Then things got very complicated.

"Paul wanted to move to Orlando and live with his parents until he found work. They didn't want Paul's parents to know that Kit had been married before, not right away. When they came back from their honeymoon, they decided to leave Billie with a sitter for a few weeks until Paul found work, and could muster the nerve to tell his family about Billie. That was your mama's first big mistake. She should have never left Billie, even for a couple of days."

"So, she abandoned her."

"Yes. But that's not the whole story. She was so deeply in love with your daddy. This was the first time in her life that anything good had really happened to her. She would have done anything he asked her to do."

"So how does that make it better? The bottom line is she left Billie with a stranger and took off."

"Not a stranger, Jackie. The sitter was a long-time family friend. She lived in the same apartment building that your mother and I lived in. She had been watching Billie since Kit left St. John. No, she didn't leave Billie with a stranger. She was well cared for, and the woman was willing to watch her for Kit."

"But she still ran off without Billie."

"I think your daddy had a hard time finding a job. A few weeks dragged into months. Then Bill St. John filed for custody. The state put Billie into a foster home, while the case wound its way through the courts. Two years after your mama left with your daddy, the courts awarded Bill St. John custody."

"Two years!"

Glory Jean looked away from me and at people who crossed the street. "I know it doesn't sound good. But your mama loved Billie. She was also deeply in love with your daddy. And your mama was in a home where no one knew she had a child. She couldn't talk about her or get in touch with Billie. It must have been horrible for her."

"If she truly loved Billie, she would never have agreed to marry a man who wanted to hide her. If she truly loved Billie, she would never have agreed to leave her behind. If she had been your child, what would you have done?"

She stared at me for several minutes. "I would never have left her. But I didn't go through all the things that your mother went through either."

"She dumped her. She ran off on her. She deserved to lose her. Two years! I can't believe it." I was furious. "I understand she had gone through a lot. But nothing excused just leaving Billie like that. Nothing."

There was a long silence. Suddenly, I could see that my words had troubled her, and made her feel uncomfortable. "I'm sorry, Glory Jean. I didn't come here to vent my anger on you. I came to learn what I could. And you've been most helpful."

She grabbed my hands on top of the table. "Kit was a fine woman. She loved Billie. She would never have done what she did without good reason."

"Do you know what that good reason was?"

"When I went to see Kit before she died, I was going to ask her about it. But she was in so much pain that I didn't have the heart to bring up old wounds. She had enough trouble without me adding to it."

"Well, are you two lovebirds finished with your lunch?" Carlo began to clean the plates off the table before we had an opportunity to answer.

I looked up at our host. "We'll take a check, please."

"On the house, I just want you to know that there are no hard feelings about you stealing the love of my life from me." He rubbed the back of my neck and winked at me. "My beautiful Glory Jean. It was such a pleasure having you with us. Not so long next time, or I come to your house myself to escort you."

"I'm sure your heart will heal and you'll find someone else, perhaps not as beautiful as me."

"To be sure." And with a flourish of his hands, he left to tend to the rest of his flock.

Walking back to her house I asked her, "So what of Billie?"

"After Billie left your mama's, the only time I had seen her was at your mother's funeral. She would call or write a couple of times a year to learn if I had heard from or talked to your mama. She moved around a lot; California, New York, Georgia. It seemed like every year she was somewhere new. After your mama died, I didn't hear from her again. I'd send her Christmas cards, but they would be returned. After a couple of years I stopped trying to send her things." She stopped and turned to look at me. "Now there's a child who's had it hard. Poor thing."

"Billie always seemed so upbeat and together. The world could be falling apart around her, and she was always the one providing encouragement."

We passed the square that we had stopped at on the way to the restaurant. "Whew, I need to stop for a minute. You walk too fast for an old broad."

Glory Jean aimed her backside at the park bench and sat down with effort. Pigeons filled the square, cooing and scratching around, begging for handouts. The pleasant afternoon sun warmed the skin and my mood.

I took in the sight of this frail bird of a woman and realized how much I had enjoyed my time with her. I suddenly felt guilty that I had not visited her more often. She and Ruby were the only relatives of my mother still alive. Since Mother's death, the only effort I had made was to answer the many cards she faithfully sent each year.

"What happened to Ruby?"

"She ran away, south to Jacksonville. She bolted before Joe O'Connor had the first thought of visiting her room late at night. I encouraged her to leave. An old friend of O'Connor's, a guy named Barnes I think, lived south of Jacksonville and had stopped in Charleston with his family to visit Joe. He had a daughter Ruby's age. They took Ruby in. Joe was furious when she left, but Mama finally caught on to what Joe was doing and threatened to expose him if he went looking for her."

Glory Jean patted my knee. "Enough unpleasantness. Tell me something about my famous nephew."

"What do you want to know?"

"Everything. When I tell all my friends that you're not my gigolo lover, they're going to want to know who you are. And, when I tell them who you really are, they are going to want to know everything. A bunch of old hens with time on their hands and all they have to talk about is their families, and the good old days."

"I was born . . ."

"I know all that. Tell me about your writing career."

"Like what?"

"Are you married?"

"What does that have to do with my career?"

"Just tell me."

"I thought we weren't going to talk about unpleasantness."

"You're not happy?"

"I'm not unhappy. Well, at least not with Emily. She's not happy. She left me four days ago."

"You have a girlfriend on the side and she found out?" She almost licked her lips at the prospect.

"Nothing like that."

"What did you do?"

"Why did I have to do something? Let's talk about something pleasant."

"What did you do?"

"Nothing!" The word came out almost angry. Recovering, I said, "Well, doing nothing is probably why she left."

"Couldn't get it up? Oh, I'm sorry today they call that erectile dysfunction."

"What is it with you?" I looked at her and her eyes danced with delight.

"That's it, isn't it?"

"No. It isn't. Well, not entirely." I scrambled for an answer. "I've been pretty depressed. Can't write.

Can't do much of anything. I guess she finally got tired of it and left."

"Tell me about her?"

"Nothing much to tell."

"Sugar, for a writer you sure are short on words. Where did you meet?"

"About nine years ago when my editor retired after working with me for twenty years. I called Stetson University's English Department to see if I could find a promising English major, someone I could train. The receptionist who took the call was just graduating with a master's and asked if she could interview for the job. She had gotten a divorce and gone back to school for her master's."

"Was she pretty?"

"Astonishingly."

"Big-breasted blonde?"

I turned and looked at her.

"Well, that's what all the female characters in your books are."

"Emily has a lot more class than that. When she came for her interview, I thought she looked like Jaclyn Smith. Midway through the interview I decided that she was even more beautiful." I could still picture her sitting across from me in my studio. Small oval face, high cheekbones, olive skin, light brown eyes, and flawless makeup. She had worn an autumn-colored skirt and blouse. "I kept stumbling over my questions I was so taken with her. I kept saying to myself that I would never be able to write with her around. I'd be looking at her all the time."

"She sounds young?"

"She was twenty-nine. Eleven-year difference."

"Was she a good editor?"

"Awful. Missed too many of my errors. But, she had a real knack for plot development. She could come up with real inventive twists and turns that made my work so much better. That was her real strength. Before she was divorced and went back to school, she had worked as a legal assistant to an attorney/agent who handled athletes. It turned out she was an exceptional business manager. Within six months, she became my manager and my editor. And she excelled at it."

"So how long was it before you started chasing her around the desk?"

I stared at her again in disbelief.

"You wouldn't deny an old woman a little vicarious pleasure, would you?"

"My life isn't a romance novel, woman."

"Sugar, all of life is a romance novel. If anyone should understand it, you should. Romance is the juice of life, the glue holds atoms together. So when did you decide that you wanted her?" Her eyes may have been a little cloudy with cataracts, but there was no mistaking the mischief. She had hit the nail on the head. It had been a long time since I had romance in my life, about as long as it had been since I had written anything meaningful.

"I want you to understand that Emily looked like a model in just about everything she wore. She always came to the house dressed professionally, wearing a skirt and heels. I told her she didn't need to dress so formally, that she could wear casual clothes. She never did, until she had been working with me for four months. She came to work in tight-fitting jeans, smelling of citrus, and wearing a long-sleeved starched white shirt that buttoned down the front. We had been openly flirting with each other for several weeks, but I just never got up the courage to confront it. As the day progressed, she would nonchalantly unbutton another button on her shirt until it was opened almost to her waist. I finally took the hint and attacked her." Just thinking about that day brought a smile to my face.

"You still love her, don't you?"

"Deeply."

She reached for my hand, pulled it into her lap and held it. "You'll work it out."

"Emily can be as hard as granite. That's what made her such a great manager and agent. When she made up her mind about something, she was immovable. No, I don't think she'll be back."

"So, are you just going to roll over and let her leave? Aren't you going to try? If you don't try to get her back, she will see that as proof that you didn't love her. At least that's how I would feel. Of course, right now I would just settle for having someone around, much less wanting to leave them." She shooed away a pigeon pecking at her toe. She squeezed my hand and seemed content to let silence settle for a moment.

A horse-drawn carriage's metal wheels clattered against the brick pavers no doubt carrying tourists on a guided adventure through the old restored section of the city. With an air of bored condescension, the driver looked down at us as they passed by only briefly halting his narrative of the history of the city.

"Why are you so unhappy? You have everything."

"It's hard to explain. I just feel dead inside. No emotions. It's not Emily's fault. I just don't feel anything. As much as I love her, I just can't express it. She is better off without me. It's just like writing. I want to write. I just can't write. It's as if I have no power. No power to write, no power to keep Emily, no power to keep going."

Glory Jean turned and perched herself on the edge of the bench. "I've been where you are, Jackie. It's like being in a dark hole and you can't pull yourself out. Those feelings are the most awful feelings you can have. I can only speak for myself, but when I was in that dark hole, it was if I wanted to be there. And the only way out, was to make a decision that I wasn't going to hide there anymore. It was as if I decided to be miserable, and the only way to end it was to decide not to be miserable anymore.

"There aren't many things that I have learned in my lifetime that are very important to me right now. When I was younger, I had the mistaken notion that the world was here for my enjoyment, and love's purpose was to make me happy. We aren't complete until we love someone else. It's our purpose. We need to express love to someone else more than we need to someone to love us. We need to give ourselves to someone else to be happy. Sugar, it's a privilege to have the Emily's in our lives. We need someone to whom we can give our love, not the other way around. It's not what we get that completes us, it's what we give."

She reached out, took my neck, pulled me close to her, and held me, and I languished in it. "Now, you go find Emily. You make sure you don't lose her. Nothing in your life is more important."

Nineteen

Mount Dora, Florida
1995

I felt like the Spanish moss that hung from the limbs of an ancient oak by the lake's edge: shredded, lifeless, tossed by the circumstantial winds of my life. A pontoon boat glided along the shore of Lake Dora. Partygoers on the festive vessel talked loudly and laughed. Music, sounding like Linda Ronstadt echoed softly on the water from the boat, a ballad as smooth as a sip of Merlot. The horizon still burned with the oranges and reds of sunset, but the water was dark and the air was cool.

The drive from Savannah left me drained. Except for landscape lights along the drive and front walk, the house was dark. After a short tour of the house, it was apparent Emily had been there for selected furnishings. The master bedroom furniture was gone. A clock radio, a lamp from the nightstand, a chrome tray that I put pocket change on that sat atop the dresser, and my clothes from the dresser were all that remained.

Throughout the house familiar landmarks were missing, just the things that one would need to fill an apartment. A note was tacked to the refrigerator door with a magnet.

"Jack, I helped myself to some things I'll need until the divorce is settled. I hope you don't mind. I called Jack Spears and he suggested that we attempt to mediate a settlement first before we get our own separate attorneys. He suggested David Huff in Eustis. I called him and he's available in two weeks. I booked the appointment. Let me know if it will work for you. I put my address and phone number in your computer. Em."

Emily, was always efficient and professional. A woman who always knew what she wanted and she wasted little time acquiring it. She was moving quickly. I gave my own chances of dissuading her from her course as low. But, Glory Jean was right, I needed to try. Emily turned pages in her life quickly. I needed to do something very soon or I would lose her.

I turned on my computer, and pulled up my address book and found her number.

I got her answering machine.

"Em, it's me. I just got home. I . . ." I heard someone pick up.

"Jack, I'm here."

"You okay?"

"Yeah, I'm fine. What's up?"

"I just got home. The place looks empty."

"Jack, I tried to be as judicious as I could." She was defensive.

"I'm not talking about the furniture, Em. The house is empty without you."

Silence.

"Your note sounded like there is no hope here. Mediators, attorneys. Sounds pretty final."

"It is final, Jack."

"Can't we get together and talk? This is tearing me up."

"There's nothing to talk about. Nothing's changed."

"I went to see LuAnn. She believes my depression is tied to unresolved anger with my mother, and how she handled my sister, Billie."

"Billie?"

"I told you that my mother had been married before. Billie's my half-sister."

"Okay."

"LuAnn suggested I dig into why my mother threw Billie out of our home when I was a child. I went to Savannah this morning. Now I'm going to try to find Billie."

"Uh-huh. And she thinks this is going to help?"

Her skepticism wounded me.

"Listen, Jack. We've been down this road before. You know what I'm saying? She hasn't helped you a bit. It's the same old stuff. You go to her. You come home with new things to think about, and a week later, I'm scraping you off the floor. I'm over it."

"It's hard to explain everything that happened in her office and what I learned in Savannah. If we could just spend some time together, and let me explain."

"I've heard it all before. You're not happy. You're not happy with your work. You're not happy with yourself and you're not happy with me. You're miserable. It's making me crazy, too. I won't do this anymore."

"You won't even give me an hour?"

"No. I'm sorry."

"You owe me that."

"I owe you? I owe you? Let's talk about what you owe me." Her breathing was heavy on the phone. "How about paying me back for all the time I've wasted in counseling? How about all the nights we spent home when we could have been out having fun? How about paying me back for the friends that we've lost because you wanted to be alone. How about paying me back for all the sex I've missed in three years. And how about all the time that I didn't get to spend with you? I owe you nothing."

"I guess I had that coming. I just wanted to see you, to talk to you. That's all. I feel awful."

"I feel awful, too, Jack. But, what has really changed? So you went to see LuAnn. That's good. But, what's different? What's changed? You know what I'm saying?"

I didn't have an answer. The longer I took to answer, the more distance I could feel. "I don't know, Em. Except that I don't want it to be over. Before, I didn't really care if I came out of it or not. I don't want to live like this anymore. I may not know how to fix it, but I don't want to live in a pit anymore."

The silence extended longer than I felt comfortable. But I was determined to wait until she responded. "Jack, I know this is difficult for you. I know you're struggling. But things have been bad for so long that you've got me in that same pit with you. I feel like I'm losing it. The longer I stay with you, the deeper I get myself. I feel like you're sucking the life out of me. I have to think of myself right now. I can't help you. The only person I can help right now is me, and it's taking every bit of energy I have to do that." More silence. "I have to go."

"I love you, Em. I'm sorry I've put you through all this. It hasn't been fair, I know."

More silence, then, "I hope you figure it out and get a handle on your life."

"Just give me some time before you file for a divorce. That's all I'm asking right now. You don't even have to talk to me. Just give me some time."

"How much time?"

"A month or two, until I get Reynolds and Ryan off my back."

"And what will happen in a month or two?"

"I don't know. If I'm still the same then divorce me. I just need a little more time."

"Two months?"

"Just two months."

"Alright, two months. But I make no promises, Jack."

"I'm not asking you to. Do you need anything?"

"No. I'm fine."

I hung the receiver on the wall phone and watched the long cord swing back and forth until it came to a rest. Suddenly, I felt like an adolescent child who wet the bed and was horrified it would continue, embarrassed beyond comprehension at my affliction, and powerless to stop it.

Was the solution as simple as Glory Jean had suggested, just deciding not to be depressed anymore? Could it have been that simple for Hemingway and for Helen Holland? Could Mother have simply decided one morning that she would no longer live in her self-created pit of worthless feelings? Could she have avoided years of alcoholism, and ill health by simply deciding to take a different path? If it was that simple, why was it so hard to do it?

Or was it as LuAnn described? Are we merely programmable vessels into which our parents deposit a code? Like computers that are programmed with certain information, are we programmed through instruction and circumstance mostly at the hands of unwitting and untrained mentors? Was LuAnn right? That the only way out of the pit is to figure out where the ancestral programming mistakes were made, and write some new code, an emotional patch written around the glitch, or was it just as simple as deciding?

I wished Emily knew how much I hated living as I had been. My depression was a self-made prison. At least with her, she had made my existence those past months tolerable. It frightened me to think of being alone, without her standing watch, to guard me from myself.

I struggled to find a way to explain it to her. It was as if I was an actor, living out a life and a part I didn't choose, hating the role, wanting it to be different, but powerless to walk off the stage. It was like driving down the road with a wheel stuck in a track, and as hard as I tried to turn the wheel, the car continued on its own course, at its own speed. If Mother had felt like this, then I understood why she hadn't wanted to live anymore. She hadn't had the courage to take her own life. Instead, her emotional state infected her body with a self-inflicted cancer. She may not have used a gun, but she killed herself just the same, horribly and painfully, one cell at a time.

Billie held the key. Billie's departure was the downward turning point in my mother's life. It is when my feelings for my mother turned to anger. I was afraid to see Billie. I was embarrassed that I hadn't made more of an effort to find her before now. Would her feelings for me still be the same or had she painted me with the same brush she no doubt had painted my mother? If I had suffered at Mother's hands, what of her? My problems paled in comparison to what she must have gone through.

I used an Internet personal search program and found four Billie St. Johns. I located her in Key West on the second call. The ease with which I found her, and the fact that she lived so close, both added to my guilt.

"Billie St., John?"

"Yes."

"Does the name Kit McNamara mean anything to you?"

Long silence. "Who is this?"

I could tell from her voice that it was Billie. "It's your brother, Jack."

Another stretch of silence. "Jack?"

"It's me, Billie. I feel awful that I've waited all these years to call you. I feel terrible."

"And how old were you when I saw you last?"

"Fourteen."

"I must have been seventeen or eighteen years old."

"Seventeen. Thirty-four years ago."

"Why are you calling me?" Her voice had a very sharp edge.

"I need to see you."

"What about?" I didn't have any expectations of how she would react when I called, but I wasn't prepared for this.

"Personal things. I just need to talk to you."

"What could be so important that after thirty-four years you suddenly need to talk to me?"

"I just need some help - your help. I'm having some personal struggles and you may be able to help me."

She roared with laughter into the phone. "This is amazing. Where were you when I needed help? Where were all of you? And now you're having some personal problems and you call Billie." She nearly sang the words, personal problems. "This is truly amazing. Thanks for calling, brother, but, you called at a bad time."

"Then when should I call?"

"Thirty years ago. Now leave me alone." She hung up.

I called back and reached her voice mail. I hung up and tried to call again, with the same result. This time I decided to leave a message.

"Billie. I've been depressed for months. My life seems to be falling apart. My counselor thinks that it has to do with Mother. I have never forgiven her for throwing you into the street the way she did. I need to understand what happened. I know you're angry with me. You have good reason. I should have called long ago. I hope you can find it in your heart to forgive me." A beep came over voice mail signaling that time had expired. I called back again and waited to leave a second message. "Billie, I want to come see you. Please call me back and let me know it's okay."

I hung the phone up, and hoped she would return my call.

I went to the store for food. When I returned Billie had called and left a message on my machine.

"Jack. Billie. I'm not crazy about you coming. The last thing I need now is you dredging up old wounds. But you're my brother. I owe you that much. I live on Whitehead Street across from Mel Fisher's Museum. It's near Mallory Square in the old section of Key West. Alex is on a trip, so this would be a good time for you to come. I'll plan on seeing you tomorrow morning."

The message was cold, impersonal. And, I was thankful she agreed to see me.

Twenty

Key West, Florida
1995

The salt air filled my nostrils and cleansed me of the mainland as I ascended the bridge leaving Marathon for the lower Keys. I was once again taken aback by the surreal greenish-blue waters that served as a backdrop for small Key islands and mangrove swamps. I grew up around the blue-gray waters of the Atlantic Ocean. As a child, I played on the white sand beaches of South Florida and swung from the fronds of coconut palms that lined Hollywood Beach. But this was man's created version of paradise. The Keys were God's version.

Amid the abundance of water, the Keys had an arid appearance and unlike the rest of Florida, rainfall was sparse. Sea grape, mangrove, buttonwood and Australian pine found abundant life in the high humidity and infrequent rainfall. As I drove south, jutting out from US-1 were long fingers of land formed from shifting sand and mangrove root. These thin and infrequent peninsulas became winter havens for the rich who created their version of paradise behind gated entrances and sun-bleached asphalt.

It had been nearly thirty years since my last visit to the Keys, and as I passed through Islamorada,

Marathon, and points south, I became uncomfortably aware that the cancer of explosive growth that had ruined the rest of Florida had devastated this most delicate of Florida environs. Like a beautiful woman, the Keys could not hide its beauty with the makeup of developments and resorts. I still found Florida's strand of pearls astonishing in its raw unabridged beauty; the blues, greens and grays of water struggling for control of the reefs and sands only a few feet from the surface of the briny water.

The evidence of the lower Key's dependence on the mainland abounded with high power-lines and telephone cables that escorted the concrete and macadam road to Key West. I tried to fill up with gas at Big Pine Key and discovered that a construction crane had unwittingly swung a boom into a neutral line and had taken down two spans of wire, cutting power all the way to a place called Kokomo behind the Casa Marina Hotel close to the southernmost point of the United States.

Impatient drivers, pulling boats, RVs and piloting big rigs suffered the clogged two-lane highway, the only link to Florida's mainland. Although the speed limit was fifty-five, the convoy never made it above forty-five, exasperated drivers passing me only to get stuck behind another slow-moving car only two or three vehicles in front of me.

Parallel to the highway was the abandoned remnants of the first overseas highway constructed on the bridges and infrastructure of the abandoned Florida East Coast Railway, first constructed and completed in 1912. The Hurricane of 1935 destroyed huge sections of track and isolated the lower Keys. Henry Flagler abandoned plans to rebuild the railroad in favor of deeding over the right-of-way and remaining track to the state of Florida. The state modified the old railroad bed for vehicular traffic and created the first road covering the 150 miles south from Miami to Key West in 1938. Standing relics of concrete and iron quietly bespoke the engineering marvel of connecting such a far-flung collection of islands. The rhythmic click of my tires on the expansion joints of the new seven-mile bridge became accompanying music as I watched span after span of abandoned concrete and steel of the old seven-mile bridge, and thought about the significant human effort that went into its creation. Pelicans used the structure as a resting place between their graceful flights foraging for delicacies from the deeper channels that led to the Atlantic Ocean and the Gulf of Mexico.

The road widened at the naval air station at Boca Chica and ushered me into the heart of the narrow palm-laden streets of Key West. It was not the Key West I had remembered as an adolescent. In the 1960s, I had seen an island desperate to survive;

an island in need of restoration noted for its cheap motels, sailors, and fish camps. As I drove west along North Roosevelt Boulevard, the evidence of Key West's adulthood became evident. Key West had taken its proper place with Miami, Naples, Orlando, and West Palm as a tourist trap. The once sleepy fishing village had been transformed into a bustling resort town.

There had always been a war in Key West between bawdiness and respectability. A part of this boisterous city had always catered to the vagabond youth who have for decades prowled its streets in search of spirits and an overnight companion. But there had always been a part of Key West that had attempted to make itself into something finer. Like zirconia, it had only created the appearance of something refined. Like Charleston and Savannah, Key West had a quaintness and charm that its age and architecture created. But unlike Charleston and Savannah it lacked lineage. Key West had the distinction as the southernmost city without the pretense of the Deep South. When I walked the narrow streets and alleyways south of Broad Street in Charleston, I knew that my name would never appear in her social registers. While I could have owned property in this most venerated of neighborhoods, I would not be a part of her ancestry; I did not have the right blood coursing through my veins. Unlike her blue-blooded Georgia and South Carolina sisters, Key West was accepting of those who lacked nobility and warmly received those who wished to make zirconia into diamonds.

While Key West struggled desperately to direct the focus of her visitors on the rewritten history of its checkered past and guide them past the homes that spoke of its flashes of opulence, the limelight was greedily purloined by bars and nightlife along Duval Street. Ships from around the world still moored at her docks as they had for more than three centuries, and filled her streets with many tongues from distant continents. And the city showed her gratitude and satisfied those seeking the warmth of her climate and quenched the thirst of her many visitors in her bars. Military men and women from the backwater towns across the heartland still journey her streets in search of freedom from morals imposed by parents and to lose their innocence.

Therefore, the war between the city's need for respectability clashed with its visitor's desire to buy T-shirts and drink youthful quantities of beer. As I drove the streets of Key West in search of my half-sister, I was easily distracted by this island with multiple personalities. I would have preferred to sojourn her streets than face the spotted elements of my own history. My heart longed to dig into the history of this unique island rather than dredge up the coral of my own past.

The house on Whitehead Street was unexpected. I had only sketchy details about my sister's life in Key West. The home and its location advertised significant wealth. I drove past the two-story structure, awestruck and nearly ran over a pedestrian who cursed me in some Hispanic dialect, no doubt a passenger on a day visit from the cruise ship docked nearby and visible from my sister's house. Tourists clogged the streets. Drivers double-parked cars waiting impatiently for people to vacate the metered parking spaces. I parked my car a block away near the old navy base directly in front of the Harry S. Truman Little White House and walked the short distance back to my sister's grand home.

The house was fitted with white clapboard and mint-green shutters and faced the wharf. Beyond the Maritime Museum that was directly across the street, the Hilton Resort neared completion next to the aquarium. To the right, just off Wall Street, the behemoth old Customs House with deep red brick and Elizabethan architecture underwent restoration.

I turned to take in the breadth of my sister's home. Porches wrapped around the house on both the first and second floors. Ornate Bahamian-style woodwork added elegance and shade to the front of the house and enormous Boston ferns displayed in woven rope hangers softened the porches and made them warm and appealing. Attic dormers in the silver metal roof provided a vantage of the harbor.

244

I stood across the street and worked up the courage to cross the short distance to my sister and answers to questions that had haunted me the majority of my life. Words that so easily found their way to my lips were lost in a heart afraid to find the truth. I leaned up against a power pole and looked up and down Whitehead Street like an animal that searched for a route to escape. The demons that haunted me would not be exorcised until Billie revealed what had happened to her.

A white picket fence surrounded the house. A forty-foot Banyan tree with its spider web of above-the-ground roots had taken up the entire front yard. I pushed open the wooden gate, which had a sign warning against trespassing and made my way to the gray, freshly painted wooden steps. I reluctantly knocked on the front door and peered through the leaded glass windows on either side of the solid white door. Vague shadows flashed across the glass and the door opened with a bolt.

"Can't you see the sign on the fence young man?" the elderly woman said with a thick German accent. The woman was noticeably agitated as she looked over my shoulder to a group of Latino tourists who had stepped inside the gate that I had left open to take pictures. "Now look at what you have done." She hobbled down the steps, shooed the picture-takers from the yard and secured the gate. Then she turned her attention toward me as she struggled to climb the two steps onto the porch.

"I'm Jack McNamara. I'm here to see my sister, Billie. She is expecting me." My announcement had not changed the irritated look on the woman's face.

"Of course you are," she said as though she were disappointed that I had some legitimate reason to stand on her private porch. "I guess you will want to come in?" she asked, not expecting an answer as she pushed in on the heavy wooden door and entered the house. "Please sit down and I will tell her you are here," she said over her shoulder as she disappeared into the depths of the house.

The bare hardwood floors squeaked as I made my way from the foyer into the living room. White wicker furniture and the colors of spring flowers on the upholstery and window coverings gave the room a bright appearance. A ceiling fan labored silently above my head. I walked to the window that faced the side of the house and was impressed with the courtyard and garden that flanked the house.

"Jackie?"

Turning to face her, I was astonished at how she resembled our mother. Shortly cropped red hair aside, her green eyes were the centerpiece of an oval face. Thin expressive lips renewed fading memories of how my mother had looked. The woman standing in front of me was the same age as our mother when she had died nearly eighteen years ago. At age fifty-two, Billie looked remarkably the same as the Billie who had hugged me and kissed me goodbye so many years ago.

"So how's the famous writer?" Her voice displayed none of the animosity that laced our conversation yesterday.

"Juiceless."

She looked puzzled for a moment. "Ah, juice. Hemingway. Your mother and her juice. I don't think I'll ever forget that." Suddenly, tears streamed down her cheek. "Lots of memories, Jackie. Not all of them are bad."

I forded the distance between us and hugged her. Then she cried softly. The embrace was long and silent like the gulf of the years that had separated us. I pushed away and took in the sight of her. The years had been kind to her. She had our mother's facial features and coloring but she was taller, her face more youthful. Although she looked like Mother, and each of the features of her face matched our mother's, the arrangement of these features on Billie's face did not match the allure of our mother's. Billie wore faded denim jeans, a Banana Republic T-shirt, a small scarf about her neck, and plain Birkenstock sandals on her small feet. The only jewelry she wore was a gold wedding band on a hand that was small and delicate. Her bearing spoke of confidence and the sincerity of her smile was endearing. Billie may have been fifty-two, but she looked thirty-five.

At forty-eight, the years had not been as kind to me as they had been to Billie. Fifty pounds overweight on a medium build and a gray balding head, I long ago stopped declining vendor's offers for a senior's discount. I wondered how two people who shared the same half of the gene pool could have had such dramatically different results. We shared the same green eyes and some of the facial features, but she had inherited our mother's disarming smile.

"You don't know how good it is to see you. I can't think of a sadder day in my life than when you left. I don't think I ever got over it," I said. I withdrew from her embrace and scrambled for a place to put the pieces of our relationship back together.

"Believe me, Jackie, I mean Jack, had it been up to me I would have stayed. I desperately wanted to. But your mother couldn't handle it," she said. Her words had a hard edge to them; a hint of anger.

The heavyset German woman appeared at the entrance to the living room. Billie turned on her heels and gestured to me and then to the woman who carried a serving tray. "Jack, this is Mrs. Berger, my housekeeper and friend. Helga, this is Jack McNamara, my brother."

Mrs. Berger nodded her head toward me dutifully. Her earlier scowl remained. She labored toward the glass-topped coffee table, pushed aside the vase of fresh flowers and set the tray on the table. Billie motioned for me to sit in the small chair she had pulled up to the table. She sat down opposite me on a wicker couch.

"Coffee, Mr. McNamara?" she asked with a hint of contempt. It seemed illogical that her irritation with me for leaving the gate open would have extended to this moment. I felt an animosity and an air of mistrust as Mrs. Berger occasionally eyed me. She positioned the silver coffee pot over my cup and poured.

"Yes, please," I said. Both Billie and I began to speak at the same time. "Go ahead. You go first," I said to her, then pulled my coffee cup to my lips and sipped the brew that had a slight touch of Bailey's in the taste.

"I always knew you would become a writer. I still have a copy of the story that appeared in the newspaper. It's yellowed and worn on the edges, but it has a place of prominence in my scrapbook. I have first editions of all your books. I want you to sign them for me before you leave."

"I'd be happy to, Billie." I was pleased she approved of my work.

"I love your stuff, Jack. And I'm very proud," she said genuinely.

"And what of you?”

"Well, I may be doing okay today, but it hasn't always been that way and it may not be that way in the future; something I'll have to tell you about later. I moved to the Keys when the Keys were on their hands and knees begging for handouts. For those of us who have been through the lean times, we know that life in the Keys is either an economic feast or a famine. That you enjoy life while it's good, but you learn to take the good times with a wary eye since you know that the bad times will come as well."

“Kind of like the writing business. Ten lean years of hard work and then you're an overnight success.”

“Exactly.”

“I love your home.”

She looked around the room, surveying her possession with pride. “That's a long story all by itself.”

“Tell me.”

“This used to be a rooming house. Someone had taken this beautiful old place and cut it up into four apartments. This is where I first stayed when I moved to the Keys. The place was infested with roaches and mice, and termites had eaten half the foundation. I remember making myself a promise that if I ever had the money I'd restore the place. The old woman who owned the house and rented the rooms passed away. Her children lived in New

Jersey and couldn't be bothered with a rundown eyesore. A realtor friend of mine contacted them with an offer shortly before a hurricane came across the lower Keys. You know how the television blows the damage from these storms out of proportion. Well, the family saw the coverage on the television about how the hurricane destroyed half the Keys and they accepted my offer immediately.

"There was an old set of blueprints between the rafters in the attic. The paper was very dry and brittle, but in good enough condition to make reasonable copies. We gutted the interior and had it built back to the original prints except for a kitchen, baths, and closets in the house. Originally, the garage out back was the kitchen. The outhouse was torn down long ago."

"How long has it been since the house was finished? It looks brand new."

"Little over a year ago. I just love it."

"The yard is so big. Most of the houses I saw driving in have no yard at all."

"We were very fortunate. The land came with the house. I've been offered over a million for the place. Because of the land, the commercial value of the property is staggering. But, I won't sell it. In fact, I may have to turn it into commercial property."

I waited for her to tell me why, but she didn't.

"You look terrific, Billie. Life must be treating you well."

"Alex makes me very happy. And there's the restaurant. It keeps me pretty busy."

"Restaurant?"

"I have a place on Duvall Street near Hemingway's house. Have you eaten?" It was after lunch.

"No. And I'm starving."

"Good. Let's go there and eat. I have to take care of a small problem anyway. We can talk about why you're here on the way."

Twenty-One

"This is the only bad part about living near the port and Mallory Square; so many people." Billie led me out the garden gate and onto the sidewalk in front of her house. There was a line to get into Mel Fisher's ship treasure museum and Front Street was a throng. "Duval Street will be a mess. Let's go the back way."

I followed Billie past my car, the Truman Annex and along Whitehead Street toward the eastern end of the island.

We walked past Kelly's, a restaurant owned by actress Kelly McGillis, then Whitehead Street became a mixture of nice, restored homes and clapboard cottages in disrepair, some with porches butted-up against the sidewalk. "It's a shame to see what the city has done to this street. These old conch houses will never be restored with them sitting right on the street like this."

"Conch houses?"

"You don't know what a conch is?"

"A shell, isn't it?"

"In the Keys it is much more than that."

"Conchs are like clams. They were so plentiful in the waters here that, in the old days, conch was a staple here for the natives. Conch chowder and conch fritters were the most popular. Conch shells were sold to the tourists, and exported. Natives were called conchs. Today even if you are a long-time resident, you earn the title of conch. There is even a small group of militants who want Key West to secede from the United States to form the Conch Republic. The tourists think it's cute, but these guys are serious; petition signing and everything."

"You're serious."

"I am. Conchs can be strange. Maybe that includes me, too."

We had to split up to pass a slow-moving group taking up the whole sidewalk, talking and laughing loudly. We rejoined.

"How did you come to settle here?"

"It was about ten years ago. I was working in New York managing a restaurant. That's where I met Alex. Alex complained that the food was cold and I tried to calm the situation down. We talked and one thing led to another."

"What does Alex do?"

"Airline pilot. Alex transferred to Miami. By the time the job change rolled around, I couldn't stand the thought of the separation. So, I came south, too. We settled on Key West. Alex takes the puddle-jumper to Miami to go to work."

"I assume you like it here?"

"I just love it. It was hard when we first moved here, especially getting the restaurant started. If it hadn't been for Alex's support, I never would have made it."

Before we reached Olivia Street, I recognized the crooked red brick wall surrounding Ernest Hemingway's home, from the many pictures I had seen. As we walked closer, I could make out the outline of his green stucco home and a small line of people purchasing tickets to enter. The house was directly across the street from the lighthouse, a fitting place, I thought, for a man who spent so much of his time on the sea. We turned on Olivia and walked along the side of the Hemingway house.

"I want to go through the house before I leave. I think of all the places Hemingway lived, he was happiest here."

"Never been in there, Jack. I walk by it almost every day, but never been in. Hemingway is such an icon in Key West, everything with his name on it is mobbed by tourists. I guess I get enough molestation at the restaurant without going to the tourist haunts."

We walked to Duvall and turned to the left toward the center of town. "Well, there it is." Billie nodded in the direction of the open-air restaurant to the left. We walked along the front until we reached the open-air entry and hostess station. Two huge Banyan trees covered what was once a front yard and now a courtyard filled with linen-covered tables.

"Hey, Ms. St. John." The host, dressed in black trousers, white shirt, black vest, and black bowtie, stood sentinel at the entrance. Billie led the way to the back of the courtyard. Large wooden frame umbrellas covered in dark green canvas shaded all the outside tables. Brick pavers and extensive use of tropical plants and shrubs transformed the front yard into a most elegant setting. Billie pulled director-type chairs from the table and offered me a seat. A long, thin building along one side of the front yard served as a bar, and the house had French doors along the front that opened directly into the courtyard. A moderate breeze tossed the Banyan trees, sunlight danced across the courtyard; the wind flapped the canvass material on the umbrellas and played with the cloth napkins and tablecloths.

"This is charming." I scanned the restaurant from front to back again for her benefit.

"This place has been a work in progress ever since I opened it. Ten years ago, the foundation of the house was crumbling; the roof had leaked for so long the plaster ceilings were crumbling and falling in places. It was a dump. Reluctantly, I signed a five-year lease. Then Alex and I did the best we could with the money we had. We covered the roof with a plastic tarp, patched the plaster and started a small breakfast and lunch diner. We catered to the locals then; business owners and workers along Duval. That first year I didn't think we would make it. Alex's salary as a pilot helped pay the bills until the business was established. By the end of the first year the place was packed. By the time the lease came up for renewal, we had the house restored, and opened the dining rooms on the second floor. That's when the troubles with the landlord began."

"Troubles?"

"Jack, this place should have been condemned when we first rented it. Its location on Duval Street was the only plus the place had. At the end of five years, after all the work we did on the place, the bastard doubled our rent. He said that the restaurant was worth more because of the improvements we made. Then I tried to get a longer lease. But he wouldn't budge. Five years was the best we could do. By then, we couldn't keep up with the growth in the business. You've heard the expression 'in for a penny, in for a pound?' At that stage, we had so much invested in this place we couldn't stop expanding if we were going to handle the growing numbers of people."

"There's more, right?"

"Our lease is up in three months. And he won't renew it." Her smooth face turned to a grimace.

"Why? At this stage it sounds like even if he doubled your rent again, it would still be better than you trying to find another location."

"He's selling it."

"Why?"

"Key West is changing. The great economic boom of the nineties has created wealth. People are coming in record numbers to spend it here; especially the cruise ships. Sometime within the past ten years, Americans discovered cruises. Now, record numbers of people go on them. Ships need destinations. Disney even built their own island in the Bahamas just to have a place to take their ships. Key West is perfect. They have a deep-water harbor, Mallory Square and Duval Street is an easy walk from the pier. Sometimes we have two or three ships in here a day."

"That would seem to be a good thing."

"Well it is. But all this business has attracted big money. It used to be that Duval Street was a string of T-shirt shops and bars, with an occasional restaurant thrown in for good measure. Now corporate America is buying up Duval Street, putting in Hard Rock Cafe, Planet Hollywood, and outlet stores. Duval Street has become big business. We've been discovered. The sharks of big business circled to find places along Duval, and they found my landlord; he wants to sell. He even put a sign out front. My regulars are wondering when I'm going out of business."

"Well, why don't you buy it.?"

"The last few places that have sold along Duval have gone for over two million, but they were closer to Mallory Square. This place would be well over a million and a half. I'd have to pay out over four thousand a month just in principle and interest. Even with an average meal price of fifteen dollars, after costs we'd have to serve five-hundred meals just to cover debt."

"How many meals are you serving now?"

"Anywhere from one-hundred and fifty to two-hundred a day during the season, one-hundred to one-hundred and fifty a day in the off-season."

"I'm not much of a businessman, but those numbers sound like they would work."

"Yeah, but one and a half million dollars, Jack."

I looked around the restaurant. It was first class, from the wait staff uniforms to the furnishings and decor. It was obvious that Billie managed the place well.

"A multi-millionaire friend of mine told me once that it isn't what something costs, it's how much money you can make. And if Key West continues to grow, the property and the restaurant will continue to grow in value with it."

Billie fiddled with a white cloth napkin wrapped in an oak ring. "Enough of my problems. What's going on with you?"

"Well, let me see. My wife left me a couple of days ago, my publisher wants a book that would normally take four months to write done in forty-five days and I can't write one decent sentence. To top it off, the night that Emily left, I seriously thought about blowing my brains out. Just another typical day in the neighborhood, I'd say."

My flippant attitude scored no points with Billie. Her silence made me feel every bit the sick shit I was.

She regained composure. "How does any of this involve me?"

"It may not, I don't know. Let me see if I can explain." I racked my brain trying to come up with a twenty-five-words-or-less explanation of the problem, when I wasn't sure what it was. It was like the dust cover on a novel where writers condense an entire 100,000-word novel down to a few sentences. I've often thought, why should I even bother working for months writing an intriguing story when some dustcover writer can say it better and more concisely. Where would I begin to explain everything to Billie?

"I never forgave Mother for the way she treated you. My relationship with her was never the same after. At the funeral, I couldn't even cry for her. She never would tell me why you left. She wouldn't even discuss it with me. I'm angry with her for hiding you for all those years, and for not keeping you in the first place. I've been going to a counselor for a couple of years. She thinks that there is more to the story than I know. She believes my unresolved anger with Mother could be one of the causes of my depression. She suggested I try to find out what happened."

"So you came to see me."

Her statement hit me very hard. I was embarrassed. After all the years I hadn't seen her, then to look for her for purely selfish reasons suddenly seemed petty and insensitive.

"I'm sorry I haven't made an effort to find you. But you had the same opportunity to find me and you didn't. You had an advantage. You knew where I was."

"Touché. I was angry, too. One day everything was going so well, I suddenly felt like I was part of a family. The next day I'm on a bus to nowhere. I was angry with all of you. It took a long time to get over it. Even now, when I think about it, it makes me angry."

"Why were you angry with me?"

"I was angry because I got dumped again. I was hurt. When I did get over it, I thought about looking you up. By then you had become this famous writer. I felt like I would have been intruding."

"It's good to see you, Billie. You look terrific. And you've done so well for yourself."

"You too, Jack." Billie signaled to a waiter who scurried to our table and took our orders.

The maître d' came to the table to ask about a private party that was booked later in the evening. Billie gave instructions, dismissed the man then surveyed the restaurant grounds. "You wouldn't believe how much work this place is. It's a twenty-four seven job. But I love it." She turned and looked directly at me. "I remember when Alex and I first came to Key West. I was almost at the same place you are right now. Very angry. Very depressed. For the first forty years of my life, I couldn't do anything right, and nothing went my way. When I left on that bus in 1961, I started running, and didn't stop until I met Alex. I ran from your mother, I ran from my own family, and mostly I ran to get away from myself."

"I have always remembered you as a pretty positive, upbeat person."

"The realities of life chewed that to pieces. It was Alex who got me into counseling when we first arrived here. It was Alex who paid the bills and encouraged me."

"You sound like a woman in love."

"I am. I can't wait for the two of you to meet." The waiter brought appetizers, poured our wine, asked if we needed anything and then left. "After four years of counseling, I finally realized that my hatred of your mother had consumed nearly twenty years of my life. And, if I let it, it would deny me the opportunity to love Alex fully. I finally let it go. I had a difficult time accepting myself, too. I figured, how good could I be if no one in my family wanted me around? I got past that, too. And I had pretty much put the McNamara's out of my mind until today."

She became tearful, pulling the white napkin from her lap and dabbing at her eyes. "Unfortunately, you are a representative of a past I would prefer to forget. They are painful memories. Please understand if I'm not enthusiastic about reliving them."

I thought to tell her that we had been down similar paths, but thought better of it. I had no idea what she had been through. "I suspect that there is much about Mother that you and I don't know. I'm angry, too. And I've been angry for a long time. Like you, if I can't let it go, it's going to ruin my life, if it hasn't already. I can't let go, though, unless I know what happened. My mother kept that part of her life a closed topic. My father refuses to talk to me about any of it. You're the only person that I can come to."

Lunch was a chicken and pasta dish in a fruity-tasting cream sauce that was marvelous. The Chardonnay was dry and potent, and took the edge off our conversation. Billie told me she wanted to walk and suggested we work off our lunch with a walk on the south side of the island. We retraced our steps back down Olivia to Hemingway's, then turned south, past the lighthouse to the marker for the Southernmost Point. Billie explained that the marker attracted tourists and traffic, and that it really wasn't the Southernmost Point anyway; that it was somewhere on the nearby navy base. The city was thinking about moving it to relieve Whitehead Street of a traffic problem.

We walked through the parking lot of the Casa Marina Hotel, once a Henry Flagler-owned hotel. The Spanish architecture, similar to other Flagler-built hotels in St. Augustine and Palm Beach, made me think of the forgotten Florida, with which I had grown up. It was built near the turn of the century to coincide with the completion of Flagler's Florida East Coast Railroad from Miami to Key West. It wasn't until the railroad was completed, Billie explained, that Key West really began to grow. Until then it was a simple fishing village, and a haven for smugglers and pirates.

At Monroe County Beach, an enormous black man stood completely naked in the doorway of a dilapidated Dodge van, changing his clothes. With his back to us, he looked like a large, chocolate manatee. According to Billie, Monroe County Beach was one of the few havens for the homeless on the island.

Our final stop was the White Street Pier, a solid concrete structure that looked like an abandoned and half-finished bridge that might have been built to Cuba. I was surprised that the bridge was vacant of fishermen. We had the place to ourselves. We walked out to the end of the pier. Occasionally you could smell dead fish where fishers had cleaned them atop the square concrete rail that ran the length of the pier.

"I walk down here just about every day. I come out to the end of the pier, take in the salt air and the sounds of the water lapping against the pilings and remind myself of how lucky I am to be here; to have had the success that I've had."

She rested her elbows on the railing, leaned out, looked at the water, then the horizon, and turned to look at me. The smile, on her face a moment ago, was gone. "There is much about me, Jack, that you don't know. We have a lot to talk about before Alex gets home tonight."

Her words had an ominous tone. I had no idea what she wanted to talk about, but I sensed it was connected to her reluctance to have me visit her.

Twenty-Two

"I brought you here because I want to talk to you about something very personal. I want to talk about my homosexuality, Jack." Billie leaned on the guardrail. The wind off the water sent her red hair into boiling flames.

I was shocked. Nothing in the past three hours had prepared me for this moment. She combed through her hair with her fingers and walked to a nearby park bench and sat down. Billie looked like this was the last place she wanted to be. She leaned forward on the bench with her elbows on her knees and hands clasped. Head down, she studied the pavement between her feet.

I remembered Billie as being a comely girl, my friend, and confidant. The thought of Billie being a lesbian didn't square with the memories of Billie I wanted to archive. I was stunned by her boldness. I walked from the guardrail and sat beside her. I was uncomfortable. "You don't need to explain anything to me, Billie," I said, almost wishing she wouldn't.

"I want to, Jack. You're my brother. If I can't talk to you about it who can I talk to?" She looked up from the pavement to me and waited for me to show signs I was listening.

I didn't know how to respond. I turned sideways on the bench to face her and folded my arms across my chest.

"How do you feel about homosexuality?" She sat up straight, turned in her seat, and brought a knee up on the bench seat in front of me.

I felt trapped. I thought about the countless times I had heard my father use the term faggot to describe anyone he felt was uniquely different. I remembered the jokes I had heard and told of fruits, men light in the loafers, flamers, and limp-wristed faggots. No one had ever asked me a question like this before.

"You're serious?"

"I am serious."

"Honestly?"

"Yes, of course."

"I don't know, Billie."

"I want to know, Jack. Be honest with me."

"I feel uncomfortable with it."

"Why?" she asked coolly.

"I thought you had something you wanted to talk about?" I turned on the park bench, away from Billie.

"I do, but I want to know where you are first." She was insistent.

I paused for a moment and looked away from Billie, trying to find the right words. "Alright. I guess I don't like it very much. I guess you could probably say that I'm a typical homophobe."

"Have you ever known any homosexuals, Jack?"

I stood abruptly to my feet. "What is the point of this, Billie?" I said with unmistakable irritation.

"The point is that your sister—half-sister—is a lesbian, a homosexual. I just want to know how you feel about it."

"I barely know you. I've been here for less than three hours. You have a beautiful home, a great restaurant, and you live in a charming city. Now you're telling me you're a lesbian. I don't know how I feel about it, Billie. I don't know enough about you to make that judgment. But I'm still here. I haven't gotten up and left. So I must be alright with it," I said, not totally honest with her.

When I was a teenager, I worked for a gay man. He owned a small business, and I did odd jobs and made occasional deliveries. The man was a toucher. Not that his touches carried any importance. He was this way with everyone. I was terribly uncomfortable around him. Mostly it was his overt feminine mannerisms, and his verbal sexual teasing that made me the most uncomfortable. Sitting here with Billie, I stretched my memory. The only thing that my former boss did that merited my discomfort was to tell me that he thought I had a cute behind. At sixteen, I was not altogether sure what gay men did or how they made love to each other, but I did understand the implications of the overture. I pulled this long-forgotten memory to the surface and renewed the feelings of disgust and repulsion that I tied to it.

"But I want to know how you feel about it," she persisted.

"It doesn't matter what I think," I said, now angry. Standing, I waved my arms for emphasis and Billie sat on the edge of the park bench looking like she would spring to her feet at any moment. "What matters is what you think about it. I don't have to live your life. So what do you think about being homosexual, Billie?"

There was a long stretch of silence. Every fiber within me could not agree with the life-choices Billie had made. If I told her how I really felt, if I explained the revulsion, I knew I would lose her. Something in me softened. Who was I to stand in judgment of her? There was nothing Billie could do or say that would change how I felt about homosexuality. But, she was my sister. I didn't have to agree with her sexual orientation to accept her.

Billie looked from me to the ocean. She stared at the horizon. The soft sea breeze, the blue-green waters, pelicans flying in formation inches above the water, all had a calming effect on the moment. I sat down opposite Billie on the bench and resumed my listening position. The salt spray felt good against my face.

Billie looked away from the ocean, slid back into her seat, and looked down at the concrete. "I am what I am, Jack," she said with conviction.

"And I accept what you are, Billie. I don't understand it. I won't pretend to agree with it. But I accept it," I said, pleased that I could be truthful and supportive in some measure.

"What don't you understand?"

"That's easy. I don't understand how two people of the same sex can be physically attracted to each other."

"I'll try to explain."

"Billie, you don't need to explain anything to me." We had already moved into areas I never dreamed of discussing with her. We could stop now and it would suit me fine.

"I want you to understand. It's important to me." She turned on the bench to face me. She pulled both of her small feet up on the bench between us and wrapped her arms around her knees. "I've been in therapy for many years trying to understand this very question. One of the nice things about being in your fifties is that you finally accept things about yourself.

"I don't know how much you know about your mother's involvement in my life. I was only two or three years old when she left me—I should say abandoned me. I was left with a sitter right after your mother married your father."

"Yes, I know. Aunt Glory Jean filled me in on the details."

"There is much she doesn't know." She looked away from me and combed through her hair with her fingers. "I can't remember anything around the time your mother left me in Charleston. As a small girl, my father would tell me that I looked just like your mother, as though this were an assault on him. I would close my eyes and try to picture what your mother looked like. When I was twelve, I called Glory Jean. She met me downtown at a drug store with a soda fountain and gave me a picture of your mother. I smuggled it into my bedroom. I still have that picture. It's ragged from having been folded and unfolded so many times, and worn from being handled so much."

"I have plenty of photos of her I could send you."

"I really don't want them. My made-up memories of your mother from that picture are far better than the real ones. I would rather remember her the way I wanted her to be."

Her bitterness toward Mother tapped into my own, touching off feelings of anger. "She should never have let you get through her fingers. I hate her for what she did to you, Billie."

She looked at me without acknowledging what I had just said, either because she didn't believe me or she was deep in thought. "My father remarried when I was five. Ella worked for my father at the antique store. She was thirty-five, had never been married before, and had little use for children. The older I got, the more I resembled your mother. It was as if I were your mother in some incarnate form, a figure that he could hurl abuse and hatred toward. During some of the worst beatings I got from him, he would say things like, 'You're a whore just like your mother.' Or, 'You're a worthless piece of shit, just like your mother.'

"More than the beatings and insults from my father, Ella's ignoring me hurt far more. I was worse than dirt to her. In her mind, I didn't even exist. It was rare that she even spoke to me. I don't know all the reasons your mother left my father and abandoned me. From what little I did know, she was caught in some difficult circumstances. It doesn't excuse what she did, but it will never compare to how Ella treated me.

"When I was twelve, my father and Ella began traveling to Europe to buy and sell antiques. At first the trips were short, a week or two at a time. They would hire a sitter to stay with me. By the time I was fourteen, their travels would extend for long periods. I'll say this for Ella, she was a businesswoman. She knew how to make money.

"Ella hired a governess. With the governess in place, she wouldn't have to deal with me at all. They could extend the length of their trips to Europe into months, not weeks. Your mother may have abandoned me as a toddler, Jack, but nothing your mother did, could compare to the feelings of abandonment and loneliness I felt when my father and Ella took off and left me for six months with a total stranger.

"At first, I hated Stella Regent; she was the governess they hired. She was eighteen years old, and had never been a governess before. She worked part-time in the store for my father during high school. When she graduated, she was looking for full-time work, and Ella suggested looking after the house and taking care of me in their absence.

"Stella became more than the mother I never had. We were lovers, too. Stella was the first person in my life that I felt truly loved me. Having sex with Stella was the most natural thing to me. I had never been with a man. And no one had ever talked to me about sex before Stella. She was my teacher, my friend, my lover, the family I never had.

"I had never been in love with anyone before Stella. I was hopelessly in love with her. The hardest times were when my father and Ella were home, and we couldn't sleep together.

"When I was sixteen, Father and Ella returned one night, earlier than expected. Father found Stella and me naked in bed together. I begged him not to call the police, but he beat me black and blue. Then Ella suggested that a bargain might be struck. If I agreed to leave their home and never return, then Stella would be spared. My father literally threw Stella and I out the front door on my word that I would never see him or Ella again.

"Stella and I rented a tiny two-room apartment. She got work as a cocktail waitress, and I waited on tables. Within a year, we were broke and on the street. Stella couldn't deal with that and left. I was stranded, deeply hurt, and had nowhere to turn. That's when I called Glory Jean and got your mother's number and called her for help."

"That must have been hard to call her."

"I was desperate, Jack. I would've called anyone, if I thought I could get help. My heart was broken."

"And then your own mother throws you out."

"It's a real mystery. A few days after I came to Hollywood to stay with you, I told your mother everything that had happened. Everything. I needed to talk to someone. Your mother was wonderful. I expected her to be upset. But she hugged me, told me she loved me, and gave me hope. Except for my time with Alex, I can't think of a time in my life that I've been happier."

"Then why did you leave?"

"I didn't just leave. I would have stayed there forever. I had you. I had everything I needed. The night before I left, your mother and I were in her bedroom talking. I had just put on my pajamas, and she was ready for bed. I was telling her how much I loved being there and what a fine boy I thought you were. Then she gave me one of the warmest hugs I have ever gotten. Your father came to the doorway. He had turned off the television and readied to go to bed. When he saw I was in the room, he walked back out. Your mother told me it was time for bed, kissed me, and then I went off to my room.

"I could hear their bedroom door slam as your father went into the room. Then all hell broke loose. They were yelling and screaming at one another. I couldn't understand what they were saying, but I knew it was about me."

"Yeah, I remember that. I just wrote it off as one of their many intense arguments. How did you know it was about you? They fought like that all the time."

"It was the very next morning that your mother told me I was going to have to leave."

"Did she tell you why?"

"No. I'll never forget what she said, though. Her face was all puffed up from crying. She said, 'Darlin', as much as I would like them to, things are just not going to work out. I want you to know that I love you very deeply, but you're going to have to leave.' With that, she gave me an envelope filled with money. She told me that she had been saving it for a long time. It was her escape money, but that I needed it more than she did."

"That's it?"

"That's it, Jack. I pleaded with her to tell me why, but she wouldn't. She just kept saying that things weren't going to work, and that she was sorry. Did she ever tell you why?"

"No. I'd asked her many times. I even brought it up with my father, but he refused to talk about it."

It occurred to me that my father may have had more to do with Billie leaving than I had thought. "Do you think my father could have had something to do with it?"

"I asked her that question just before she passed away. But she was under so much medication I didn't get a very clear answer. But, I never felt like your father liked me. I always chalked it up to the stepchild thing. After all, I did show up unexpectedly and then became this unannounced houseguest. He was always pleasant and courteous. I just got the impression that he would have preferred that I hadn't come."

"What happened after you left Hollywood?"

"When I got to the bus station, and after she left, I found ten thousand dollars in that envelope your mother gave me. I don't know how long it took her to save it, but I was dumbfounded."

"So where did you go?"

"Your mother gave me enough money to go to school somewhere, to make something of myself. But I just pissed it away."

"So where did you go?" I asked again.

"When Stella left me, it broke my heart. When your mother asked me to leave, it broke my spirit. She was everything I expected her to be: warm, caring, affectionate, and loving. How could she be all these things, then turn around and throw me out? I felt like she loved me. I felt like she really wanted me to be there. And then wham, out on my ear. That was the lowest point in my life. You talk about wanting to kill yourself? For the next two years, I tried to do it with alcohol, drugs, and sex. When the money ran out, I found myself in New York, living in a rooming house. I wanted to die, but didn't have the courage to do it. The next twenty years were survival years. I feel like I went through them on autopilot. Married and divorced twice, I was just going through the motions. The only good to come out of it is I learned the restaurant business and I met Alex."

At the mention of Alex's name, her face brightened and she straightened her back. "She was a gift. Even when I first met her at a restaurant I managed, when she was angry about her food being cold, and annoyed at her server, I liked her immediately. She was there alone. The night before she had broken up with a woman with whom she'd had a five-year relationship. I could tell she was hurting. After I had gotten her food squared away and I came back to her table to let her know the meal was on the house, I sat down at her table and tried to console her. She broke into tears and poured out her heart. I suggested that we get together when my shift ended so we could talk some more. I could relate to her deep hurt. We began seeing each other, and within six months, we were partners. We had been together for almost a year when Alex's transfer to Miami came through."

I was moved by Billie's story. I wasn't repelled or turned off. Here was a woman who had suffered rejection in ways I would never understand or relate to, who, at last, had found happiness. While I couldn't understand or agree with the sexual attraction, I could understand the emotional need, and the fulfillment of love.

"Are you happy?"

"Now. And it's been a long road for me from there to here."

She stood and gestured to me to follow. We walked in silence all the way to the end of the pier and found a lone bench. Billie brushed some debris from the seat, sat down and patted the seat next to her. I sat and turned toward her.

"After we got to the Keys, my struggles really began. Thank God Alex was there to help pull me through."

The wind began to blow in gusts. Pelicans struggled to hold their glide above the water and turned into the wind.

Bill Cronin

I felt badly that I had not been there for Billie. My heart ached at the thought of her in New York alone, hurt, and scratching out a living. But mostly I felt loss that I didn't have her in my life all these years.

Both of our lives had been broken, the path of destruction different, but the cause the same. I thought of Mother and wondered if she had had any idea of the pain she had caused.

Twenty-Three

An old man, bent over at the waist and supported by a cane, hobbled the length of the pier. He led a small boy who carried two fishing poles, a tackle box, and a small brown paper bag. The entire pier was vacant, but the old man chose a place at the very end of the pier, ten feet from where we sat. The boy leaned the poles against the guardrail, set the tackle box on the concrete, handed the brown bag to the old man, and then stared at us. For protection, he grabbed the hem of the old man's shorts, and then explored the inside of his nose with his forefinger.

Billie looked at the boy, twisted her face into a disgusted look and then looked at me. "Ready to start back?" A smile caught the corner of her mouth.

"Might as well. Seems we've lost our privacy."

We vacated the bench, which the boy seized quickly. The old man took sandwiches from the bag, handed one to the boy, then sat on the bench and began to eat his. The old man never looked at us or acknowledged our presence.

To Billie I said, "Friendly sort."

We walked back on the tongue of concrete toward shore.

"Soon after we moved to Key West, Alex and I were married." She looked over at me and saw a puzzled look on my face. "Not a state-type of marriage, but we had a ceremony, invited our friends and made all the promises to each other that we would have made in a legal ceremony. Soon after, Alex and I began to have problems. Jealousy consumed me. When Alex was on trips, I would imagine her cheating on me. Alex is extremely beautiful. I couldn't completely accept that she would be satisfied with me."

I looked at Billie. At fifty-two, despite small signs of age, she was striking. "Why would you feel that way? I think you're very attractive."

"You're kind, Jack. But I still felt that way. After one trip, I found a note from another woman in the coat pocket of her pilot's uniform. The note was a simple thank you from a passenger, but toward the end of the note was a postscript. 'If you're in Minneapolis sometime, give me a call, and I will return the favor with dinner.' The woman's telephone number was written hastily on the bottom of the note.

"We had a terrible fight, and Alex left our apartment and stayed at the Holiday Inn on Duval. The next morning she came to the apartment and told me that she thought I needed help. I was crushed. I started counseling a week later. After three years of counseling, I learned that every person that I ever loved had rejected me, and that I feared Alex would do the same. I had a lot of hurt inside that I needed to unload. I hope I never have to go through it again."

"What about the note that you found in Alex's pocket?"

"It was exactly what I thought it was. The woman was hitting on her. Alex told me that it happened a lot, mostly with men. She told me that she couldn't help being hit on. That she loved me and had no interest in offers elsewhere. I didn't see it then, when it happened. We'll be sitting in the restaurant, and men will come up to our table and ask her out. Without a man being with her, they just assume she's available. Doesn't bother me now. I know she loves me. The way she stuck with me while I worked out my problems is all the proof I'll ever need."

"Alex sounds like a gem."

"She is. I just didn't want you to meet her until you understood the situation."

We had slowly walked the length of the pier. Billie stopped, grabbed my hand, and turned me to face her. "I worried about your coming here and not understanding my relationship with Alex. She'll be home in about three hours. Are you sure you're comfortable with it?"

"Yes, I'm fine." I was surprised by my answer. I understood the journey she had been through, and I saw Billie's happiness now. It helped to set aside the moral and ethical conflicts that fought for my attention.

"I also worried your presence would dredge up all the hurt feelings from long ago. But I feel good, Jack. It is really wonderful to see you." She hugged me and kissed me on the cheek. "I'm glad you're here. I'm sorry that I didn't make more of an effort to find you sooner."

I returned her hug enthusiastically. "I'm sorry, too, Billie."

As we retraced our steps toward Whitehead Street, I picked through the details of my discussion with Billie regarding the night before she left. I wondered if Mother had shared with my father the story of Billie and her au pair. Knowing my father's bigoted attitudes, I began to wonder how much of a role he might have played in Billie's departure in 1961.

"Billie, when my father came into the bedroom the night before you left and you and Mother were embracing, did he say anything?"

"No. Nothing."

"Did you see his face? Was there any expression?"

"None."

"When they fought after, did you hear anything that would give you an idea of what they fought about?"

"Sorry. I could hear them yelling, but their voices were muffled."

"The next morning when you woke up, did he say anything to you before Mother took you to the bus station?"

"No. When I got up, he had already gone to work. Do you think he had something to do with it?"

"I don't know, but I want to talk to him about it."

We found our way back to Hemingway's. The line to get in was ten deep along the crooked red brick wall. We stood across the street in the shadows of huge ficus trees.

"Have you ever been to the Keys before?"

"Once as a teen. I remember fishing boats and bait shops but that's about it."

"Then you've never seen Hemingway's?"

"Only in pictures. I'd like to see it if we have time."

"I need to go to the restaurant to set up the dinner menu. If you want, this would be a good time to go. When you get done, just come to the restaurant."

Billie started to walk across the street. "Oh, I've been meaning to tell you about something since you called yesterday, and I keep forgetting. Do you remember Jody Holland?"

"From Hollywood?"

"The same. I was at the host station, and this woman was in line. I sat her and her party, thinking to myself that I knew her from somewhere. I racked my brain for forty minutes. Then I finally put a name to her face. She is still as pretty as she was when I introduced the two of you."

"Was she visiting?"

"After I put the name to the face, I went over to the table and introduced myself. It turns out that she has a place here in Key West. She asked about you."

"Is she married?"

"She left me her name and telephone number and suggested that we get together for a drink sometime. She came to the restaurant with an older woman. So, I have no idea what her status is. I still have the number. When I get to the restaurant I'll look for it."

"Please. I'd like to see her."

Billie crossed the street, walked around Hemingway's house, and disappeared down Olivia Street.

I crossed the street and found a place at the end of the line. As I waited to get a ticket into Hemingway's house, even though I had never been through his home, I felt like I knew it well. My earliest thoughts about writing were linked to Ernest Hemingway. From my mother's interest as a fan and admirer, Hemingway had always been more than an idol to me. Mother's early words of encouragement to write came from wanting the same success for me she saw in Hemingway. It didn't matter that writing was the most difficult art form in which to make a living, as my father so accurately pointed out to me on many occasions. She read the many articles written about Hemingway, his flamboyant lifestyle, his travels all over the world and wanted that for me. From the construction of the very first sentence I had ever written, Mother shared Hemingway's wisdom to young aspiring writers from the many interviews he had given. His goal was to write, 'one true sentence.' Mother's interpretation, which I shared for many years, was that a novel was written one sentence at a time. She chided me to focus only on the sentence at hand and avoid looking at the yet unwritten 80,000 words ahead. Later in my career, Hemingway's one true sentence came to mean an inspired collection of words that would produce that one sentence above all that paints the perfect mental image or makes a clever point. Although it was Hemingway's continuing goal to write that one true sentence, it was not his work that gave meaning to the phrase.

Midway into my career, Pat Conroy had already risen to literary heights with his work The Great Santini. The Prince of Tides had received critical acclaim in the late 1980s. In the prologue to Prince, Tom Wingo, the central character, then a ten-year-old boy, had illegally killed an endangered American bald eagle. Tom's father had made a makeshift Indian headdress from the dead eagle's feathers and made Tom wear it to school as punishment for breaking the law. His father made him wear the headdress for weeks, until it began to fall apart. "Those feathers trailed me in the hallways of the school as though I were a molting, discredited angel." Conroy's one true sentence leaped off the page, and echoed back through the years to the first time I had heard the phrase which now, for me, had a career of meaning.

Following my intersection with Conroy's one true sentence, hard as I tried, I could never duplicate his feat, until I realized that to each writer only a few true sentences were allotted. It was like wealth. Those who had it came by it accidentally, and those who pursued it as a single goal found it elusive. These literary gems—a unique turn of words, the odd combination of phrases, that, once put together, created that one true sentence—were rare indeed. For every writer that one true sentence is a uniquely personal humbling experience. For when it is your fortune to write it, all past and future work pales. Henceforth, you strive to duplicate the accomplishment, and fear you will never write another. "One true sentence." For me, it means that every time I face the keyboard, borrowing a phrase from Hemingway, I hope I have enough "juice" to create one. Every time I think about it, I think of him.

After paying my entry fee, I was impressed almost immediately by the lush gardens and landscape. The house seemed small compared to the stately manors and estates that accompanied celebrity today. But writers enjoyed a sort of anonymity, even though they may have been on the New York bestseller list. Even Stephen King, the king of American prose, lived on a quiet suburban street in Bangor, Maine, complete with wrought iron fence decorated with bats, to discourage the curious. Hemingway had lived in Key West seven years before his fame had made his home a point of interest for tourists. Once they became a nuisance, his jack-of-all-trades, handyman Toby Bruce erected the crooked brick wall, sans bats, from used street brick to discourage the gawkers.

While the house was of interest to me, I naturally migrated to the room above the carriage house where Hemingway wrote, To Have and Have Not, and started the manuscript for, For Whom the Bell Tolls, my favorite work, next to The Old Man and the Sea. The bridge from the second-story bedroom of the Spanish-style home built in the late 1800s to the second story of the carriage house was gone. Hemingway used to walk the bridge from his bedroom to his study atop the carriage house. Over the years, the structure fell into disrepair and was removed. Now a spiral wrought-iron staircase from ground level to the carriage house second floor replaced the bridge so that tourists could access Hemingway's study. The staircase deposited me at the exterior of a small room decorated in a manly style. What caught my eye was a typewriter sitting on a large table opposite from the door. A railing prevented entry into the room. Although the chair matched the description of an uncomfortable cigar-maker's chair with a leather seat he liked to sit in, I knew Hemingway had written with a number two lead pencil, and his wife Pauline typed his manuscripts for him, so the typewriter seemed staged to me.

People behind me would not let me tarry, but I could see quickly why this place would have suited him. Good ventilation and light, and privacy. Like Hemingway, my best time to write was early in the morning, the quietest part of my day.

Just as I turned in the doorway of Hemingway's studio to leave, a cat meowed, rubbed up against my leg, and swished its tail high in the air. The longhair smoky gray cat was a polydactyl, a cat with more than five toes. The cat's feet looked like a catcher's mitt. Polydactyl cats along with other varieties rule the grounds of the Hemingway estate in large numbers. It reminded me of Emily. She had read about the cats at Hemingway's house and found a female polydactyl at the pound, named it

Hemingway, and gave it to me for my birthday. The cat was an ever-present fixture in my studio whether I was in it or not.

When Mother entered "The Doorman," my first short story, in the Hollywood Sun-Tattler contest and after they announced that I had won the contest, Mother took me to meet the editor of the newspaper. I'd long forgotten his name, but I'd never forget the words he spoke to me. He was talking to Mother, and said, "Mrs. McNamara, you may have another Ernest Hemingway on your hands." Then he reached out, shook my hand and congratulated me.

I stood at the gate on Olivia Street, and looked back at the grounds and wondered why Hemingway had been such a lifelong obsession. Over the years, I had collected first editions of all of his published works, some even signed by him. I had original copies of all the magazines that had chronicled his many short stories and serials. Perhaps it was Mother's constant comparisons to him as a youth, or his untimely death during such an embryonic state of my own career. Unmistakably, he had been as much a part of my development as a close relation. His suicide haunted me still.

I started writing when I was twelve years old. It was been part of the ebb and flow of my life, an extension of my soul and being. The emotional short circuit that prevented me from writing now drained me of life. I thought about Hemingway's visits to the Mayo Clinic, and his experiences with electroshock treatments that annihilated his memory and decimated his concentration; doctors killed one part of his brain in order to save his life. When they destroyed his ability to write, though, they took his life just as surely as the disease they tried to cure.

Physical injuries suffered in a plane crash and mental illness had cut Hemingway off from a normally active, boisterous life. Worse still, he was severed from his number two lead pencil and pad of paper. I had tried, then, to imagine what life would be like if I couldn't write ever again. In 1961, Hemingway's suicide and my father's insensitivity to the needs of a fledgling artist almost discouraged me from a career that had brought immeasurable pleasure to my life. Now, seeing his home, seeing the place where he lived during some of the happiest times he knew, having stood in the doorway of his studio, the place where so many of his finest works were conceived or written, made me realize how intertwined my writing was with my own happiness.

I left the Hemingway House and turned toward Billie's restaurant. As the last of the crooked brick wall around Hemingway's house disappeared, I knew I did not want Hemingway's fate to befall me. I had to write again, even if it was only one sentence.

Twenty-Four

Billie took me down Duval Street, past Sloppy Joes. The lyrics to Jimmy Buffett's, "Why Don't We Get Drunk and Screw?" brought cheers from the patrons at the chorus. T-shirts with a bearded Hemingway's face, adorned windows in Sloppy Joe's gift shop.

"Hemingway would roll over in his grave, if he understood how his name was being used." Billie stopped at one of the many portals to the famous bar, shook her head as a college-age boy stood on one of the flimsy tables, danced, and sang the words of the Buffett song to the barmaid delivering his drink order.

Billie said, "There was a side of Hemingway that would probably have thought it funny."

After pushing through the streets thronged with tourists, we turned at Front Street and made our way to Billie's home. Mrs. Berger met us at the door, a grimace stretched across her flabby face.

"Miss Alexandra called. She is at the airport. Shall I pick her up?"

"No, Helga. Jack and I will go get her."

Mrs. Berger scowled and waited impatiently while Billie found the keys to her car. She looked at her shoes, the floor, the walls of the foyer, anywhere but at me. To the delight of Mrs. Berger, Billie appeared with her keys.

The eighties-something beige Volvo sat disheveled at the curb some fifty feet from her front door. The vehicle was badly rusted, windows foggy with age, leather seats split and cracked, but it started as soon as she turned the key.

"It doesn't pay to have a decent car here. What the salt air doesn't destroy the tourists will." The beat-up Volvo ran smoothly across the uneven road surfaces. We took almost the same route we had walked earlier, avoiding Duval and U.S. 1 altogether.

Even in her airline captain's uniform, Alex was unexpectedly beautiful. With a gold-braid cap in her hand, she had already let her long black hair down and loosened her black tie. Billie pulled to the curb. Alex looked at me without expression, aimed for the rear door before I could get out to let her sit up front with Billie.

Alex's 'I wish you weren't here' look made Mrs. Berger's ice-cold reception seem warm. She patted Billie on the shoulder. "You okay?" Then she looked back at me, leaving no doubt the question was for my benefit, like I were Ted Bundy and Billie a potential victim.

I guessed Alex's age to be mid-forties. A trim, fit figure was overshadowed by a face that could grace any fashion magazine. She was hard not to look at.

"How was your trip?" Billie pulled away from the curb, looked over her shoulder and smiled broadly at Alex.

"Had a bout with severe turbulence over New Mexico. Dropped ten thousand feet like a rock. Shook up some passengers. Other than that, same old grind. You hear from that asshole landlord of yours?"

"I was telling Jack all about it. No, he didn't call. And he won't. We're wasting our time. He's not going to change his mind." Billie looked at me, then at Alex. "Jack thinks I should buy the place."

Without looking at me, Alex said, "And did you ask Jack what you would use to buy it with? Or maybe he has invented some tree that produces money."

Billie looked at me and gave me an 'Alex is not in a good mood' look, and the rest of the trip back to the house was spent in silence.

At the house, Mrs. Berger showed me to one of the second-floor guest rooms with the enthusiasm of a funeral director. The only crack in her icy persona appeared at the mention of the door to the widow's-walk. With her German accent and monotone voice, she instructed me that a widow's-walk was used by the women of the house to survey the waters of the harbor for the return of their sea-going men. She acquainted me with the location of linens and the telephone, then informed me that Billie, Alex, and I would be dining out and to be ready at six. Then she hobbled down the back stairs to the kitchen, each step creaking under her weight.

Alex's almost rude reception suggested that she and Billie needed to spend some time alone. I thought about checking out the widow's walk, but a nap, after the events of the day, seemed more appropriate. Alex's physical beauty and dark coloring reminded me of Emily. I slipped off my shoes and stretched out on the feather mattress of the four-poster bed. As I drifted off to sleep, I regretted I had let Emily slip through my fingers.

Loud voices from the kitchen below roused me from sleep. After a shower, I pulled on casual slacks and a shirt from my travel bag and descended the back stairs to the kitchen. An argument between Billie and Alex ensued and quickly found silence as the creak from my first step on the stairs announced my presence.

They were sitting in the kitchen at a small table, half-filled glasses of red wine stationed in front of them. Alex had changed into a fuchsia short-sleeved blouse and white slacks, and Billie still had on what she had worn all day. Billie looked exhausted. Alex made no effort to hide her anger.

"Sleep well?" Billie wearily pushed herself up from the table.

Before I could answer Billie said, "Well, I'm going to get ready." She nodded toward Alex. "Since both of you are ready, why don't you go to the restaurant and have a drink, and I'll join you shortly."

I felt as one might feel alone in a cage with a lion. Still slouched in her chair, Alex stared at me for a few moments, exhaled sharply, and summoned the energy to descend to my level.

"Am I dressed appropriately?"

"Your birthday suit is appropriate just about anywhere in Key West."

"Well, that's comforting."

"The evening is young. Follow me. It's only a block away. Ever eaten at the Rooftop?"

"Haven't been to Key West in many years."

"Well, at least the food will be good."

With equal sarcasm I said, "I can't wait."

The Rooftop was a block away from Billie's on the second floor. The bar and restaurant were divided. The bar was open-air and gave you the feel of a tree house. The restaurant was enclosed, but windows around the entire dining room made it feel like it was a porch.

Alex led me to a barstool at the end of the bar away from a small group congregated near the entrance to the restaurant that was waiting for a table.

Alex ordered a margarita on the rocks and I followed suit. The bartender, with a flourish, delivered the festive glasses edged with salt.

"Why are you here, Jack?"

"I'm doing great, Alex. I'm so glad you asked. Trip from Mount Dora was a little fatiguing, and I'm just getting over a small cold. Other than that, I'm fit. And you?"

"I want to know why you're bothering Billie."

"Right for the jugular."

Her eyebrows narrowed, and jaw tightened. "Okay, I've been going through counseling for depression. My counselor believes my unresolved anger toward my mother is at the root."

Her face brightened into a clown-like grin. "I can't believe it. You haven't seen Billie since you were a kid. And you run into a little quote, unresolved anger, and you come here to screw up her life again. What a selfish little bastard!"

I stood from the barstool, pulled a twenty from a money clip, and tossed it on the bar. "We've only known each other for a few hours, and we haven't spoken two words. So, I really haven't had the opportunity to earn your contempt. But you've earned mine." I could barely contain my anger. It was as though she possessed the spirit of my father. I looked directly at her for a reaction. I considered explaining my departure. A waste of time. I just waved her off with my hand and aimed for the exit.

I'd catch Billie at the house, apologize for my hasty exit, assure her I wouldn't bother her anymore, and leave. I would be in Miami by ten o'clock.

A hand grabbed my arm. "Jack, stop."

I snapped around. "Why, so you can have some more fun at my expense? Ever since the airport, you've shown your ass over my being here. I get the message." I pulled my arm from her grasp. I passed through the door and then on to the stairs leading down to the street.

"I'm sorry, Jack." From the top of the stairs, she called, "I have been very rude. Forgive me, please."

Her contriteness gave me pause.

"Please come back and sit down. Please?" She extended her hand to accompany me back through the doorway.

I followed her back into the bar. Our drinks awaited us.

Once we were seated, Alex moved closer, as if to share a secret, and looked directly at me. "I'm so sorry, Jack." She paused, looking past me over my shoulder. "Billie and I have been together for a long time. No one could make me as happy as she has made me. She has made a huge difference in my life. But Billie has been through it, Jack; all the crap she went through with her family before I met her. Three years of counseling. The challenges with the restaurant."

"So how does this involve me?"

"It's just one more thing she has to deal with, and things have been going so well. Well except for the lease on the restaurant. These past few years have been some of our happiest. And now you show up, dredging up all the painful memories she has finally put to rest."

"Did she tell you I upset her?"

"No."

"Then we're dealing with your fears and concerns, not hers."

She looked away from me, looked back and then nodded.

"Has she said that she would prefer I leave?"

"Not at all. That's what we argued about during your nap. She wants you to stay."

"And you wanted me to leave."

She looked around, folded and unfolded her hands in front of her. "Nothing in my life is more important to me than Billie. Nothing. During these past few years, she's finally been at peace. She's happier than I've ever seen her. I'd do anything within my power to keep it that way."

I offered her my handkerchief. She dabbed at her eyes with the handkerchief now black from wet mascara.

I was suddenly touched by her devotion to Billie. It occurred to me that I would have reacted similarly if someone came to visit Emily and dredged up painful past memories. "I didn't come to create a problem for Billie. I just wanted to find out why my mother asked her to leave our home. I've never forgiven my mother for it."

"If there was ever a time when Billie needed acceptance and love it was then. She was confused, deeply hurt, and vulnerable. It has taken years for her to unwind from all that hurt. I'll never forgive your mother for what she did to her."

"I'm not defending her, but there would have been few places Billie could have gone in 1961 and received unconditional acceptance as a homosexual. There is no question my mother was wrong to send her into the street, but acceptance of Billie's sexual orientation at any level would have been very hard in those times."

"You seemed to have accepted it, and you're a half-brother. This was her mother for Pete's sakes."

"I accept Billie, but that doesn't mean I necessarily buy into the lifestyle. And the times are different. And I suppose your parents wholeheartedly supported you in your sexual choices?"

"Well, not immediately. But they wouldn't have asked me to leave their home."

"How many brothers and sisters did you have?"

"None. Only child."

"When you told your parents that you were homosexual, were you living in their home?"

"No. It was after I had graduated from flight training, and I was on my own."

"Ours was a Catholic home, in a conservative middle-class neighborhood, in 1961, where homosexuality was the taboo of taboos. My mother had not seen Billie in fourteen years."

"Well whose fault was that?"

"I can't speak to that, and I agree that my mother was wrong to abandon her for the second time. But Billie didn't exactly give her mother the easiest problem in the world to deal with."

"All I know is the damage your mother's indifference caused in her. Now that she is happy it frightens me to see the ugliness of her past thrown in her face again."

"Alex. I haven't thrown anything in her face. Even though I haven't done a very good job of being a brother to Billie, I do love her. We were very close once. All I wanted to do is understand what happened, that's all. In the process I've gained my sister back."

"But you still don't accept her, do you?"

"Because she's a lesbian?"

"Yes."

"Do you accept heterosexuality?"

"I don't have anything against it."

"I didn't ask you that. I asked you if you accept it."

"Not for me. But I don't hold it against someone who is."

"The moral issue aside, I don't understand same-sex attraction. I certainly don't accept it for me. Judging from the cracks in my own pillar of virtue, I'm hardly in a place to judge anyone.

"Until today, I haven't had to think seriously about how I feel about it for someone else. Billie is very happy. It is obvious that you both love each other. I don't need to understand it or accept it to be happy for you and Billie. And I am happy for her. She is fortunate to have found someone who cares for her as you do."

The wrinkles on her forehead smoothed. She put her hand on my forearm.

"Thanks for your kind words. I guess I can't expect any more than that."

"Now, can we be friends?"

"Yes . . . I think we can, Jack. I feel awful, now, for jumping on you like I did. Again, I'm very sorry."

"Don't worry about it."

She licked a large section of salt from the rim of her glass and polished off the rest of her margarita. "Have you found out everything you needed to know?"

"My counselor said she felt there was more here than I knew. She was right. Even after talking to Billie today, there is still much I don't know."

"I hope everything works out for you."

"Me, too. Tell me about the Mangrove."

"What about it?" She combed through her black hair, with long thin fingers, and pulled her mane out of her face.

"Billie was telling me about the lease situation."

"Nothing to tell, really. The scumbag is selling the place. Not a damn thing we can do about it."

"Why don't you buy it?"

"We would if we had the money. Twenty-percent of one-point-five million is more than we have right now. Even if I raided my retirement we still come up short."

"Can you borrow against the business?"

"Already done that! How do you think the bar was built, and the restaurant restored? Good thing we had the house for collateral. We've borrowed against anything that had value. We'll lose it all, Jack, if we can't find a way out of this mess. Billie doesn't know how serious things really are. We're fried if we have to move that restaurant and leave all the improvements."

"Why doesn't Billie know?"

"Billie does a great job running the restaurant, but she's awful with numbers. All she would do is stress if she knew how deep we were. Better not to worry her with something she can't do anything about."

"How much of the down payment can you raise?"

"Maybe eighty thousand."

"Is the place worth it?"

"Jack, it's a goldmine. If we only had another two years, we would be fine."

"I have a friend in the commercial real estate lending business. Let me see what I can work out."

"What are you going to work out?" Billie's voice floated on the air as she walked to our end of the bar.

"I was just about to give Jack a kiss and hug. He's going to see if he can help us get a loan to buy the building."

Alex stood, wrapped her arms around me, and kissed me on the cheek. That's when I noticed Jody Holland.

Twenty-Five

Billie clapped her hands and giggled at my total surprise.

"Jody Holland." I knew my mouth stood open. The gangly girl had grown into a woman. Even in her late forties, with long blonde hair, her face was unmistakable. I understood now why Billie had so easily recognized her.

Jody studied my face and then extended a hand.

I got off the barstool, bypassed her outstretched hand, and hugged her tightly. I couldn't believe it was Jody.

"You don't know how many times I have thought about calling you, Jack. I have copies of all your books. Unfortunately, they don't say how to reach you."

I looked at Billie, who was still euphoric about her surprise. "Billie told me that you happened into her restaurant, and she recognized you right away. I would have, too. You look marvelous." The words came out with more enthusiasm than I had intended. She did look incredible. Even though I had grown several inches since we were kids, Jody was still an inch or so taller.

Billie had changed into a light pink pantsuit that clashed with Alex's ensemble. Jody wore white snug-fitting jeans and a pale yellow sweatshirt with Key West emblazoned on the front.

"I wish I had thought to bring my camera and caught your face when you saw Jody." Billie laughed and signaled to the maître d' that we were ready to eat. "So shocked."

I looked at Jody for signs of a reaction. She looked at me, smiled broadly, absorbed in the success of the surprise.

Billie stretched her arms out and shepherded us to the awaiting maître d'. The restaurant was sparsely filled. We followed Billie to a table that had been reserved in the corner overlooking Front Street.

I was genuinely glad we were eating. After the heavy conversations of the day, I was ready for something light. Seeing Jody brought on a flood of feelings, some surprising. She made me feel, now, as I had felt the day in the ice-cream shop when Billie first introduced us. I had that nervous feeling in my stomach, and I scrambled for something to talk about. Billie came to my rescue in an unexpected way.

After the dishes had been cleared from the table and the waiter refilled our glasses with wine, Billie looked at Jody then me, and hesitated to speak.

"You were going to say something?" Alex asked.

"Yes, Alex. But I'm trying to find the words. I realized when I saw Jody tonight, that all three of us, Jack, Jody, and I, suffered traumatically during that summer we were together and spent most of our lives trying to recover from it; Jody you most of all. All of us were hurt by the sins of someone else. We were the innocent ones, but we suffered for the crime."

Silence fell upon the table as we all reflected on what Billie had said. Jody had the courage to continue.

"For the longest time, I blamed myself for what had happened to my family. I could have saved my brothers and sisters if I had moved a little faster. A million times, I have wished that I hadn't survived. Then I got some help, and did well until my husband died in a car accident. I fell into the same pattern with his death. If only I had done this, or that, he might still be alive. It wasn't until a year after his funeral that someone convinced me that I had no control over what happened to my husband, nor the horrible things that happened to my family. For some reason, my life had been spared. I was twenty when I first realized I was making my own life miserable trying to atone for what happened to my family. It wasn't until after Barry passed away that I decided I had been given the gift of life, and that I wasn't going to waste another minute of it feeling guilty." Jody looked around the table at us chin high.

Billie put her hand on top of Jody's and gave it a gentle squeeze. "I felt guilty, too. When your mother asked me to leave, Jack, I felt worthless; that I must not be worth much if my own mother wouldn't even have me. Even my father didn't want me. My life was filled with people who didn't care if I lived or not. Alex helped pull me out of my pit. Like you, Jody, I came to realize that the things that happened to me were not my fault. Jack's mother abandoned me; I didn't abandon her. Whatever the circumstances were, I hadn't created them. I'm still not completely over it, but I'm doing much better. What about you, Jack? How did that summer affect you?"

"I can still hear my father's words, 'You're going to end up just like Hemingway.' I can't tell you how many times I have thought about that over the years. When my father told me Hemingway was crazy, a nutcase, I hated him for it. When Hemingway committed suicide and on the same day that my first story appeared in the newspaper, I couldn't breathe. Then, the only other successful writer I knew, your mother — who was also depressed — killed her family in such a tragic way. That only punctuated what my father had told me. I was devastated. Then, three women that I loved were gone. Jody, then Billie, then my mother disappeared into a bottle when Billie left. I was hurt, angry, confused, and heartbroken."

"To hurt, anger, confusion, and broken hearts." Jody lifted her wineglass.

"Hear, hear." Alex touched each of our glasses.

Jody touched me on the arm. "But you went on to write. It seems to me all those things would have discouraged you from doing it."

"With all the things that happened to me that summer, the only way I could cope was to write. I began writing letters to both of you. I had no idea of where you were or how to reach you, but it was my only outlet. Then with your mother's help, the short story appeared in print. All that attention propelled me into writing, ready or not. It was a pretty lousy summer, though."

"For all of us." Billie looked around the table for agreement.

The waiter brought Billie the check. To Alex she said, "These guys haven't seen one another in a long time. Why don't we let them talk, and get reacquainted? Besides you've had a long day." To me she said, "The back door will be unlocked. Just make yourself at home."

Alex and Billie bid their farewells.

"Another drink?"

"Let's go in there." Jody pointed to the bar.

Billie and Alex were still saying good-bye to the maître d', when we found a small table in the back of the bar where the roof was open to the stars. A gentle breeze swirled in under the huge ficus tree sending paper napkins fluttering through the air.

A waiter scurried about, picked up the errant paper, and asked us what we wanted to drink. We continued the selection of Cabernet from dinner. I had been stealing looks at Jody all night. Although the years had softened her lines, and added character to her face, she summoned long-suppressed feelings in me.

"Jack, I am so proud of your success. What is it now? Twenty-five novels?"

"Twenty-five and holding."

"Holding?"

"I haven't been able to write for months now."

"Why?

I really didn't want my time with Jody to slide into a poor-me-fest. "Just a bad case of writer's block. I just don't feel like writing."

"If you were writing about our meeting tonight, what would you write?"

"Wow. Put me on the spot. Well, I guess I would say . . ."

"No, don't tell me what you would say tell me what you would write, like you were dictating the story to me."

"Alright." Writing for me had always been an adventure. My outlines had been a frame to hang a story on, but I never knew what would come out until I put my fingers over the keyboard and things began to flow. I imagined I was sitting at the keyboard, with my hands poised over the keys, and began to dictate. "I had often wondered how I would feel if I ever saw Jody Holland again. The tragedy that kidnapped my first love haunted me in every relationship since. After a couple of years, I stopped thinking about her every day. By the time I married for the first time, I thought of her during the many struggles of our relationship and wondered how different my life would have been had I married Jody instead. Over the years, there were countless evenings when I couldn't sleep that I would wonder where she was, what she was doing, and whether she was thinking about me."

"Now it's my turn to say, wow. You certainly haven't lost your gift."

"That's what I would write. And you did ask. If I was going to say it, I'd say things like it was great to see you, you haven't changed a bit, and isn't the weather great in Key West."

"It is great to see you, Jack. And you do look great."

"You're too kind. You look old when your publisher uses old pictures of you on the dust cover. They haven't used a current mugshot of me for eight years. I'm forty-eight and look like an AARP poster person. You're the same age I am and could be on the cover of a magazine. Life is so unfair."

"If you're trying to make me feel good, you're doing a great job. And I think you're just as handsome as the day we first met at the pool."

"And isn't the weather great in Key West?" I smiled.

She laughed.

"We have so much catching up to do, Jody. The last time I saw you, you were in the hospital."

"Those were some bitter-sweet times. I would have forgotten them entirely, except that I couldn't put you out of my mind. I was emotionally destroyed. I was so in love with you and hated my aunt for taking me away. My heart was broken. In one day, I had lost everyone in the world that I loved. Love mixed with unbearable grief; it was a potent and deadly drug."

"After I left the hospital, I tried to call you from home. But they said you had been discharged."

"That's what they told everyone, but it wasn't true. I didn't leave until the next morning. My aunt showed up shortly after you came to see me, but the police wouldn't let me leave. Can you believe they actually thought I was the one who had killed my family? I was in complete shock. And, the grilling they gave me, as though I were a suspect. My aunt went nuts, found a lawyer, and got me released and we drove straight to Atlanta."

"I was surprised I didn't see you at the funeral."

"I'll never forgive my aunt for that. With the bout I had with the police and the throng of press attracted to the case, she decided it would be better for me not to be there. In truth, she was the one who didn't want to stay. At the time I was just plain angry with her, but later I realized she robbed me of the only chance I had to say good-bye to my family. The last mental picture I have of them, they were lying in a pool of blood. Even today, this picture haunts me. I could only imagine what they looked like in their caskets, ready to meet God. She robbed me of that. It was the closure I needed. And I wanted to see you again."

"How did you deal with the grief? It had to be unbearable."

"I didn't. I just suppressed it. Until your first novel came out, that is."

"The Disappearance of Laura Talbot?"

"That was about me, wasn't it?"

"Yes, my way of dealing with my own broken heart. Your mother's magazine encouraged me to write the story. I was seventeen when I finished it. It was awful. It took the editor a lifetime to re-write half of it. When I go back now and reread the story . . ."

"Don't say another word about that story. It's my favorite. It may not be your most eloquent work, but there is more of you in that story than anything you've ever written."

The waiter came and refilled our glasses, a large party from the street crowded around the reception stand, and waiters scurried, rearranging tables in the restaurant to accommodate. The partiers were ushered into the restaurant, quiet returned and Jody continued.

"I was so angry. My poor aunt deserved some of my hostility. It was clear I was an unwanted burden. I was a wild kid, Jack. Most parents worry about their children being with the wrong crowd. I was the wrong crowd. By the time your first book hit the stands, I had already been arrested four or five times. The last time they arrested me, it was for trying to rob a convenience store to get enough money to leave town. I was twenty-three. Fortunately, a detective did a background check on me, learned my history, and concluded I needed help. I was in the county jail, awaiting trial, when an inmate came around with a cart of reading material. Your book was on it. When I saw your name on the cover, I turned the book over, and there was your smiling face. I couldn't believe it was you. Even though the book had been out for a while that was the first time I had seen it."

"I wondered if you had ever read it. I dedicated it to you."

"I know. That was sweet. My heart was so hard then. It was the only thing that got through."

"It was your story. I made us older and changed the circumstances, names, and locations. But it was your story. I just made the ending come out the way I dreamed it might have if you had stayed."

She looked at me directly as though she wanted to ask me something then shook her head. "That story moved me in ways you could never understand. I was in my cell and read the whole story in one sitting. I cried through the whole thing. I just crumbled emotionally. It was like I had relived the horror of it all over again."

"I'm sorry, Jody. Even when I was writing it, I worried whether it was the right thing to do. It was your story after all, not mine.

"The only person in the world who could've gotten through to me then, was you. That book made me feel again. I had been seeing a shrink at the jail without much success. Your book opened me up. It helped me see that I wasn't at fault. And between the lines, your love for me was the light I needed to find my way out of my emotional cave."

"It was therapy for me, too. It was the only way I could turn the page on that part of my life."

"I often wondered what would have happened to us if I had stayed in Hollywood."

"Me too."

Our conversation fell into a silence; the years of separation melted away like it had only been yesterday since I had kissed her for the first time.

"So what happened then, after you read my book?"

"My aunt hired an attorney, who cut a deal with the prosecutors. I got two years, but the sentence was suspended if I agreed to remain in counseling. The criminal record thing haunted me for a few years, but, looking back, it was the best thing. I got everything on track until Barry died."

"Children?"

"Had Clarisa when I was twenty-five and Barry Jr. fifteen months later. Clarisa has an interior decorating business in Mobile. Barry, Jr. is an engineer with the power company in Atlanta."

"You still live in Atlanta?"

"When Barry died, I needed a change of scenery, so I sold our place and bought a house in New Hampshire, near Concord, a little town called Warner. Barry and I toured New England, and happened on this little village and fell in love with it. Most summers we would end up there, driving around imagining ourselves living in one of those saltbox antiques with a huge barn attached to the house by a summer kitchen. Once I got our affairs settled I went up there and found a small farm with an 1800s farmhouse on it. Then I discovered how severe the winters were. Especially in an old drafty farmhouse."

"Then you came to the Keys."

"We tried several places, but found the Keys to be almost paradise, except for the traffic. I can do without that."

"We?"

"Me and Rex, my golden retriever. We found this cute little story-and-a-half conch house that hadn't been restored yet. Just about have it done."

"Into old, aren't you?"

"Yeah, there's hope for you, then." She smiled. "The house is on Simonton, a couple of blocks from Billie's restaurant. I go in there all the time. I couldn't believe she recognized me after all these years."

The waiter found our table and Jody declined a refill of her wine. "Children?"

"Sorry?" I didn't understand her question.

"Do you have any children?"

"No, but I wanted them, though. I'm afraid I'm the problem. Emily and I have thought about adopting. The last couple of years, though, I don't know of any kid who would benefit from me being a father."

"Emily?"

"She's my wife. She left me four days ago. Apparently she had overdosed on my sparkling personality."

"I'm sorry, Jack." She must have sensed touching an open wound. "Let's walk. You haven't really seen Key West until you walk the waterfront at night."

I paid the check, and we took the stairs down a flight to the street. The breeze was stronger, sweeping us along Front Street toward the Old Customs House. Jody put her arm through mine and led me in the direction of the Hilton. Seeing her sent my emotions swimming. Her touch at my arm brought me back to Hollywood Beach when life was so simple and first love feelings dominated without competition. For a few moments, I felt fourteen again, and for the first time in months, my heart was light. It was like a dream that I had had many times, that I was with Jody again, and none of the horrible things of our youth had really happened. I had no idea where the night was headed, but being with her now, I knew I didn't want it to end.

Twenty-Six

The Customs House looked haunted, abandoned, fenced off, barricaded, and boards covered the windows and doors. Even with scars and wounds, the enormous multistory structure that dominated the view down Front Street toward the waterfront looked stately and elegant.

"They'll never finish restoring this place. If I were the Hilton, I would be screaming about the eyesore. But, they say it will be restored soon. It's taken forever."

Next to the Customs House, the Hilton Resort sat at the end of the point made where Green and Front Streets met. The Hilton grounds were constructed around the marina and along the southern end of Fury Dock. We walked through the Hilton Resort grounds to the water. The dock had been renovated from the Hilton north to the sunset deck at the Ocean Key House.

"See the island there?" Jody pointed to a dark outline of an island. "The Hilton purchased it. It used to be called Tank Island, but they changed its name to Sunset Island. They've sub-divided it into lots going for a half a million or more. The conchs are in an uproar over it. Sunset watching is a major deal here. They say it spoils the view."

All I saw of Sunset Island, a good quarter mile offshore, was a scattering of streetlights and dim light from one or two houses. "How do residents get over there?"

"By boat." She pointed to the marina on our left. "The houses they're building out there are amazing. They even have their own private beach. Well, somewhat private. Residents of the Hilton Resort can take the boat out to the island and use the beach, too."

"Hate to live out there in a hurricane."

"You don't want to be anywhere in the Keys in a hurricane."

We walked along the empty dock past huge iron cleats used to tie off cruise ships. As we neared Mallory Square, the dock opened into an expansive courtyard that ran away from the water, then down to a lower courtyard. Red brick pavers, and concrete trim, gave the dock the look of a park, with planters, benches, and odd trees scattered across the grounds. We stopped and leaned on a concrete railing and looked out at the water.

"At sunset, this place is a carnival. Street people perform all along the dock. We have a sword-swallower, a juggler who tosses knives and fire sticks, mimes, gymnasts, and we even have a guy who balances a stove and a moped on his face." She turned away from the water and looked at the area in which they performed. "The most amusing part is watching the performers jockey with one another for space to perform. They yell at each other, then

at the crowd. 'Over here, my show is just starting.'"
She turned back to the water and leaned on the rail
with her elbows. "But they do draw the crowds. At
sunset, this whole area is jammed with tourists.
Reggae and island music from the Ocean Key House
and Pier House sunset decks floats down and
mingles with the ruckus from the street performers.
It's unique. I've never seen anything like it
anywhere."

She pulled at my arm, and we aimed for the
northernmost point on the dock. The sunset deck of
the Ocean Key House jutted out into the water
several hundred feet. "At sunset, conchs and
tourists alike walk to this end of the island and
watch the sun set. I must confess, it is one of the
nicest customs of the island. No matter what I'm
doing I always manage to find my way here at
sunset and have a drink."

We walked across the square to a small bench
near the aquarium.

As we approached the bench she said, "Tell me
what's eating you, Jack. You've been talking around
it all night."

She sat on the bench first, and I sat perched on
the edge of the seat and turned toward her. She
tried to straighten her hair, but the wind was too
strong. "Why spoil such a beautiful night with
listening to my garbage?"

"I know you're in the dumps, and I know it has something to do with Billie. Come on, spill your guts."

I said, "I can't write a word. My publisher is breathing down my neck for two books they have already advanced me money for, and Emily got tired of the bullshit and left. Short version."

"And how does this involve Billie?"

"My counselor thinks my anger with my mother for what she did to Billie is at the bottom of it."

"At dinner tonight when we had our little impromptu group therapy session, you didn't mention a word about Billie. It was your father you talked about. How he told you that you would end up like Hemingway if you continued to write. Do you remember?"

"Yes."

Jody asked, "Why did you bring that up?"

"I don't know. I guess to acknowledge that my father was right. That I have ended up like Hemingway."

"Hemingway committed suicide. Just because he was depressed doesn't mean you're going to end up just like him."

"I did try to commit suicide, the other night. A cop interrupted me before I had the chance."

"Jack, this is serious, isn't it?"

"Yes." I had finally admitted emotionally the seriousness of what happened.

Bill Cronin

"You know, I remember when your dad gave you such a hard time about writing, especially the day Hemingway died. You were so hurt. We sat on the beach and you cried like a baby. 'I hate him,' you kept saying over and over again. I tried to console you, but all I could do was sit there and listen."

I tried to remember, but couldn't. All I remembered was Father reminding me that he told me Hemingway was a faggot, and I would end up like him if I wrote.

"I never did like your dad. I think he was hateful to you. I couldn't believe he gave you such a hard time about writing. You were so proud when that story appeared in the newspaper. And all you got from him was a ration of crap."

"And when your mother took your family away, I knew what he was thinking. 'She was a writer, too, son. Just like Hemingway. And look what happened to her.'"

"Did he say that to you?" She said this through gritted teeth.

"Not in so many words. But in his own way he got the point across."

"And you don't think that has some significance. I'm no scientist, but it sure seems like it does to me."

"I hadn't really thought about it in those terms."

"After Hemingway and my mom, how were you feeling?"

323

"Afraid. When the magazine wrote me and asked if they could publish my story, I was horrified."

"Of what?"

"That my father would be right."

Jody brushed hair away from her eyes. "That what? One of these days, you would end up like Hemingway. And how did Hemingway end up?"

"He was depressed, couldn't write, and killed himself."

"Sound familiar?"

I stood up and paced back and forth.

"And what about your mom? What was she doing when all this was going on?"

"She didn't want me to stop writing. She told me not to listen to my father." Then I remembered something my mother said. "'Writing has nothing to do with depression. Depression happens when people have no hope. Your father has taken mine, but don't let him take yours away from you.'"

I said, "She was supportive and encouraging."

"He doesn't sound like a villain to me."

"Then why am I so angry with her?"

"I don't know, Jack. I don't think it has a thing to do with your writing. From what I can remember, she was a cheerleader. She wanted you to write; almost pushed you. It's not your mom. What's the situation with your publisher?"

"The publisher gave me forty-five days to have a draft of a novel to them."

"How much do you have done?"

"Nothing. Not one word. And now I have only forty days left."

"How much can you write in a day?"

"When I'm on a good stretch, I can write about twenty-five hundred words a day."

"How many words in a novel?"

"Seventy-five to one-hundred thousand."

"Forty days if it's one-hundred thousand. Looks like you have just enough time."

"I don't know, Jody."

"Jack, you are a talented writer. Even when you were a child, your mother recognized the gifts that you had. It's like your life has been on this course since you were a child. You were meant to write. It's what you do. Don't let your dad's ignorance and bigotry keep you from it." Jody stood up and put her hands on my shoulder. "Hemingway's death had nothing to do with his writing. He was sick. My mother was very sick. What happened to them was especially traumatic to you because of your dad. Don't you see that?"

I did see it. "I can see it with my head, but can I get it into my heart?"

"When do you like to write?"

"In the morning, early. Even before daybreak."

"Write tomorrow morning. Write one sentence. Then one paragraph. Then one chapter."

"One true sentence," I said

"What?"

"Nothing. You're right. I'll try."

She hugged me and kissed me on the cheek. "Good. Now walk me home."

We walked out of the square and aimed at Duval Street. Hard rock music poured out of the Hog's Breath Saloon into a low-lying fog. We bypassed Duval and turned down Simonton.

"This is it." She stood in front of the small, neat, one-and-a-half story with her arms outstretched like a symphony conductor might ready an orchestra. The house was a light pink with white trim, and the tiny front yard tropically landscaped.

Parked at the curb was a mid-sixties Ford van filled to the roof with junk. The right front tire at the curb was flat. I looked it over with curiosity.

"My storage shed. Billie gave me the idea. These old conch houses have small closets and no storage. The yard is so tiny, there's no place to put a shed. Some of the conchs buy old vans, park them at the curb, and use them for storage. As long as I keep a current tag and insurance on it, I'm okay.

"Well, I'll be."

Jody walked over and touched the side of the van, then turned toward me and leaned up against the old vehicle.

"Jack, in your story about me . . ."

"Disappearance . . .?"

"Yes. There was a love scene at the end of the story. Do you remember it?"

"Uh, huh." The rest of the book was awful, but that scene was one of my favorites.

"Were you thinking of me when you wrote it?"

"From the first time I kissed you, I had dreamed what it would have been like to kiss you again. After you left, and I grieved for you so, it was what sustained me, a daily fantasy; a recurring dream. It was the easiest scene I had ever written, because I had been there so many times."

She moved away from the van, put her arms around my neck and hugged me. "I've read and reread those words for a lifetime," she whispered in my ear then she pulled away enough to look me in the eyes.

The need in Jody's eyes matched my own. Everything in me wanted to follow her up onto the porch and into her home. She must have seen the hesitancy in my eyes.

She lowered her eyes, then looked back up at me and stepped back slightly her arms still resting on my shoulders. "I understand, Jack." Then she pulled back and her arms fell to her sides. "You go home and try to work things out with Emily." She hooked her hair over her ears, looked down at her feet, and then back at me. "I've never stopped loving you, Jack. Still do. You know where to find me if things don't work out."

I stepped forward and hugged her fiercely. "I will always love you, Jody. Always. You have helped me beyond words."

Jody pulled back from my embrace, kissed me, looked me in the eyes, released me, walked up on to the porch, unlocked the door and disappeared into the house.

I made it to Billie's shortly after midnight. My time with Jody had been food for a hungry soul. Her insights into my father's role in my current maladies blew reality into my failed thinking. I had been surrounded by the truth of my father's culpability and hadn't seen it. His loathsome prophecy had come true in every detail. My life had paralleled Hemingway's, perhaps not in specific detail, but certainly in course and direction. When I looked back on almost an obsessive curiosity with all things Hemingway, the power of the stigma my father had placed on me was clear.

If Hemingway's death had added force to the blow of my father's prophetic words, certainly Helen Holland's tragic choices added weight. Even now, as I pulled my laptop computer out of my briefcase, and put it atop a small desk in my room, I could recall my feelings as a fourteen-year-old as I tried to grapple with the horrendous events of that summer.

I wanted my father's approval, his reassurance. My mother's words were comforting, but they lacked power. I knew she would say anything to make me feel better. I needed him to put his arm around me and tell me I would be okay. I needed him to listen to my words of grief and assure me that I was right for feeling the way I did. What I got was that all-knowing "you know I'm right, you're all screwed up" look. The sting of his rejection and the pain of his ridicule hurt even now, as I considered the power of his words across the decades. My father's words only had power if I let them.

I opened the screen on the computer, poised my fingers above the keys.

London – July15, 1944

Supreme Allied Command Headquarters sweltered in a late July heatwave. Maj. Patrick M. O'Brien saluted senior staff officers as they departed the building. He bounded through the lobby then up three flights of stairs to an unmarked door near the head of the marble staircase. A thin, balding sergeant dressed in olive-drab fatigues looked at O'Brien's nametag and said, "The colonel is expecting you," then waved O'Brien through the door to Colonel Aubrey James' office.

The blonde-haired James, flanked by a Brigadier General William Scott hovered over a map table illuminated by a bare, clear light bulb hung from a wire in the ceiling.

James's age belied his rank for he hardly looked thirty. Tanned skin, sunburned face and athletic body confirmed to O'Brien the scuttlebutt that James was a hands-on field operative well experienced in special operations. Unlike James, Scott appeared a holdover from World War I. The massive unkempt man in a disheveled uniform chomped on an unlit cigar and broke off his conversation with James as O'Brien entered the room.

One sentence. One paragraph. I set the computer aside and slept soundly if only for a couple of hours. At first light, I was back at work and by ten the first chapter was written.

Twenty-Seven

The door to the stairs leading to the widow's walk was only a few steps from my room. After five hours at the keyboard, I needed to be outside.

The stairs led up to the peak of the roof; the door opened out through the gable. A catwalk, three feet wide, stretched across the ridge of the roof from one gable end to the other. A simple white wooden rail lined both sides of the walk. A bright sun in a cloudless sky reflected off shiny leaves of the Banyan and palm trees flourishing in the gardens around the house.

A cruise ship, guided by two tugs, moved sideways toward the dock. One of the crew blew a whistle that announced the ship's arrival. Ship's crewmembers and hands on the dock threw ropes in each direction as the ship nudged the pilings. The gangplank dropped from a portal to the dock, and an invading pedestrian army, equal in number to the population of the small city, descended on the Conch Republic, prepared to conquer her drinking establishments and plunder her T-shirt shops.

Emily occupied my thoughts. I missed her terribly. When I wrote that morning, my first thought was to wonder what Em would think of it. It was for her that I wrote. She was my encourager and coach. When I was stuck, and I'd written myself into a corner, Em found me a way out. But it wasn't just her skills as a literary physician that I missed.

Emily brought balance to my life. Where I had incredible shortcomings, she had strength. Where I had strengths, she had a need for me. Our conversations flowed smooth like a waltz, and our times of silence together felt like old flannel. We shared space like Fred Astaire and Ginger Rogers might have shared a stage, and, until two years ago, the music of our relationship was like a symphony.

But mostly I missed the intimacy. I isolated Em like a rose separated from the sun. I robbed her love's nutrients, and she withered. In doing so, I cut off my own life's blood, just as surely as a physician might cut off life support to a dying patient. Em was more than just a part of my life she was part of me. I just prayed that I was not too late.

I decided to call and share the good news of my writing again, and hoped the development would soften her resolve to leave me.

Mrs. Berger had already been through my room, made the bed, folded the clothes I had draped over the foot of the bed, and placed them in a chair.

I decided to leave after lunch. This would give me time to say my good-byes. First, I needed to deal with Billie's landlord problem. I picked up the phone on the nightstand and called my banker friend in Mt. Dora.

"Bob, this is, Jack McNamara."

"I'll be ready in ten minutes, just let me run home and get my clubs."

"I'm not calling about golf. I need your help with something."

"When are we going to get together? You're my excuse for sneaking out. A week without golf is a pretty dull week."

"Next week, Bob. I promise."

"What can I do for you?"

"My sister . . ."

"I didn't know you had a sister."

"Long story. She owns . . ."

"You're an only child."

"Would you shut-up and listen, please?"

"Sorry. Go ahead."

"My sister owns a restaurant in Key West. The owner of the building will not renew her lease and has the place up for sale. If she doesn't buy it, she'll have to shut her business down. And, Bob, this is one classy restaurant. I want you to help her buy it."

"Well, I can't make any commitments until I see some numbers."

"I'll guarantee the loan."

"You sure you want to do this?"

"Yes. Can you make it happen?"

"How much are we talking about?"

"Little over a million. They'll be short on the down payment, too."

"I may have to use some of your assets as collateral."

"That's fine. Just do whatever it takes."

"Are you in the Keys now?"

"Yes. I'll probably be home tonight or tomorrow."

"I'll take care of it. Just have . . ."

"Billie St. John."

"Just have her call me."

"Thanks, Bob. You're a good friend."

"Whoa, whoa. I heard you and Emily split. Is it true?"

"I hope not. I'll explain everything when I get home. Gotta run."

I hung up the telephone and sat on the edge of the bed, and thought about my time with Jody. Her observations the night before helped me divide my woes into manageable portions. With her assistance, I understood that I needed to place my writing woes at my father's feet. Although I felt my depression could have been part of a misplaced association with my father's predictions, a fact I understood with my mind, understanding the cause of my depression at an emotional level would be far more difficult. But I knew its origin and its cause, something I felt equipped now to deal with.

I had still not resolved my anger with my mother for how she treated Billie. But from what I had learned from her and having a lifetime of experience with my father's prejudices, I was beginning to feel he had much more to do with Billie's departure than I had thought. I needed to have another talk with him. The sooner the better.

I thought about going to see Jody before I left, but rejected the option of calling her. Leaving her last night had been hard on both of us. There was no need to multiply her difficulty or mine. I pulled paper from my briefcase and began a note to her.

Dear Jody,

The complexities of life can fog our path and make the way difficult. Sometimes we need a guide, a person with clear sight, who can see where the path has escaped us. Your insight helped me beyond measure.

This morning I wrote the opening chapter to my illusive novel. It is glorious to write again. With less than forty days, I can say with confidence, I am up to the challenge and have you to thank. I'll dedicate the book "To Jody: who gave me eyes to see, and hands to write."

We are entitled to experience first love, but once. To experience it twice is a gift. Our time together last night was beyond any dream, a memory for a lifetime. I hope you share my feelings.

But, I still love Emily. I owe her my best effort at reconciliation. I can't fault her for the distance in our relationship. The fault rests with me.

Until the course of my relationship with her is clear, it would be unfair of me to make commitments to you beyond the present. As you always have, you will continue to occupy a special and important place in my heart.

With love,
Jack

With a shower and a change of clothes behind me, I packed my remaining things in my overnight bag and descended the back stairs to the kitchen. Alex sat at the solid oak pedestal table reading the newspaper and picked at a plate of cut-up cantaloupe pieces. Her long black hair was pulled back into a ponytail. Khaki shorts and a white sleeveless T-shirt complemented her dark olive skin.

"I came by your room earlier to offer you breakfast, but you were writing away. I didn't think you wanted to be disturbed." She folded the newspaper and laid it on the table. "About last night . . ."

"I had a wonderful time."

"I gave you such a hard time. I feel just awful."

"You demonstrated to me, in a very profound way, how much you care for Billie. You were just looking out for her interests."

"Then you're not upset with me?"

"Of course not."

"After we came home last night, I told Billie that I had treated you dreadfully. I worried that your being here would upset her. But she is really happy to see you."

"I wish I had come a long time ago. When I think of all the time we could have spent with one another, I get angry."

"She said the same thing. Can you stay for a couple of days? I'd like to make up for the cool reception I gave you."

"No. I'll be leaving after lunch. I wanted to spend some time with you and Billie before I left."

"Billie already left for the restaurant."

"Can we go there? I really need to talk to you both about something."

"Are you ready to go now?"

"All packed."

"Well, let me put on some makeup and I'll be right with you."

It was almost one o'clock when Alex and I reached the restaurant. The host showed us to the table Billie and I had sat at yesterday.

"Tell Billie that we're here, will you, George?"

Alex had pulled her hair down and applied just enough makeup to manage gorgeous. Billie came out from the side of the building, gave Alex and I each a peck on the cheek, and sat between us.

"Well, did you and Jody have a good time last night?" She winked at Alex and grinned at me, then pinched the hairs on my arm. "Details, man, details."

"Nothing to tell. We just had a lot of catching up to do. I do have some good news."

"Spill it. I'm in the mood for some good news. I just heard from our kind and generous landlord. He wants to show the restaurant to a prospective buyer this afternoon. I need some good news."

"I'm writing again, thanks to Jody."

"I like the sound of this. Billie hugged Alex. I'm a sucker for a love story."

"Nothing like that. I admit it was good to see her. But she helped me see that my father's repeated warnings about the doom and gloom my life would suffer if I continued to write could be part of the cause."

Billie said, "I remember the day your story came out in the paper. He gave you such a hard time about Hemingway. I hated him for the things he said to you. I think Jody's right."

"On my way home I got angry. Angry that more than thirty years later his words were still hurting me like they did then. I made up my mind that I wasn't going to let him ruin my life. I started writing this morning with something to prove to myself. It was great. The words came out like water from a faucet. I've been thinking about this story for so long the story is already written in my head. All I have to do is put it on paper."

Alex touched Billie on the forearm. "He's leaving after lunch. I told him how sorry I was about last night."

"You've got to stay. I have so much to show you. We have so much to talk about."

"I have less than forty days to get the first draft of this novel finished, or I'm shark bait. And I have to turn the page on my mother."

"Afraid I haven't been much help."

"You've been more help than you know. As soon as I get this draft done and off to my agent, I want to come back and spend a week or so. Would that be alright?"

"That would be wonderful!" A genuine smile stretched across Alex's face.

"Now, I need to talk to you about this restaurant. As soon as I leave, I want you to call your landlord and offer him full-price for the place. Tell him you'll have a contract to him today. Get a hold of the realtor and get an offer to him this morning, before someone else buys this restaurant out from under you."

Billie shook her head. "We don't have the money."

"I called a friend of mine with a bank in Mt. Dora. This guy is a miracle-worker." I wrote Bob's name and number on a napkin and handed it to

Billie. "I explained the situation to him. He said he will do the deal."

"Just like that?" Alex looked at Billie.

"Yes. You just need to call him today. He will get the paperwork moving."

"You're serious, aren't you?" Billie smiled.

"I am. But, you need to act right now. Don't waste one second."

I looked at Alex and she was in tears. She got up from her seat, came around the table, put her arms around my neck, and kissed me on the cheek. "What can we say?"

"Nothing. I'm just glad I could help."

"I couldn't have asked for a better brother. It's just too bad it's taken this long for us to get back together."

"We'll just have to work twice as hard to make up for lost time."

I pulled my note to Jody out of my shirt pocket. "I have a note here for Jody that I would like you to give to her. Do you have an envelope I could put it in?"

"I'll get it." Alex headed to the main building.

"Why can't you stay tonight? I know you didn't get a lot of sleep last night. It's an eight-hour drive home."

"I wish I could. But I want to confront my father while I still have the courage and anger."

"It doesn't matter anymore. I'm over it. I'm happy and content. If you're doing it for me, it isn't necessary."

"I'm doing it for me. I don't want to be angry any more. As soon as I finish this story, I'll come back. You have my word."

Billie leaned over and kissed me.

"I think this will work." Alex handed me a plain white business envelope and placed a bottle of champagne on the table with three, fluted glass. "We need to celebrate our purchase of the restaurant before Jack leaves."

Alex popped the cork and poured while I put the note to Jody in the envelope and handed it to Billie.

"I'll be sure she gets this."

Alex held up a glass. Billie and I stood and held our glasses up to hers.

"To writing chapters. And may they all be happy ones." Billie touched her glass to mine then to Alex's. We drank the dry bubbling wine and basked in the warmth of the moment.

Twenty-Eight

The drive from Key West was long and tiring. Ten miles south of Florida City on a stretch of two-lane highway north of Key Largo, a tractor-trailer jack-knifed on the highway and blocked both lanes. The wreck had traffic in and out of the Keys blocked for nearly two hours while wreckers cleared the road. I got home just after midnight.

I had used the time waiting for them to clear the vehicles from the road to outline the next five chapters and write most of chapter two until the batteries went dead in my laptop. I felt good for the first time in months. I was on a smooth stretch, and I was hoping to finish the second chapter before I went to bed. But I was fading fast.

I put the car in the garage, and made my way to the kitchen. On the countertop, there was an envelope, marked simply, JACK.

I opened the envelope.

Dear Jack,

I've been through the house one final time. I don't think you'll object to anything I've taken. I've packed all my things, and there is nothing left in the house that I want.

I've considered the commitment I made to you not to file for divorce for sixty days. I will keep my commitment, but I will not be coming back. Even if you were to put things back together, and I hope you can, I don't think I could make it work. Somewhere along the way, in the past two years, I stopped loving you. I care for you deeply, and if I can help in any way, I want to. I'm just not in love anymore.

I'm in no hurry to file papers. You let me know when you feel up to it.

Emily

In the envelope were her keys to the house. While her letter was devastating, it wasn't totally unexpected. I put the note down on the counter and walked through the house. Everything was as I had left it before my trip to see Billie. Only an odd knick-knack or picture was missing.

I picked up the phone in the kitchen and dialed the number she had left me.

Emily answered the phone and sounded like I had awoken her. Then I realized how late it was and regretted calling her.

"Em. Jack. I didn't think about how late it was. I'm sorry I woke you up."

"You just get back from the Keys?"

"I just found your note. Is this a bad time?"

"No. After I left the note, and left my keys, I thought that I should have told you this in-person. I'm sorry. I shouldn't have done that."

"Are there any conditions that would change your mind? I'm writing again. Finished two chapters. I think I can meet the deadline."

"I'm happy for you. I've never loved anyone as I've loved you. You were unhappy, though. Most of it vented on me. You just beat the love out of me. A person can only take so much."

"I'm sorry, Em. You're right. I was angry, and down, and I took it out on you. That was a dreadful mistake. Won't you give me a chance to make it up to you?"

"I'm sorry. I was going to wait and tell you all this once you pulled yourself together. I didn't want to add to your burden, but I have a right to be happy, too. As I said in my note, I'll do anything I can to help. If you want me to continue to manage and edit your novels, I'll be happy to do it. But I don't want to give you false hope."

"You mean there isn't anything there at all?"

"Sure there is. I love you, but it's not the intimate love we once shared. I care about you. I'll always worry about you. I'm just not in love anymore. I'm sorry. I wish it weren't so."

"Well, Em, it isn't as if you haven't tried. I know you have. I can't tell you how much I regret the way things have ended."

"But do you understand?"

"Yes. I understand."

"If you want to talk face-to-face, I'm willing. Writing you a note was insensitive. I'm sorry."

"Actually, Em. It would have been harder in person."

"Do you want to get together, then?"

"No. I'll be okay. Right now, I actually think it would make it worse."

"If you have stuff that you want me to work on, I'll come and get it."

"I'll let you know."

"I feel awful."

"Me, too." I hung up.

Suddenly, I was exhausted. The late hours the night before, the long drive home, and Emily's note brought me low. I found the bed and flopped in, too tired to change out of my clothes. As sleep descended on me, I felt badly that I hadn't done more to keep Emily, but I also knew that I had tried everything that I could to shake my depressed state-of-mind. If I could have done something, I would have. I didn't blame Emily for her decision, but, as badly as I felt, I knew that I had done all I was capable of doing. I had given it my best. I couldn't control the fact that I was emotionally sick. It was not like I had deliberately set about to make Emily unhappy. I began to feel myself sliding back down into the emotional pit that I had begun to climb out of these past few days. I didn't want to go there. I had been in a personal hell for two years, and I had no intention of a second visit. It would be hard to adjust to life without her, but I was not going to let it send me into another tailspin.

My heart was broken, but not my spirit. As I drifted off to sleep, I felt better about myself than I had in a long time, despite Emily's decision to leave. I would survive it. I would finish my story, and I would take things as they came.

Twenty-Nine

I hadn't slept that well in ages. It was early afternoon when I awoke. I called my father and asked him if I could come by and see him after dinner. Then I finished chapter two—and the opening paragraph of the third chapter to get a head start on the next day's work.

Orlando's traffic was in its usual snarled state. A trip that should have taken forty minutes took well over an hour.

I rang the doorbell to my father's house and heard him yell that he was in the bar. I found my way to the Florida room.

"How's it going?"

"Can't complain. Emily called me yesterday. Said you were on some psycho wild goose chase."

"Is that the way she said it?" I sat down on a stool next to him, but just as quickly, he was up and behind the bar for a refill.

"Beer?"

I nodded.

He pulled a longneck bottle from the small refrigerator along with a frosted mug and set the pair in front of me before sitting next to me at the bar.

"Is that the way she said it?"

"No. She said you asked her for some time to work things out. That you were trying to find out why you were sooo angry with your mother."

"I have some problems I'm working through," I said defending myself.

"Your mother used to talk that psycho crap all the time. She made herself sick with it. Emily said that she wasn't coming back to you. You sure blew that one."

"Well, this is a great way to start off this conversation," I said to myself. "You know it's a good thing I don't expect understanding from you, because I would be sorely disappointed."

"What's that supposed to mean?" he said with irritation.

"What Mother needed from you was understanding and help. All you gave her was criticism. If Mother was sick, you helped to make her so." Now we were having our usual argument.

"We're not here to talk about your mother, Jack," he said, his face turning red and the pupils of his eyes dilating.

"She was hurting when I was growing up. She needed to talk to someone. She needed help, and all you gave her was all this crap about 'pulling herself up by her bootstraps.' She was drowning in her troubles, and what did you do? You handed her concrete blocks to swim with."

348

"She was depressed, and now you're depressed," he said in a singsong tone of mockery. "And I suppose everyone in your life is expected to stop theirs and stroke your head and pay you some attention. Is that the way it is, Jack? Do you want some attention?" He reached over and tried to pat me on the top of the head.

I swatted his hand away. I got up from the barstool. It was all I could do not to hit him. I took a few deep breaths, trying to focus on why I had come here to start with. I let some time pass to let the tension from the moment drain. When I had cooled sufficiently I again sat beside my father.

"I'm angry with her. I've been angry with her since she threw Billie out of our home."

"She didn't throw that faggot out. That was one queer, sick bitch."

"And Mother threw her out in the street."

"There was no way that little tramp was going to stay in our home, Jack."

"Why, Dad? What did she do that was so horrible?"

"That sicko-bitch tried to put the moves on your mother. I saw it."

"What did she do? What did you see her do?"

"I don't want to talk about it. Believe me."

"Well, I want to talk about it. We are going to talk about it." I could see the rage building. I had seen it many times as a child. His right hand was balled into a fist, and he ground that fist into the palm of his left hand. "What did Billie do that was so awful that Mother threw her out?"

He was silent. The veins in his neck bulged and his face and forehead were very red.

I yelled at him. "What did she do that was so disgraceful that Mother threw her out into the street?"

Through clenched teeth he said, "I came home from work late one night and found the two of them in bed together. There, are you satisfied?"

"What were they doing in bed?"

"Your mother was in bed with Billie. They both had nightgowns on. Billie had her arms around your mother for Christ's-sake."

"And?"

"Billie had her head lying on your mother's shoulder. They were in an embrace. Can you imagine?"

"What else were they doing, Dad?"

"They were watching television and cozying up together in my bed."

"That's it?" I asked incredulously.

"What do you mean, is that it? They were in their nightgowns in an embrace in my bed. It was clear to me that little bitch was trying to get your mother to turn."

"Turn to what?"

"She was trying to seduce your mother. You know, Jack, one of those lezo deals. I certainly wasn't going to let her seduce your mother. And I certainly wasn't going to let that little queer corrupt you."

"So, you threw her out!"

"No, I told your mother that Billie had to leave."

"And she was in agreement?" The weight of the revelation had begun to penetrate my anger.

"No. We had a hell of a fight, though. She was taken in by that little whore, but I wasn't. It was plain to me what was going on. Our marriage was never the same after that. But it was for her good that I did it."

"And you had a fight over it?"

"It was the worst fight we had ever had. I told her that she could choose the street or me."

I was ready to explode. "You bastard," I said to myself. But I wanted to find out more. I knew now if I provoked him further I would never find out what really happened.

"Why did Mother abandon Billie when she married you?"

"Is this what this is all about, Jack? Finding someone to blame for all your problems?"

I ignored his question. "I want to know why my mother abandoned Billie."

"I don't want to talk about it. That's between your mother and me. It's none of your business."

"It is my business. Mother would never talk about it, but I think it destroyed her."

"That's bullshit, Jack. Your mother destroyed herself with booze."

The anger crept up into my throat, and my head was filled with years of hatred and pain. "You're going to tell me what happened if I have to beat it out of you. There are many lives at stake here. There is a fifty-two year old woman in Key West, my sister, who thinks her mother hated and rejected her. And I listened to Mother's emotional problems for most of my childhood, because you were too much of a man to put up with her whining."

Before I knew it, the back of my father's hand had taken a full blow at my cheek, knocking me to the floor off the barstool. The bones in my face exploded with pain. I could taste blood in my mouth. From the floor I said, "What are you hiding, Dad? What was so horrible that you would beat me to keep it a secret?"

"THERE IS NO SECRET," he yelled, and was preparing to strike me again. I put my arm over my head to protect myself, but the blow never came.

I looked up from the floor, and my father eased back to the barstool, the rage slowly draining from his face. His face contorted into extreme sadness. He dropped his head almost to the surface of the bar. "History repeats itself," he said at the point of tears.

"What?"

"This girl continues to haunt me."

"What are you talking about, Dad?"

More in control he said, "I lost your mother in fights just like this over that little bitch, and now I'm losing you, too."

"You haven't lost me, Dad. I just want the truth. I've spent most of my life angry with Mother. I would like to understand why."

"You want to know the truth?" he said, the anger returning to his voice.

"Yes, once and for all," I said, pulling myself to a standing position, rubbing my cheek where he had struck me, and finding the barstool next to his.

"Your mother didn't abandon Billie, Jack."

"What?" I said, shocked.

"I loved your mother. She was the most beautiful creature I had ever seen. She was lovely beyond description," he said, and I could see his mind wandering to sweeter, younger days.

"About Billie," I said, trying to pull him into the present.

"I wasn't ready for children."

"What does that mean?" I asked sarcastically.

"When I met your mother, I didn't know she had a daughter. It wasn't until we had fallen in love that she told me that she had a child."

"You mean she lied to you about it?"

"No, she just never told me, not until things became serious. After she told me, I broke up with her. But I was hopelessly in love. I couldn't bear to be without her," he said. He was calmer now, reflective.

He walked around the bar and produced another beer. He poured it for me, refilled his own glass from a bottle of Smirnoff's, and sat down again.

"I asked your mother to marry me. It was right as the Second World War ended. The navy released me in Charleston, but I had no work lined up. I didn't want to leave Charleston without your mother." His eyes began to fill with tears. As quickly as they came, they were gone.

He went on. I was silent. I drank my beer and listened.

"I suggested to your mother that she leave Billie with a sitter, a lady your mother knew, while we went on our honeymoon, and I brought her to Orlando to meet my family. When we arrived at my parents' house, I didn't tell them that Kit had been married before. They were devout, old-fashioned Catholics and wouldn't have understood what their son had done; marrying a divorced woman. I decided that we would stay with my folks until I found some work."

"Did you send for Billie?" I asked knowing what the answer would be.

"No."

"Did Mother go along with this?"

He dropped his head, and tears began to reappear in his eyes. "No. It upset your mother terribly. But I only intended to leave Billie with a sitter until I found some work."

"Let me see if I have this straight. You brought Mother to your folks' home with the understanding that you would return for Billie. Once you were there, you don't tell your parents about her daughter and you decided to stay. So Mother was prevented from returning, and she couldn't tell a soul about the pain she was suffering."

My father sat there looking blankly at me. He looked straight at me, but reliving the horror of the past.

"Okay, so you temporarily left Billie with a sitter. How long did it take for you to find work?"

"Nine months."

"How did Mother communicate with her, if your parents didn't know about her?"

"I wouldn't let her call her," he said, tears streaming down his cheeks.

"When you found work, what then?"

"Since the sitter had not heard from your mother, she called Billie's father. He got an attorney and filed for custody."

"Did Mother go to court?"

"No"

"Why not?"

My father was sobbing at this point. His shoulders quaked. His head was down.

"What happened, Dad?"

Silence, there was only the sound of my father crying. He placed his arms on the bar and put his head face down into the crook of his arm.

"What is it, Dad? What did you do? Tell me. What the hell did you do?" I yelled, pounding my fist on the bar next to his head.

"I hid the court notices from her."

"So she didn't even know that Billie was being taken away?"

"No. Not until after custody was given to the father."

"You bastard!" I said aloud.

"It was better for the girl to be with her father. He was in a better position to support her than I was."

"You bastard!" I said again, almost yelling.

"In the end it was for the best."

"You bastard," I screamed at him. "It was best for you, you selfish son-of-a-bitch. What about Mother? What was best for her? How did all this make her feel? You heartless, cold-blooded bastard. Why didn't you just kill her? Because that's what you did. You should've just put a bullet in her head, because you destroyed her just the same. You pitiful excuse for a husband."

"Get out, Jack. You have your truth now get out of my house."

"This is not over, Dad."

"The hell it isn't."

"What about the poor woman in Key West who thinks her mother hated her?"

"You tell her."

"You're going to tell her, Dad."

"I'm not telling anyone anything." His crying had stopped. He regained his composure.

"I took my pen from my pocket and wrote Billie's name, address, and phone number on a notepad on the bar. "You screwed up Mother's life. The least you can do is apologize to Billie for what you did to her." I said, as I made ready to leave.

"The subject is closed. You found out what you wanted to know, now get out of my house."

"Did it ever occur to you that Billie just needed affection from her mother that she was denied by your selfishness?"

"Get out!" my father said with anger that was barely under control.

"Did it ever occur to you that Billie just needed affection from her mother, when they were in bed together?"

"Get out, Jack, or so help me . . . ."

"Did it ever occur to that small bigoted brain of yours that Billie needed love from her mother, and that Mother needed to heal a wound that could only be mended by holding her daughter?"

He exploded, "GET OUT OF MY HOUSE OR I'LL THROW YOU OUT!"

As I left my father's home, my thoughts were not for my father, Billie, or myself but for my mother. As I drove back to Mt. Dora, it suddenly became clear to me why my mother's life had taken such emotionally devastating turns. As I sat alone by the pool that night, I began to relive what my mother must have gone through.

I envisioned Mother in Orlando, my father preventing her from returning for her daughter. My heart broke at the prospect, as I placed myself in this unthinkable position. Why hadn't she done something? I could only speculate. Times were different then. She was in a strange city, probably with no money, and probably fearing what my father would do if she did do something. Or maybe she was so much in love with my father that she feared losing him.

Why hadn't she told me any of this? I'd never know the answer to that question. My mother, despite emotional problems, never criticized my father to me. She did talk about his cheating on her, but she always made excuses for him. She presented my father as a good man. It was not in her character, I concluded, to criticize him. Perhaps it was that she also felt guilty. Even though he tricked her and prevented her from going after her daughter, maybe she felt shame and guilt from not having done something more to prevent it.

But, my feelings for my mother were changed. Through a different set of eyes I began to see her as a woman of strength. I could not have endured what she had endured and survived.

When I thought of Billie and Mother in bed together, embracing each other after being so long separated, and then to have had the horrendous deed of Billie's abandonment repeat itself in what my mother was forced to do, I understood my mother and all the things she did in an instant.

My mother was not a strong person in many ways. My father dominated her, making her feel small, helpless, and trapped. To have endured those catastrophic events and not have lost her mind completely showed me the depths of her strength. Yes, she was depressed. Yes, she was an alcoholic. And, yes, she burdened me with her problems. But compared to the load she carried, what she burdened me with seemed small now. I doubt I would have survived what she went through. Even with the booze and the drugs, I didn't think I would have made it. It didn't forgive entirely what my mother did. She had some measure of control, control she didn't exercise. She could have left my father and forced him to act responsibly, and she didn't. She was just as wrong as my father was, but I understand now how it happened. My father victimized both Billie and my mother. My anger with my mother melted. Had I known then the hurts that my mother had suffered, I would have done much more than I had to help her. I didn't know. My mother probably was wise in keeping the truth from me. There was no telling what I would have done to my father had I known.

What of Billie? Would this information about her mother change her bitterness and anger? Would she feel better about herself knowing it wasn't Mother who rejected her? That was my hope.

I knew my father would never make the trip to see her. And if he did, he would bulldoze over her feelings in the process. I would call the airlines and book a flight to Key West. First, I needed to set things straight with Mother, and I needed to finish my book. I had to find a way to salvage my relationship with Em.

Thirty

I needed help to find my mother's headstone. I could picture the green canopy that covered her gravesite eighteen years ago, the gathering of mourners, and my retreat to the back of the service. Flowers adorned the markers of those around Mother's. Hers was painfully plain and unadorned.

I wished she were here. I had so much to tell her, but mostly I needed her forgiveness. She had carried a terrible burden. It must have been excruciating for her to dispatch Billie from our home. It was even worse for her to have lived with losing her daughter, and that my father had prevented her from returning to get her. Yet, she loved my father enough that she didn't want me to know the truth. She knew that if I did know the truth, I would hate Father for it.

The sun sought its way through the twisted branches of the many water oak trees around Mother's gravesite. I placed a small bouquet of flowers on her stone that lay flush with the ground. I knelt sitting on my feet, trying to find the words I would say to her if she were here. All I could think to say was 'I'm sorry.' I regretted that I hadn't had this opportunity when she was still alive.

I began to cry. The weight of the dilemma of my mother's life came to full awareness. Her world had not been a perfect one. She had done her best with what she had been given. Within moments, I was inconsolable. Suddenly I missed her terribly. I felt horrible that she had gone to her grave thinking that I hated her. Intense sadness came over me at the prospect of her spending eternity without knowing my remorse.

A mockingbird began to sing in the tree above and behind me. It sang its repertoire of songs in melodies all too familiar. The song of the mockingbird penetrated to my soul. I knew Mother was there with me. And I knew now, that even on the day of the funeral, she had tried to console me with her songs of love. The peace I had felt then, and misunderstood, was Mother trying to reach me in the only way she could. Now, she had an open channel to my heart. She could hear my contrite words and feel my grief. She could feel the love and forgiveness that I felt so deeply, and my remorse for taking so long to grieve for her as I should have. I knew, from the peace I felt, that she had forgiven me.

THE END

Ruby's Story

The next novel in the "Jack McNamara Chronicles."

Here are the first three chapters.

One

The sun breached the horizon and bled out on the still water of the lake. Wisps of fog formed by frozen air and warm lake water drifted across the path of the sun and diffused its brilliance into opaque yellows and oranges. Through the misty vapor, the Lakeside Inn across the water appeared to be on fire as the sun rose directly behind it.

I stood on the end of the sixty-foot, T-shaped, frost covered dock my beloved Lake Dora laid resplendent before me. To my left, the city of Mount Dora was a silhouette on the horizon. To my right the shoreline wended westward in an arc to a point beyond which darkness still lay on the lake in slumber. Immediately in front of me, on the bottom of the lake, with only the windshield breaking the water was our ski boat, neglected and abandoned. Weathered nylon rope still tied off to cleats on the dock led to frayed breaks where the weight of the sinking boat had broken the tethers fore and aft.

The dock on which I stood was once a point of pride. Now its treated-pine decking, posts and rails were a collection of warped, rotted and nail-exposed hazards slick with frost. I stood in flannel pajamas, a fleece bathrobe and flip-flops, my uniform over the past forty-something days, I hugged myself, shivered, wanted to tip-toe my way back to the safety of shore, but held on to the rickety structure by the importance of the moment and the significance of this particular setting.

Em and I had brought a bottle of Chardonnay in a bucket of ice with two glasses to this very site and toasted the completion of the draft of every new novel. And with the toast, my work would end and hers would begin. It was a ceremony during which the bottle was emptied, the baton was passed, and on most occasions lovemaking followed. Em was not only my wife of eight years she was my manager, and my editor. She was still, technically, my wife. This morning there will be no wine, no Em, and definitely no lovemaking. Em left me more than a month ago and, out of compassion for my state of mind, would not file divorce papers until I was in a more stable emotional state. She finally realized that she could no more raise me from the bottom of the pit I was in than I could single-handedly raise the boat whose waterlogged, rotted remains lay on the bottom of Lake Dora. Her efforts were courageous and selfless. Despite her hardened steel will and relentless drive to lift my spirits, she failed, lost hope and finally gave up.

The boat was emblematic of my life over the past three years. While the process of sinking took a while, multiple projectiles to the hull of my life slammed it to the bottom in a matter of hours. Although my life was shredded months earlier, the events of November 14, 1995 tipped it into the emotional abyss.

It has been forty-one days since my publisher threatened to cancel a million dollar contract if I didn't complete a draft of a long overdue novel. Forty-one days ago, my publisher Reynolds and Ryan summoned me to New York and threatened me with a breach of contract if I didn't deliver a draft of the second of three novels by December 27. On my return from Gotham, Emily had backed a truck up to the door of our home in my absence and emptied it of her belongings after eight years of my mercurial personality. Em told me she was finished watching depression ruin my life and career and wanted out before it ruined hers. It was less than ten minutes following her announced departure that I sat on the side of the road and reached for a Glock 9mm that I kept in the glove box of my car with the intention of ending what little life I had left. Her rejection was the final indignity, the last grain of despair that could be poured into my desperate life. Only a state trooper, curious about a car parked on the side of a major highway in the fog of early morning, intervened and disrupted my hastily conceived exit plan.

At the very moment the trooper rapped his knuckles on the window of my car, as I reached for the gun in my glove-box, I felt my life crash to the bottom of the pit I had been freefalling in for the three years. It had been forty-one days since the state trooper told me to "move on." The weight of that command carried more meaning than I wanted to admit to myself then. Now it seemed so clear. The young kid with the Smokey-the-Bear hat was an angel unaware. From the grimy bottom of the darkest place I had ever been his knock on the window of my car was a good-Samaritan, last second grab at a man who had jumped from a building. It was only a moment, but so much happened in that wisp of time.

I had been crushed, broken into nothingness by the weight of my life. Never had I ever felt so insignificant, helpless and fearful. Everything that I loved had been taken away from me. I was nothing and had nothing. I cried out to God. "Help me." I had no solutions for any of my problems, no idea of direction or how to get there. The horror of it, the memory of having nearly lost my mind and the cold, dark loneliness frightened me beyond description. Something in me changed. In the very core of me, my "want-to" was transformed. There were two things I knew in that instant: first, I wanted to live, and, second, I wanted out of the darkness and never wanted to return to that miserable God-forsaken place again.

There was the faintest of light at the top of the long black tunnel above me; only visible with great effort and concentration — but light none-the-less. As the trooper extinguished his flashing blue lights, pulled around me and accelerated on to highway 441, it marked the point at which I began to make a conscious effort to climb out of the pit I had excavated for myself. Until then, writing was just out of the question. It required energies from sources in me that had long ago been extinguished. I looked at my submerged boat in front of me and realized that it was on-the-bottom because I lost interest in it — I didn't care whether it survived or not. Forty-one days ago, I didn't give a rip about anything in my life, including me. But in that instant, when I realized how close I had come to the end my life, the wind changed. In the days that followed, with help from my sister Billie and my childhood sweetheart, Jody, I began to write again and with the writing came hope.

I don't know how long I stood at the end of the dock before the numbing cold registered. It was Christmas morning. While I could celebrate the completion of my novel, there was still the collateral damage of the emotional destruction I had caused those around me; Em in particular. Selfishly, I had a book that needed editing. I had no doubt in my mind that as soon as I delivered the draft of this book to my agent, Lisa Catera, Reynolds and Ryan, my publisher, would demand the final installment with the same threats and intimidation of forty-one days ago. Normally it took 3-4 months to write a novel and that with my full focus. Usually, my publisher was happy to get two completed works a year. This gave me 3-4 months to rest, fill my creative tanks, research and think through future projects. To get another novel written in 45 days or less would mean writing ten hours a day, seven days a week. To finish this novel I had been chained to a keyboard day and night for the last month. And while I had been a slave to my writing, it had done more than any counselor or therapist could have done to extract me from my funk. "Death in the Desert," was more than just another novel in a string of action/adventure tales, it was an integral part of the gear I had needed to break out of my emotional prison. Yes, it was an escape, as my writing had always been a departure from the realities of life that were often more than I could handle. However, while I was deep in the imaginary Sahara Desert, ready to coax a fifty-year old B-24 Liberator bomber into flight, I worked through all the emotional issues that had sandbagged my life and had brought my writing career to a dead stop. In the long hours hunched over my keyboard I mourned Em's irreconcilable departure, wrapped my mind around the reintroduction of my half-sister Billie into my life after nearly a thirty year absence, forgave myself for a long misplaced feud I had had with my long-deceased mother and gave recognition to new wounds I had created with my father. Writing had always been therapy until my energy had been sapped, the words disappeared and then the spiral downward began in earnest. Writing had always been my interface with the world around me. When the words ran out so did my ability to cope. Once I understood that which held me captive emotionally, and I moved past it, only then did the words pour from me as they had for so many years.

The sun stretched out in the sky and drew the yellow and orange mist hovering on Lake Dora away like one would pull a curtain from a window to let light fill a darkened room. Bass cleared the surface of the water nearby with a slosh. A gaggle of black and white headed Canadian geese splash landed on the glassy water formed a line near the dock and headed off into what was left of the fog. Even in the depths of my depression, early mornings on this most hallowed dock kept me from falling off the edge of sanity. From this very spot when there wasn't an emotional drop of water left in my life, I found a canteen here even among the ruins of my boat and this beloved structure.

I wanted to call Em. It was not because I needed her professionally, every bone in my body ached for her. I wanted to tell her that my life was on the mend and ask her for another chance. But I had done that and she rejected that option out of hand just over a month ago and I hadn't called her since. I wanted to tell her that, despite my loneliness, that I felt better than I had felt for a long time. I wanted to share with her the good news that I had completed my story in record time and strategize my next novel as we had done on my previous sixteen books. Em told me when I talked to her last, that despite the fact that she could not live with me anymore, she would continue to work for me if I felt like I could handle it. That was the rub; could I handle it? Probably not. Aside from her professional competence, she was the most desirable woman I had ever been around. She was, until I destroyed it, the best friend I had ever known. I don't think I could be with her without the total oneness we had enjoyed together. It would be a wall I could not scale.

I needed to call Lisa Catera. Lisa was more than an agent. For the past twenty years, she had been a friend, confidant and champion of my career. Em and Lisa had been closer than sisters. Lisa, however, was also a pile driver of a boss. As soon as I called her to let her know that "Death in the Desert" was finished she would begin to pressure me to complete the next one.

The cold finally penetrated. I knew I wanted Em back in my life. I knew the odds were long, but I had to try. I needed to find an editor. I did not want to ask Em to do it unless I could have all of her back and I knew that would take time, perhaps a lot of time and I needed an editor now. Before I turned to go to the warmth of my home and studio, I looked at the dock and pledged to myself that I would have my boat raised, replace it and my dock rebuilt as soon as businesses reopened after the holidays.

Two

Lakeshore Drive separated many of the homes along Lake Dora from the water. Owners of these homes had deeded access to the lake. They constructed docks or boathouses on the water directly across the street from their homes. While some felt it an odd arrangement I valued the southern exposure and views of the lake from my studio.

I walked across the street to the redbrick structure I called home. The house was the shape of a square C with the open end tilted slightly toward the lake. The main house was located in the lower leg of the C and my studio in the upper where a plate glass window gave me an unobstructed view of the lake. By day, the many angles of the sun gave life to the water, and by night the lights from Mount Dora brought an atmosphere to my secluded work space. During the worst of my depression, I never left my studio. I would sleep in it for days on end, doors locked, and cell phone off. When I first bought the place cell phones still looked like bricks with an antenna and wired phones were still a necessity. I did not want a phone in my studio, so I installed an intercom system between the house and the studio. When I was writing Em would save me from the phone and only signal me if a call was crucial. When I couldn't write she would plead with me over the intercom to come into the house and eat, or to get out of the "hole" for a while, her name for the studio.

One afternoon she had an accident in her car and could not get through to me. She demanded that we install a second line that had an extension in my office. There was no bell to ring, only a red light would flash then stay red if a call had come through. Since Em was the only one with the number it was always her and she would only call with something important. Then cellphones came into vogue, became irreplaceable and she made sure I had it at all times

When I approached the door to the studio, through the reflection of Lake Dora on the plate glass window, the red light blazed on the old telephone set that sat on my desk.

"Em, is everything okay?"

"Merry Christmas to you too, Scrooge."

"Merry Christmas, it has been so long since you used this line. I just thought there was a problem."

She said, "I tried your cell, but it went straight to voice mail. You must have it turned off. I decided to give the old landline a try. Guess it still works."

I pulled the cell phone from the pocket of my robe, checked it and the phone was dead. I tried to turn it on without success. "The battery must have died."

"When did you use it last?"

"I can't remember. I've been too busy. Maybe a week ago, I really don't know."

"Your aunt has been trying to reach you. How she got my number I have no idea, but she has trying to call you for several days."

"Em, I haven't even been in the main house to check messages. Anything serious?" Ruby never called me. Never. I tried to call her at least once a month and Em and I tried to see her two to three times a year. Ruby and Glory Jean were my mother's sisters and on opposite ends of the personality spectrum. Glory Jean was an irreverent, non-conformed, wild woman. Ruby was deeply religious, serious, and gracious down to every fiber of her southern roots.

"Actually, it was St. Vincent's Hospital in Jacksonville. Someone in administration called for her. Apparently, she is there and asking for you. They wouldn't tell me anything other than that. I hope it isn't serious." Em's concern was genuine. She had grown close to Aunt Ruby over the past eight years and they connected at a level that I didn't comprehend.

My Tabby, polydactyl cat, Hemingway, jumped up on the desk and surveyed his vast domain then inched his way across the desk and nudged my hand for attention.

"I hope nothing is wrong as well. As soon as we get off, I will call the hospital." I had resisted calling Em as I neared the end of my story. Part of it was stubborn anger that she had left me, rejected me even. The other part; I found it difficult to deal with all the emotions regarding the enormous role she had played in my work and life. Even though Em had told me that she was finished with me, I had held out a sliver of hope that I could still piece together my relationship with her. I was afraid that if my conversation with her drifted much past hello that I would learn that my hope was displaced. No sooner had the words, "I finished the bomber story" left my lips, I regretted it.

"That's marvelous," she cooed. "When did you finish it?"

"This morning, actually an hour ago. I wanted to call you and share the good news." There was awkward dead air.

"My offer to continue to edit for you still stands . . . that is if you still need me . . . or that is — if you want me to."

We came instantly to the place that I did not want to go.

"Em. I need to ask you something." My stomach felt like a caldron into which someone had just poured a pot full of hot pasta. I wanted Em around me very much, I wanted to see her, smell her and be absorbed into the warmth of her being. But I knew that if I were around her or had constant interaction with her it would irritate the open wound she created when she left me. I barely hung on emotionally as it was. The fresh coat of paint I had applied to my life was so green it had to be protected, perhaps even defended.

"Shoot," she said. And, I could picture her perfectly made up mouth as she said the words.

"I'm much better. I'm writing and enjoy it. I feel good. I know you had to leave to get away from me. I needed to get away from me. If I continue to progress as I have for the past month or so, I will be back to my old self . . ."

"Jack, I know where this is headed and I don't want to go there. In fact, I had planned to wait until after the first of the year to send the divorce papers to you. I promised I would give you some time. You're writing, doing better and I'm proud of you. And I'm willing to help as long as you need me."

"But getting back together?" The question hung in the air like a guillotine.

"No, Jack. That will not happen. I'm sorry."

"Em, I don't think I could handle working with you right now. It would be too hard. I'm still in love with you."

I could hear her breathe into her cellphone. "I understand, Jack. We all have to do what we need to do. Let me know what is going on with Ruby. I want to call her or send her flowers. I'll let you go now."

"Bye, Em." I laid the antique phone onto the receiver base, scratched Hemingway behind his ears and considered whether this was the final nail in the coffin of our marriage.

I looked around my studio. The sleeper-sofa against the wall that I used as a bed stood disheveled; none of the linens had been changed in two weeks. Books, magazines and printed-paper from the internet and remnants of fast food meals warred with each other for control of the space on the desk in front of me. Guest chairs in front of the desk were topped with dirty clothes, and the single counter kitchenette was overrun with dirty dishes, an overworked and under-cleaned coffee pot and what little space there was left in my studio was covered in dust. Little flecks of dust swirled in the air as the sun fought its way into my corner of the world.

I could feel myself backslide into darkness and my resolve not to call Lisa dissolved. I thought about calling her on the old landline, but I knew she would not recognize the number on caller I.D. and there was no chance she would take the call at home. I pulled my cellphone from my pocket, reached for the charging cord that had fallen on the floor, plugged in the phone and called her New York number. I didn't want to call her, but I needed to talk with someone.

"Lisa! Merry Christmas!" I thought I sounded desperate, lonely.

"Jack, do you realize what time it is?" Her voice was filled with sleep, and her groans equal to the effort the sun made as it struggled to rise above the fog on the lake.

"I just wanted to share the good news. I finished the book this morning."

"That's wonderful," she said and yawned. "I talked to Em the other day and she is ready to edit as soon as you're finished."

Lisa Catera was my friend. When nothing else had gone right in my life, she had been there for me. But she also worked for me and made a handsome living as my agent. There was no question in my mind that she was my agent first and my friend second. I had always wondered how long our relationship would last if our business dealings ended. I didn't have that many friends that I could be picky. It was comments like these that reminded me of her place in my life. Despite the glamour that goes along with the profession of a novelist, it was very lonely work. Vast amounts of time are spent alone huddled over a keyboard. You have to be somewhat introverted to do the work. I have relationships with other writers, but I have not reached out to them in a while. I had become so isolated with depression that I had cut myself off from just about everyone. Lisa was one of the few people I let in.

"That's why I called, Lisa. Em and I just got off the phone. I don't want to use her. In fact, I can't. It would be too hard."

"Jack, we are up against it. I get daily threatening calls from Reynolds on your progress. You know they're going to tap dance on my head for the next novel as soon as we meet their deadline. They have already told me that you have to have the third and final novel in draft by February 15. We just don't have time to look for someone else."

I considered the dilemma. "If I start right now and do all-nighters for the next month and a half, I might, just might, meet their deadline. I do not have time to find another editor and I am not going to use Emily." I stopped short of saying something like, 'earn a little of the ten percent you get and find one for me,' but I held my tongue.

Lisa breathed on the phone; heavier, deeper. "Jack, these are the holidays. How can I find someone now?"

"Lisa . . ."

"Alright. Alright! I'll take care of it." More breath, less labored. "How are you and Em?"

"That is the point, Lisa. We aren't. Em has no interest in reconciliation. None. She will serve me papers any day now. She would have done it six weeks ago if I hadn't asked her for a little time. She told me then that there was no chance. But I wasn't ready to hear it. It's done." The finality of the words hit me hard, unexpectedly hard.

"I was afraid of that. I feel bad, Jack. For both of you."

We finished our conversation. She wished me a Merry Christmas and said that she would get to work on an editor. Those would be big shoes to fill. I could not worry about it. It was in Lisa's hands.

Three

I turned my attention to the scribbled telephone number of the hospital in Jacksonville. I called and talked to a social worker assigned to my aunt's case. She relayed the same message she had given Em; that Ruby was asking for me. She said she wanted to meet with me when I came but was evasive about the nature of the discussion. Another novel by the middle of February. As much as I loved Ruby, I just didn't have time for this.

Late in the morning of Christmas day, the lobby of St. Vincent's was sparsely populated and heavily decorated for Christmas. Tinsel hung and Christmas music played softly in the elevator and the nurse's station on the third floor had a North Pole appearance. The door to room 301 was ajar. I poked my head in. A curtain had been pulled around the far bed in the semi-private room.

"Oh, honey, I'm so grateful for this. A woman has to smell pretty to feel pretty."

A nurse's aide looked out from behind the curtain. "I'm sorry sir, but you'll have to wait in the hall until I'm finished with Mrs. Johnson's bath."

From behind the curtain, "Is that you, Jackie?"

I answered, "Yes, Ma'am."

"The nurse won't be long. Besides, you don't want to see an old woman in her all-together."

"I'll just be out in the hall." To the aide I said, "Take your time. I'm in no hurry." On the outside I may have given the appearance of calm, but on the inside my stomach was roiled and all I could think about was the plot to the next novel and all I had was the kernel of an idea.

Ruby's hospitalization was an untimely and unfair intrusion into the madness of my life. She was 85.

Ruby's voice echoed off tiled walls and found its way into the hall. The banter between Ruby and the nurse's aide was comfortable and casual, like they were sipping iced mint-tea together on an open porch. But that was the place all of Ruby's conversations ended, a waltz of words where her guests were made to feel uniquely special. As the aide bathed her, it was the aide who had become a guest in Ruby's room, woven into the fabric of her hospitality.

Light footsteps from behind approached. I turned and caught the doctor before she entered Ruby's room.

"Excuse me. Are you Mrs. Johnson's doctor?"

The small elderly woman in the white smock, and the name badge that read, "Alicia Sommers, MD," stopped and inquired, "Are you a relative of Mrs. Johnson's?"

"Nephew. But we are very close."

"Well, she's been through a lot. Doing quite well, though."

"What's the prognosis?"

"You mean from the surgery?"

"I just wondered if you were able to get all of the cancer."

"And your name is?"

"I'm sorry. Excuse my manners. Jack McNamara." I extended my hand and enfolded her small delicate hand. "I'm her health surrogate."

"Ah, you must be the author she talks about all the time. She's quite a fan of yours I'd say."

"Ruby's a character."

"That she is." She paused, and looked momentarily distracted. "I usually get a cup of coffee after rounds. Let us in the cafeteria in about thirty minutes. I'd like to talk to you about Ruby and some options about her care."

"That would be great."

She patted me on the arm, gave me a warm look and then disappeared into Ruby's room.

Ruby lived in Jacksonville, Florida. Ruby and Glory Jean were not terribly close. Had I moved Ruby to Savannah to live near Glory Jean, it would have been more difficult for Em and me to be involved in her care.

Ruby said behind the curtain "Oh, thank you, Juanita. You're such an angel, the bath was marvelous."

"The doctor will be finished in just a moment," the petite Hispanic aide said to me as she came through the door into the hall.

I could hear the muffled tones of the doctor's conversation with Ruby, but none of the words. Dr. Sommers appeared in the doorway. Her eyes narrowed over granny reading glasses. "It's good you're here." She reached up and squeezed my shoulder with her small hand. "She will need your support now more than ever." She looked down at Ruby's chart, flipped through some pages, then briefly looked up at me. "We will talk more in the cafeteria." She let loose of my arm, patted it and then departed down the hall. Her touch of my arm communicated warmth in a way that words could never do.

When I walked into the room, the curtain had been opened and furled against the wall and the room was on fire with orange and red Gladiolas Em had sent her last night. Ruby had her head turned toward the window and was startled by my entrance as though she had forgotten I was there.

Her face brightened. Her tightly curled grey hair surrounded her round, fleshy countenance. Reluctantly, her lips formed a crooked smile. "Oh, Jackie, honey. Come give your Aunt Ruby a hug."

I slipped my hand under her neck and shoulders bent over and kissed her on the cheek. She trembled at my touch and began to cry, first softly, then with abandon. I held my embrace until she gently pushed me away. "You're so precious to me. The last thing you need is a blubbering old woman slobbering all over you." She patted her hair down, wiped her wet cheeks, and tried to sit up in bed, but was beaten back in pain from her surgery. "Jackie, honey, find the switch on this contraption that raises my head, will you?" she said through clenched teeth. "I've got enough stitches in my stomach to open a quilting store." She made a significant effort to smile at her own joke.

I found the bed control just out of her reach and raised the top half of the bed to a half-sitting position. "You O.K.?" I took her hand and put it between mine. Her fingers were gnarled from rheumatoid arthritis.

"It'll take more than a little surgery to get this old gal down. Remember, you're talking to the Bionic Woman."

Ruby had had both of her hips and knees replaced to counter the ravaging effects of her crippling disease. Bionic Woman is a title no doubt given to many patients who have undergone joint replacement. But the honorary title stuck with Ruby, who wore the moniker with pride.

"What did the doctor say? You seemed pretty upset when I came in?"

"Isn't Doctor Sommers a jewel? I don't think I've ever met a doctor with the sensitivity she has. She cares so much about her patients. Always takes the time to explain things so that even I can understand. I just love her." With difficulty, she pulled tissue from a box on the rollaway table next to her bed and mopped up her eyes. "I want to talk to you about our story."

I had no idea what 'our story' was there were so many of them. "O.K., let's talk about it."

I always found it of interest the vein of artistry that had woven its way through my mother's family. Ruby was an accomplished artist. Her oil painting skills blossomed late in life, oddly enough after arthritis had rendered her hands and fingers useless for anything more than the most rudimentary endeavors, one of which was to sketch and paint. Her favorite subjects were floral scenes painted to perfection with her unusual sense of color, eye for composition, exacting detail and subtle emotion.

Whenever I visited her, she had a slew of ideas for stories. She stubbornly refused to let me leave her company until I promised to use one of her ideas in a short story or novel. She would have written them herself, she told me many times, but found it difficult to write or type with her hands.

Many of her ideas were good. Unfortunately, none of them lined up with material publishers felt had any commercial value. I didn't have the heart to tell her that I couldn't or wouldn't use them. So I wasn't surprised when she wanted to talk about 'our' story.

For a writer to use the ideas of others is a mortal sin. The last thing a novelist needs is to be sued by someone who claims you have used one of their notions and then have to share royalties. In fact, at the end of every one of my books was a statement that, "I do not want story ideas from anyone and all the material I write is my own." She leaned forward and whispered to me. "I've got an idea for a novel you will love. I know every time we get on this subject you think I have diarrhea of the mouth. But this is different. This story has been in me for a long time. I've got the whole thing written in my head. I want you to have it. But I want it to be ours."

"I'm always open to a blockbuster idea," I lied.

"Jackie, I'm serious about this one. I want this to be a legacy, my swan song. I ask a lot, I know, but you're the only one I can turn to. I want you to promise me you'll write this story."

"You know I will," I lied again.

"No, Jackie, I mean for real. I want you to promise me."

"Publishing a story isn't always easy. It depends on the topic and whether a publisher will go for it."

"They'll go for this. I have no doubt. God gave it to me."

"God gave it to you?" Ruby had told me many times that she and God talked to each other. I understood the prayer part it was the God talking back part that made me wonder about my bible-thumping aunt.

"Every detail. The whole story came to me as a single thought. Sugar, it's all here. Every line." She tapped the side of her head with a twisted finger.

"What's the story about?"

The Hispanic aide who gave Ruby her bath flew through the door. "Well Mrs. Johnson, you ready go? These two good-looking guys escort you to MRI. Doc wants pictures for your photo album. She says a beauty like you needs be photographed." The aide and the two attendants rattled around Ruby's bed and prepared to move her.

"Do we have to do this now? Jackie, my nephew, has come a long way to see me. Juanita, this is my nephew, Jackie, I mean Jack McNamara."

"Nice to meet you." (You came out "jew.") She shook my hand. "This machine cost a lot of money and when people no show up, they get crazy.

Bill Cronin

Maybe Jack will wait until you be done. No take long."

The attendants moved the IV fluids to the pole on her bed, unlocked the wheels and prepared to wheel her out of the room.

"Jack, please wait for me. We have so much to talk about."

"Mr. Jack, we have a waiting room down the hall. You could be there if you want." The nurse pointed at the wall in the direction of the waiting area.

Juanita smoothed out the sheets that covered Ruby and signaled the attendants and they maneuvered her through the door then down the hallway.

The crowded cafeteria on the first floor bustled with hospital staff and visitors who queued up on two food lines. Patrons talked loudly over the din and I wondered when the doctor came if we would be able to hear one another. It was nearly eleven when I went through the line, and found a quieter table in a distant corner of the room. I loved the smell of fresh coffee. The aroma wafted from the large Styrofoam cup on the table. Ruby's emotional reaction to her discussion with the doctor did not bode well. While Ruby had always been emotional, she would tear up at the slightest joyful provocation; she seldom wore her troubles on her sleeve. She would cry when she saw you for the first time in a while. She would tear up when someone showed her a kindness, or when something from nature moved her as particularly beautiful. She had always been a fountain of joyfulness and her tears had always been an expression of the overflow. So, it was rare to see her cry from hurt or sadness.

As a child, my father all but cut us off from my mother's family. My aunt Glory Jean speculated that my father could not tolerate my mother's redneck relations, all of whom hailed from Georgia and South Carolina. As I grew older and my mother's health declined, I came to appreciate my mother's family.

Since Ruby's husband died, she had lived alone in a large antique frame home in the center of Jacksonville. Her deceased husband, who sold life and health insurance, had left her without any insurance save a small burial policy. A small, dwindled savings account and social security were not enough to rescue her from her submerged financial situation. So, four years ago, I helped her sell her home and possessions and moved her into a small, well-lit apartment so she could paint, see her friends and most importantly to continue to attend her church. Thus began my stewardship of her affairs and my three to four trips a year to see her. Then her stomach pains began.

After several visits to the doctor, tests at the hospital and the loss of a very close friend who cared for her, I convinced her to let me move her to an assisted living facility. But she insisted it be in Jacksonville near her church. That was a year ago. Actually, it was Em who handled much of this since my bouts with depression were in full bloom and her miseries, added to my own, made my life a challenge. As I tried to remember the last time I had visited Ruby I noticed Dr. Sommers as she stood in line and filled her coffee cup. A doctor was not going to take this kind of time to discuss a patient's condition unless it was serious. I knew when she asked to meet me here that the news was not good.

About the Author

After a thirty-year career in the telecommunications industry, Bill sold a telecommunications and business management consulting practice to pursue a writing career. Bill wrote for the **Orlando Sentinel** briefly following military service during the Vietnam War and made frequent contributions to the **NTCA Rural Telecommunications Magazine**. Bill has written eight novels: *Dial Tone*, 2012; *The Song of the Mockingbird*, 2013*; *Ruby's Story*, 2014*, and *The Tainted Lady*, 2014; *Letting Go*, 2015*, *Joe and the Governor*, 2016*; *Night Fire*, 2017*; and *Playing with Fire*, 2017* all of which have been released as ebooks on Amazon Kindle.

* Indicates books that are available in paperback from Amazon.

Bill and his wife Linda make their home on the East Coast of Central Florida.

Stay current on Bill Cronin's work and news about his novels at www.billcroninwrite.com or his Facebook page facebook.com/billcroninwrite. Follow Bill on Twitter at @billcroninwrite.